Unholy Secrets

by

NEIVE DENIS

Book eight in the Sonoma Whittington series

Copyright

Cataloguing-in-publication data
Creator: Denis, Neive, author

Cataloguing-in-Publication details are available from the National Library of Australia
www.trove.nla.gov.au

ISBN: 978-0-6483950-9-6 (paperback)
ISBN: 978-0-6489423-0-6 (digital edition)

Cover design: T A Marshall, Mackay, QLD Australia

CONTENTS

Other Books by the Author

Prologue

Three and a half years ago…

As night closed in, the solid curtain of rain made the house feel it was wrapped in a gauze-like cocoon. Outside, the wind howled and gusted, bringing down trees and fences. What would later be termed a 'super cell' descended on the small valley community of Tanwood without much warning. Rain bucketing down for the last two days already had the river and feeder creeks running bank-to-bank. The super cell ensured the roads became flooded, isolating the community for days.

The dark figure kept to the trees for cover. Mud squelched with every careful step, and the bag he carried seemed to become heavier with each stride. He stopped and dragged a hand across his face to clear the water from his eyes. The peak of the cap worn under the hood of his jacket offered his face only minor protection from the stinging rain. This was the crucial stage of the exercise.

He must cross open ground to reach the building. At least the storm meant all the windows and doors were closed. From the outset, his concern was about his footprints. A quick look over his shoulder eased his mind. Even when under the trees, his footprints already were lost in the shallow sheet of water across the area. Despite this, nervous tension built within him. He paused for a few deep breaths before continuing his stealthy progress towards the house.

Once on the covered wide concrete path running around all sides of the building, he would be safe. A muddy footprint left by each step lasted but a second before rain obliterated it. The soft thud and splash of his gumboots on the concrete barely discernible to his ears. A light was on inside the house. No one in there would hear him. Although it felt like a lifetime, it took no more than a minute to pick his way to the north-eastern corner of the house.

His intention, once he reached the corner, was to cut across the yard to the jumble of large boulders left in situ as a garden feature some thirty metres from the northern side of the building. From there, he could scope out the place and plan the final act of tonight's performance. He could smell smoke. 'Why not,' he asked himself. 'Tonight is a perfect night to light a fire.'

Panic set in when he reached the corner of the house. This was not scripted. Light spilled out across the path and beyond, illuminating a patch of the yard to the north of the house. The only open window in the building was the worst possible one. Now he couldn't risk cutting across to the rocks. He knew hesitation could be his downfall, and fought to control his panic. Clear thinking returned. Sure, it meant a change of plan, but an open window presented different possibilities.

The deed was done. His objective achieved. He felt euphoric as he picked his way back along the same track he used to arrive at the house. Was it really so easy? An almost hysterical giggle broke free. He forced himself to walk and not run. Falling face first into the mud at this stage of the game was not wise. He giggled again. At least, if he fell in the mud, the rain would soon wash it off. Then he was at the gate. Through the falling rain, he could make out the road in front of him and his battered vehicle parked several metres further along beside the road. Now it was critical to be gone; to be 'home' and warm, and dry again.

The village was deserted; nobody out and about on such a night. Floodwaters already trickled across the road as, spurred on by the thought of the rum toddy and dry clothes waiting for him, he drove as fast as possible through the rain.

Chapter 1

A tentative young woman cracked open my office door and peered inside, before again checking the name on the door. Still unsure about where she was, she asked, "Is this Whittington Investigations?"

"Unless someone has changed the sign on the door, that's who I am."

"That's amazing. I can get lost in a two-room apartment, but I've found this place on my first attempt. May I come in?"

"If you're wanting to talk to Whittington Investigations, perhaps you should."

The tall, willowy girl checked over her shoulder before closing the door behind her and picking her way across the bilious green carpet to my desk. "Please, take a seat and tell me what brings you here this morning."

"Uhmm … Yes … Thank you. Miss Whittington, is it?"

"Call me Sonny. It's much easier than the other mouthful. Would you like a coffee before we start?"

I directed her to make herself comfortable in one of the lounge chairs in the front corner of my office while I fiddled with the coffee machine. When I joined her with our coffees – one cappuccino with no sugar, and one black – she was perched on the front edge of one of my ancient lounge chairs and looking quite uptight. After placing the cappuccino on the table in front of her and collapsing into the other chair, I encouraged her to relax and tell me why she came.

She took a couple of sips of her coffee before running the tip of her tongue across her top lip to remove froth deposited there. So far, our meeting was going nowhere in a hurry. My frustration level was rising. A dangerous situation, as it tends to bring out my darker side. At last, while retaining a firm two-handed grip on her mug, she slumped back in her chair.

"I'm sorry. I haven't done anything like this before, and I'm not sure how to go about it."

"Well, it's not a complicated procedure. Something caused you to come to my office to discuss whatever it was with me. Now you're here, we can move onto the next part of the exercise. It's where you tell me why you've come to see me. So… Why are you here?"

"I want you to investigate a murder."

"A murder…? Has it happened, or is it one you're about to commit?"

"Oh, I'm not doing this very well am I?"

"I can't answer that. You haven't told me anything yet. So far, all you've said is you want me to investigate a murder. Maybe you should be telling the police about this murder instead of asking me to investigate it. So, I'll ask the question again: has this a murder happened, or is it about to happen?"

"No, no. It has happened. It happened about three and a half years ago. There's no point in talking to the police about it."

"Okay, that's a start. Did this murder happen here in Millhaven?"

"No … Yes … Well, sort of … It happened on the outskirts of Millhaven, up the valley at Tanwood. Do you know the area?"

My mind reminded me it was a long while since I'd been there. "Yes, I know Tanwood, but it must be at least ten years since I was there."

"I haven't been there in a long time either. It must be eight years since I left."

"Right, so far, we have established that a murder occurred at Tanwood about three and a half years ago and, for some reason, you don't think it's worth mentioning it to the police.

Is it safe for me to assume the police investigated the murder at the time it occurred?" She gave a curt nod in response. "I see. What was the outcome of their investigation?"

"There was no outcome. Nobody was charged. They claimed there was insufficient evidence to charge anyone. I believe the coroner gave an open verdict. And that seemed the end of the story as far as the authorities were concerned."

When she lifted her eyes from the coffee mug she was squeezing to death, the deep-seated pain in them tugged at my heartstrings. Perhaps more compassion on my part might pay dividends. I rescued her mug and put it on the table out of harm's way. "What can you tell me about the murder and the subsequent police investigation? I'm not looking for technical details. Just tell me anything you remember about the event."

"That's just the point. I don't remember anything about it. I wasn't even in the country at the time, and it was a while after the event before I heard about it. By then, the police investigation was over and the coroner had declared an open verdict."

It was obvious the event was personal for the young woman but, so far, she had avoided providing clues as to why. She was so tightly coiled and controlled within herself, I couldn't determine whether her reluctance to reveal those personal details was deliberate or otherwise. I decided to try a different tack. "You said the murder occurred about three and a half years ago; why wait until now to decide you want the incident investigated?"

"I had to wait until I was twenty-one. I know the age of majority is eighteen but, in my case, I had to wait until I was twenty-one years old."

Can this become any more difficult? I'm sure she thinks she answered my question, and will be dismayed to learn her answer only created more questions. "What was so significant about turning twenty-one? What was to happen when you reached that age, and why did it impact on your wanting to investigate this murder?"

"When I turned twenty-one, I was supposed to gain control of my trust fund. It was quite clear that's what should happen. But, when the time came, there was a definite reluctance on the part of the trustees to relinquish control. Some legal 'prompting' was required before one of them decided to comply with the rules of the trust. The other trustee was not so keen. Why that was so became apparent when my solicitor did a bit of digging. There was an anomaly to the tune of $20,000. It was only the threat of legal action against that trustee, a solicitor, which brought results. The anomaly was corrected, and I gained control of my money. Once that happened, I was in a position to pay for an investigation."

My 'I see' comment seemed an inane response under the circumstances. Her story wrong-footed me and, for a moment, I struggled to reinstate some direction in my questioning. "How urgent is this investigation you want undertaken?"

"Are you saying you don't want to take the case?"

"Not at all. If the murder and the subsequent investigation occurred three and a half years ago, I doubt anything of significance will occur in the next week or so. All I'm saying is, I don't know what your agenda is or how you see any such investigation proceeding."

"I'm sorry. I suppose I half expected you to tell me to go away; that I was some sort of nutcase and you had more to do than listen to stories about some long-gone murder. Do you think you might take the case?"

"At this point in time, I don't know much about it. I can tell you I have a couple of matters requiring immediate attention. After that, I would be prepared to look into the murder and the events associated with it, before committing to take the case or otherwise. Are you planning on staying in Millhaven long, or just passing through?"

"My time is my own. I am prepared to be in Millhaven for as long as required … For as long as an investigation might require me to be here."

"Right, here's my suggestion. Over the next couple of days, I will do some research into the incident. I suggest we meet again at nine o'clock on Friday morning. By then, I'll be in a better position to tell you whether I will take the case or not. How does that suit you?"

"Yes, that's fine by me. I'll be here at nine o'clock on Friday. If there is nothing more you need, I'll be on my way and leave you to get on with your work."

"It would be helpful if I had a few details before you leave. We could start with your name and how I might contact you should I need to before Friday."

"Yes, of course. I'm Lucy Telford."

A triumphant look spread across her face as she finished giving me her phone and email details. As I scribbled them in my notebook, I asked my next question. "It would be helpful if I knew something about the murder … like, who was murdered, for instance."

"Didn't I say…? Oh dear, I'm making a real mess of this. Right, details… The murdered man was Thomas Blaine, aged about forty-six at the time; a long-time resident and farmer in the Tanwood area where the murder occurred."

As I scribbled the last of the details in my notebook, I asked, "What is your interest in this? Why do you want to investigate Mr Blaine's death?"

She didn't answer. I looked up. She was almost at the door. She didn't pause her exit, wrenching open the door and starting out through it. Without turning her head, at the last moment before letting the door close behind her, she answered my question.

"He was my father."

Chapter 2

Was I stunned or intrigued – or both? Probably both is the correct assessment. Whichever it was, it kept me glued to my chair for some time after Lucy Telford left. The sound of the door opening drew me back from my long stare into the distance. Thinking it was Lucy returning, I attempted to scramble out of my chair to meet her.

"So this is what investigators do while the rest of the world slaves away all day at real jobs."

I relaxed and slumped back into my chair. "I was working. I was thinking; thinking about a client who came to see me about a new case. Anyway, if the rest of the world is slaving away, what are you doing here at this hour of the day?"

Emily Ibbotson's chirpy entrance might be just what I needed after my meeting with Lucy Telford. "It looks as though you've already had coffee. Could you go another one if I make it?"

My friendship with Emily goes back a few years. A chemical engineer working in the mining industry, she upskilled to become a forensic scientist. Then, a forensic laboratory established in Millhaven was a new state government initiative designed to ease the load on the single state-owned establishment. The mining conglomerate Emily worked for won the contract. They set up the new forensic facility as a separate wing of their central mining analysis and testing laboratory. Emily while appointed manager of the whole expanded facility, spends most of her working hours in the forensic lab. Her logical thinking has proved invaluable in many of the numerous investigations she worked with me. And, she has those 'extra skills' should I be in need of a spot of 'unofficial' forensic analysis to help with a case.

As she set our steaming mugs of coffee on the low table in front of us, Emily demanded, "Prove you were working when I came in. Tell me about this new case and the client who goes with it. Whatever it is, it seems to have grabbed you. I assume it is more than a simple errant-spouse type case."

"…And you would be correct. It's a murder investigation; a more than three-year-old murder investigation."

"You don't normally investigate murders, not even if they happened yesterday, never mind one that's almost ancient history. What's so special about this one … And why does somebody want it investigated after so long? Oh, and while I'm on the hunt for answers, are we sure it was an actual murder? …And do the police know about it?"

"It appears the murder was real enough and the police did investigate it at the time. Indications are it's now a cold case. Nobody was charged with murder. No, I don't know why that is, but I was given to understand it had something to do with a lack of evidence."

"If the police investigation didn't solve the crime, what do you hope to achieve? Or, perhaps the question is: what does your client hope you will achieve?"

"At this point, I'm not sure she is a client, or if I have a case. I told her I would look into the murder and meet with her again on Friday to tell her whether I will take the case or not. Yes, I know it sounds peculiar, but it is also intriguing. Perhaps I'll see it in a different light after some research. Putting it aside for the moment, you haven't told me why you are here at this hour of the day and not locked away with your test tubes and beakers."

"For the last two weeks, we have been flat out. I've been averaging about four hours sleep a day."

"I knew I hadn't seen you for a while, but I didn't realise there was a crime spree in Millhaven."

"No there isn't, but the locals have been running amok in Ralston. The State facility was overloaded with samples coming in, so they redirected all the Ralston stuff to us. Things have settled down in our lab, so I'm taking some time off to balance the books, so to speak. I had to go in this morning for something, but the rest of the day is mine and so is all of tomorrow. So-o, what are *we* working on today and tomorrow?"

"I have some paperwork to complete first but, if you are looking for something to do, you could start researching this murder I need to know about."

Emily set her laptop up on the coffee table. I gave her my scant details of the murder, and she began hunting for information. Her only break was to duck out to buy something for our lunches. After eating at our desks, our allotted tasks continued through to mid-afternoon. By then, I had completed the outstanding paperwork, and I was ready to join the hunt for information about the murder.

Over yet another coffee, I went through everything Emily had found. While she located quite a bit of material, it didn't tell us much. She bemoaned the fact. "I printed off all this stuff as I found it, but it's 'sketchy' at best. It doesn't provide any solid information to work with, and only confirms what Lucy told you."

"I'd come to that same conclusion. It's hard to understand why Thomas Blaine's name seems vaguely familiar. I don't remember there being a murder associated with it. I'm thinking it happened while I was on the overseas holiday I took around that time. Nevertheless, a murder in this part of the world generates a lot of interest, and the media would be packed with every morsel of information extracted from any source. It doesn't seem the case in this instance. I don't imagine the circumstances warranted a media blackout, or an embargo was placed on the release of details. If there were an embargo, the media should have been full of the story as soon as it was lifted. There is no evidence of such an occurrence."

"You might have to wine and dine your good mate Ben Richards tonight to try persuading him to let you look at the police investigation files."

"I think it might be a bit early for that. In addition to wining and dining, in this case, I think it might also require the very softest of kid gloves. After all, if the police investigation came up empty, they are not going to welcome someone else trying to show them up. Nevertheless, if Ben Richards comes for dinner, I might begin some groundwork to build on at a later date."

Just before five o'clock, Emily dashed off to do something before the shops closed. I took advantage of the solitude to leave a voice message for Ben Richards to join me for dinner. The invite probably wasn't necessary. Ben and I eat together most nights unless one of us is working. Our friendship goes back many years to when Ben was a uniformed police officer stationed here at Millhaven. Now, he is the top cop for this region. There was a time when we almost became more than friends. Then, life, work, promotions, and whatever else, separated us for a number of years. Not long after I left the public service and became a private investigator, opportunity arose to rekindle the friendship. Since then, it has proved invaluable to my investigations on a number of occasions.

A couple of minutes after I left the voice message, Ben called me. "I thought I was coming for dinner anyway. Do you have something planned, or would you like me to bring something?"

"Nothing fancy planned; just a couple of T-bones with all the trimmings. If you're inclined to something more exotic, feel free to bring it with you." He assured me a fine steak washed down with an excellent Cabernet would be most acceptable and sufficient.

It wasn't a late night. Wining and dining were accomplished with no attempt at groundwork occurring. Ben seemed pre-occupied all evening. It probably had something to do with the conference he was flying south to first thing in the morning. An early night suited me fine as I was keen to return to researching the Blaine murder.

After seeing Ben off, I headed for my office in the front wing of my home, acquiring a mug of hot chocolate on my way through the kitchen. My first task was to establish a case file. I knew I hadn't accepted it as a case yet but establishing a case file gathered everything we collected so far in one place and enabled me to make sense of it. Once that was done, I set about noting key points contained in the material.

After two solid hours of extracting information from the printouts, I still didn't know much more than when I started … not much more than the details Lucy gave me. In spite of my intention to work on until midnight, my eyes were becoming heavy and that idea went the way of many other good intentions. It was just after eleven o'clock when I crawled into bed.

*****

This morning I headed for my city office earlier than usual. Not only did I feel guilty about wasting a good research opportunity last night, but I wanted to explore a few potential resources before Emily arrived. As she had today off work, I had no doubt she would be in my office and ready to start researching by nine o'clock. While I welcome her assistance, I work better alone on this part of a case. Once I know where an investigation is going, Emily's input is most useful.

It didn't matter how I viewed the Blaine murder, I was a long way from knowing much about it, or what direction my investigation should take. After ruling a line down the centre of a page to create two columns, I headed one column *Details I Know* and the other one *Questions Needing Answers.* Then, I sat back and studied the otherwise blank sheet.

"Get on with it," I snarled aloud. I was achieving nothing at a great rate of knots this morning. Frustration was high;

output zero. I snatched up a pen and started scribbling. Things in the forefront of my mind went onto the paper quickly. Then the proverbial 'brick wall' loomed up in front of me. It was time to stop writing and start thinking. Thinking happens better when fuelled by caffeine. On my way to the coffee machine, I checked the time.

"That's unusual," I told my empty office. "She usually arrives long before this." It was 9.30 and Emily was a no-show. As I took my first sip of coffee, she called.

"Something has come up at work. I'd like to think I'll get away from here sometime later today but, if I'm honest, I don't believe there's any chance of it happening. I'll call you later in the day."

Okay, so my time is my own today. I'm not too disappointed, but now I have to plan what I'm going to do for the rest of the day. I told myself I wasn't procrastinating, just was waiting for Emily to arrive before getting on with it. There was no ducking the issue now.

What is wrong with me? I'm not one who has trouble getting stuck into whatever has to be done. In a show of resoluteness, I pulled my chair in close to the desk, squared my sheet of paper in front of me, and gave it a long, hard look. The list of facts was remarkable for its brevity. The list of questions had reached the bottom of the page. My eyes were drawn to one particular line.

In the facts column I had written *home alone at the time.* On the same line in the questions column, I had written *who else should have been there.* One of the newspaper articles indicated Blaine was home alone at the time of the murder. Nowhere else had I seen it mentioned. It raised the questions: was it unusual for him to be home alone? Did others reside in the house? Who else should – would normally – be there?

Lucy hadn't mentioned anyone else; not a mother or siblings. Was Thomas Blaine a widower living alone? That drew my eyes to the very next question on my list: why hadn't Lucy been back to Tanwood in so many years? From the information she gave me, she must've left Tanwood when she was about thirteen years old. Where did she go, and why? …And why did she never return?

One answer might be that she went away to boarding school. Tanwood is a long way from the nearest high school. At age thirteen, she was about to begin secondary school. Other students from up the valley travelled on the school bus every day to the nearest high school, but travelling the distance involved made a long day for them. Some mothers chose to drive their children rather than subject them to the extended travel time resulting from the long, meandering bus route.

If Blaine was a widower sharing a house with only his young daughter, getting her to school every day during her primary school years would not be a problem. There was a small one-teacher school in the Tanwood area. Lucy could catch a bus, ride her bike, or be collected by a neighbour driving her own children to school. It wasn't until she reached secondary school age the problem with travelling to school occurred.

While the scenario was realistic, it was pure assumption on my part. I had nothing to suggest Lucy was sent away to boarding school. But, if she wasn't, why did she leave Tanwood at such a young age, and then not return. If she was away at school, it was likely she would spend the school holidays at home at Tanwood. Such deliberations were getting me nowhere. The only relevant fact was that Lucy wasn't at home at the time of the murder. The good thing is, Lucy can answer those questions when she comes on Friday. Pity some of my other questions won't be so easy to answer.

I started a second sheet of paper. No new facts had emerged yet, but more questions had occurred to me. In the midst of it all, a revelation dawned on me: what did I know about Tanwood? The short answer is, not much. As I told

Lucy, I hadn't been to the area in at least ten years. In reality, I had never 'been' to Tanwood. It was somewhere you passed through on your way to somewhere else.

Perhaps a visit might help the thought processes dredge up something worthwhile. If I devoted the rest of today to researching in-house, I could take a trip to Tanwood tomorrow morning. I'm not sure what such a trip might produce, but it might help focus my thinking.

While I haven't accepted the case yet, it has me captivated. It's not just the murder itself and who did it, it's everything about it ... the lack of media coverage, the supposed lack of evidence for a conviction, and Lucy herself. Setting the murder to one side to spend time researching the family situation might prove useful. If I manage to speak with any of the locals during my visit to Tanwood tomorrow, it would be helpful to know the composition of Blaine family at the time of the crime.

Getting to know the family required ignoring all my usual research resources to focus on those avenues more familiar to family historians. Genealogy was never one of my passions but, in the course of some of my past investigations, I learnt the usual rudimentary procedures and processes. I suspected researching the Blaine family story would be different ... and more difficult.

Any births, deaths or marriages involved in the generations associated with the crime time period will be recent. Too recent to be found in the state's indexes. After considering the situation for a few minutes, it became apparent the most likely place I would find the information I wanted was in the social columns of the local newspapers. As a result, I found myself again searching the same resources Emily and I searched yesterday, but today I skimmed the social notes, working backwards from the most recent editions.

As the day progressed past lunchtime, I began losing hope. I was beginning to think the Blaine family never existed. So far, I had found no mention of Thomas or Lucy, or of any wife. Time to step away from my desk to buy a sandwich and juice for lunch. Opting not to eat at my desk where I'd only end up working with sandwich in one hand and a mouse in the other, I settled in one of my lounge chairs. Over lunch, one thing became clear to me: I might spend the rest of the day working back through the papers, week by week, and still have nothing more by the time I went home.

My new approach was to go to the approximate date of Thomas' murder. Maybe there was a funeral notice, or perhaps something about his death which mentioned his family. After some searching, his funeral notice appeared in a paper dated a few weeks after the crime. Even that was frustrating. The two-line notice inserted by the undertaker told me nothing more than when and where the funeral would take place.

I was beginning to doubt there was any family besides Lucy. If there were other members or relatives of the Blaine family, there was no close bond between them. Absence of any mention of Lucy was not too difficult to understand. She said she was overseas at the time, and already had been away from Tanwood for a few years.

Determined not to be put off by a lack of information, I continued trawling backwards through the papers. By five o'clock, my neck hurt and I had a thumping headache, but it was about all I had for my efforts. In disgust at having spent a fruitless day, I packed up and went home early. For one fleeting moment over dinner, I thought I might continue searching the papers after I'd eaten. Later, common sense, or some other self-preservation mechanism, kicked in and I surfed the TV channels instead.

Tomorrow I would drive to Tanwood. Who knows what I might gain from the adventure?

Chapter 3

After a quick trip into my city office to check for mail and messages, brimful of hope and little expectation, I was on the road up the valley to the Tanwood area. Farms, pockets of scrub and rainforest, houses dotted here and there, tractors doing their thing, and a few cattle and horses flashed by as I clocked up the kilometres.

It was ten o'clock by the time I passed the sign announcing I had reached Tanwood. A kilometre or so further along the road, a store occupied a cleared area on the northern side of the road. The sight of it brought back memories of the last time I'd come this way. It didn't look as though it had changed in the ensuing ten years since I last saw it. The store was the 'commercial centre' of the area.

Like Topsy, this enterprise had grown and grown over the decades. Comprised of a central building with extensions added to both sides of the building sometime during its long history, the establishment had developed to meet the needs of its surrounding community. The look of the central building identified it as the starting point for the business. Sometime later, an extension was tacked onto the western side of the building. This now hinted at a 'man's domain'. It stocked basic hardware items, paint and brushes, and containers of oil and grease. Keen home gardeners' supplies such as packets of seeds, and bags of fertiliser and potting material were available. There were also bags of chook feed, several brands of dog food, and a whole host of things required for looking after pets.

New since I'd last seen the place were the two pumps out front of that extension. Motorists could now fuel up with either petrol or diesel. For a moment, I wondered how many customers would buy fuel there. In the time it took for that thought to occur, two vehicles stopped to fill up. But, my interest was not on the extension on that side of the building. I was interested in the one on the eastern side.

Drawn in by the aroma of coffee and something sweet being toasted, I pushed open the door. My focus immediately centred on the enormous – and expensive-looking – coffee machine on the counter. An elderly woman bobbed up from below the counter. "Good morning; I wasn't sure but I thought I heard the door open. Can I get you something, or are you just looking?"

"Yes please; a large cappuccino and some of whatever that is that you're toasting or baking at the moment. It smells absolutely divine."

"I was just heating up a prune Danish. How does that suit?" Silly question; I'd been salivating for it ever since I entered the place.

It was a quiet day. The woman was keen to chat. I had nothing better to do while I waited for my coffee and Danish than to oblige her as I wandered around checking out everything on display. Apart from the enticing menu board behind the counter, anyone who dropped into the coffee shop would be tempted by the array of home-made cakes, packs of scones, and bottles of home-made pickles and jams to take away with them. A local potter had set up a stand in one corner to display a selection of her wares. Her prices were reasonable for the good quality ceramics.

There's nothing like information from local sources. I discovered long ago, it often is much better and more useful than anything other research might uncover. As the woman was in a chatty mood, I took the opportunity to find out about all things Tanwood. To ease into the conversation, I started by asking her about the origins of the store. "The central building looks much older than the rest of the place. How long ago was that built?"

"My father built the store about fifty years ago, when I was still single and living at home. The farm you can see behind the store is the family farm. It's one of the biggest in the area. We always had a large vegetable garden and a substantial orchard. They provided us with a surplus of fruit and vegetables. Dad saw the opportunity to earn some extra cash … And probably to give me something to do to help keep my mind off a young bloke I was pretty keen on at the time."

"So you opened a roadside fruit and vegetable stall. Was there a building here from the beginning?"

"Yes, more or less. To start with, we sold fruit and vegetables, eggs and milk from the farm. Then, over the next few years, we started responding to the community's needs. An increasing range of basic grocery lines was added to the shelves. We soon ran out of room, and the building was expanded. It was almost a complete rebuild. The central building remains unchanged since then."

"But at some point, further expansion has occurred. Extensions were added to both sides of the main store."

"Again, we responded to public demand. Dad negotiated to become an agent for one of the fuel companies. Big tanks were sunk in the ground and bowsers installed out front. It provided the impetus for the expansion on the western side, which allowed us to increase the range of products we could offer the community."

"So this coffee shop is the most recent addition to the establishment?"

"Yes. Throughout its history the store was always a family concern. The young bloke I mentioned earlier, I married him and we live here on the farm. He helped dad run the farm and, when we became an agent for the fuel company, he came to work in this side of the business. It's the story of an only child. When dad died, I inherited everything. My husband ran the farm, and I looked after this place with a bit of help from my mother until she became too ill. Now, my daughter runs the general store. My son-in-law looks after the agricultural side of things, including delivery of bulk fuel and oil to the properties in the valley. Our son helps his father run the farm. I decided I wanted to do my own thing. That's how this coffee shop extension came into being. A few years ago, the opportunity for a local post office agency came up. We secured the contract and then had to work out what to do with it. That's why the corner over there is now the local post office, and the front wall is adorned with banks of mail boxes."

"You and your family have been long-time residents of this area. Do you happen to know where the Blaine farm is?"

"Thomas Blaine's place…? Yes, I know it. If you plan to take a look at it, I'll draw you a map." She grabbed a paper napkin and quickly sketched a rough map. "I hope you don't mind me asking, but are you looking to buy it?"

"Is it for sale? I just wanted to have a look at the place, and find out bit about the family who lived there."

"Oh, that's disappointing. I thought, at last, someone might be going to do something with it. It's in such a sad state; so neglected. It's only a small place, but a good little farm … at least it was while Thomas was alive. Tom was a top bloke; always happy to help out. At different times of the year, things get a bit much for the men to handle on their own. They always called on Tom to help. It's a shame … a real shame what's happened there. Still, I suppose it wasn't a surprise. It's about what you'd expect."

She didn't appear to be going to elaborate, so I tried prompting. "I heard some sort of tragedy occurred on the farm. I was hoping to find out more about it. Do you know of anyone in the district who might be able to tell me about what happened?"

"Are you a reporter?"

Her tone had become icy, and I was in no doubt the locals had developed an allergy to journalists. Unsure of how much I should say, I did nothing more than shake my head. She gave me a sceptical look, before deciding it was safe enough to share some information.

"I can't guarantee he'll talk to you, but you could try old Ned Edwards. His farm adjoins the Blaine place, and he was a good mate of Tom Blaine's. Of course, he might find it too painful to talk about what happened there, but you can only try I suppose."

With her map safe in my pocket, I took my leave and drove about a kilometre further along the main road before coming to the side road to take me to Blaine's farm. I didn't know how far the farm was along the road. Her *you'll know it when you see it* comment wasn't the most helpful direction I've ever received. As she hadn't bothered to explain how I would recognise it, I was almost convinced I was doomed to drive straight past the place.

Fate smiled on me. For the first couple of kilometres along the side road, there several houses, and a couple of shed buildings off in the distance. Then, as I began feeling nervous about finding the place, I saw a home not too far from the road. With no idea whose farm it was, I needed to stop and think. I could enquire at that house. I pulled off the road and parked in a cleared area adjacent to the gate.

The comparison between the neatly mowed road verges and the state of the overgrown paddock on the other side of the fence held my attention for a few moments. The woman said the place was neglected. To my untrained eye, this looked like 'neglected'. Deciding to forgo the intended sitting-and-thinking, I slid out of my car and started towards the gate. 'Knowing your luck, the gate will be locked,' the little voice in my head reminded me.

It wasn't, but something nearby caught my eye. I investigated and I found the farm's mailbox. A rusty old twenty-litre drum, with its both ends surgically enhanced, lay in the long grass. At some time in the past, it was mounted on a plywood platform atop a couple of sturdy posts. Chewed through by white ants, the whole structure had collapsed to decay where it fell. I felt sure I had found Thomas Blaine's farm.

With my confidence bolstered, I was about to try the gate when something else hidden by the long grass caught my attention. Much the worse for a long period of neglect, the wooden sign might have been attached to the mailbox. It was just possible to make out the name of the property: Kirk Michael Farm.

Okay, Kirk is a church … And that building up there looks like a church. There was the little voice in my head again asking me if that was important. "Dunno … But I'm about to find out," I murmured as I battled to lift and drag the gate open far enough for me to walk through.

Run-off from wet season rains had scoured ruts in the gravelled driveway. The only gravel remaining was trapped by the encroaching grass and weeds as the rains washed most of it away. As I approached it, the view of the house appeared to reflect the same degree of neglect as the rest of the property. I felt sure now Kirk Michael Farm was Thomas Blaine's.

This was a beautiful small parish church in its day. The building retained its arched windows and main doorway. It probably suffered the same problems as had put many other small parish churches out of business: dwindling attendances and lack of funds. Perhaps this one was lucky. Once it was 'defrocked' – or whatever it is they do to churches when they are no longer a church – it became a home.

Whether it still stood on its original site or not, I couldn't tell. What was obvious was the work that had gone into turning it from a community-based building into a family home. The sight of it saddened me, and I now better understood some of those comments made in the coffee shop. The place shrieked *abandoned.* Trees and shrubs, now overgrown, encroached on the building. Once lovingly tended garden beds displayed a tangle of weeds.

With a strange feeling of foreboding, I forced myself to climb the two stone steps and pound on the solid wooden door. No response, so I knocked again. Still no response and, judging by the look of the place, it shouldn't surprise me. It was a long time since anyone disturbed this building. Ignoring a rising feeling of discomfort, I fought my way along the side of the building. I don't know what I expected to find, but it was unlikely anyone was inside. Something eerie about being around this house was making me feel most uncomfortable.

Back at the front door, I gave it another half-hearted thumping, and received the same response as before. Given my feeling of foreboding, it's probably just as well no one came to the door. More than likely, I would have died of fright if someone opened it after I successfully convinced myself nobody was home. Intending to go back to my car, I stopped a few metres out front of the house and turned around for another look at the place. It really was a sad sight, and yet I could see how once it was a lovely home. Time to go, I told myself ... time to find Ned Edwards if he is about. It was then I noticed I was not alone.

In the adjoining paddock, a man stood watching. When I looked at him, he began raking, or chipping, or doing whatever he wanted me to think was his reason for being there. He made it clear he didn't want me to know he was watching me. Still, I needed to ask someone about where to find Ned Edwards … and he just might turn out to be the man himself. After all, I was told Ned Edwards had the adjoining farm – and the bloke was in a paddock of the adjoining farm.

Taking my time, I strolled back to my car and clambered in. The man still stood where I first saw him. Before I saw him watching me, I had intended to drive up to the house on the next farm to ask for directions to Ned's place. Now, there was a change of plan. Instead, I drove about fifty metres along the side of the road and parked again. A track ran along a narrow headland between the boundary fences of the two farms. It might be a bit bold to simply turn onto the track and drive along it to reach the man.

Locking the car behind me, I set off on foot along the

headland. Driving over it would have been easier going. It was mown, but the stubble hid the many ruts and rocks I had to contend with. My trek, while short, almost exhausted me. …Might also be a wake-up call to do something about my lack of fitness these days.

As I neared the man, the little voice in my head warned *this might not go well.* Judging by the man's aggressive stance, I was inclined to agree with it. What the hell … I'd come this far and almost wrecked an ankle in the process. I might as well ask the question and see what happens.

"Good morning; apologies for interrupting your work, but I wonder if you might give me directions to Ned Edwards' farm."

"What would you be wanting with Ned Edwards?"

"Ah well, the woman at the coffee shop said Mr Edwards might be the right person to talk to about the Blaine property."

"What's your interest? Are you thinking of buying it."

"No, I… Is it for sale?"

"Not that I'm aware. If you're not looking to buy, why are you interested? You're not one of those journalists people are you?" I shook my head as I tried to think of a suitable reply. "So, why are you here … and why were you prowling about next door?"

"Is there an easier way to have this conversation? Yelling at each other while we stand several metres apart doesn't seem the best way to go about it."

He shrugged and came over to lean on his fence. "I'm not suggesting I have anything to say to you mind, but you never know what some straight answers might achieve."

Chapter 4

A truce was declared. I drove Ned to his house and we settled ourselves in squatter's chairs on his verandah. He opened a new chapter in our dialogue. "I fear we got off to a confusing start back there. Perhaps we should start again. And, we could begin with you telling me why you are here asking questions."

While his questions hadn't changed, his tone and demeanour had. He was still 'abrupt and no nonsense', but I detected a curiosity in him now. "I haven't been up this way in a lot of years but, in coming here today, I hoped to gain an insight into who Thomas Blaine was and what his life was like. When his murder was brought to my attention recently, I realised I didn't know anything about the incident, or about Thomas or his family. Can you tell me about his family?"

"Within reason, I suppose. I'm not one to gossip. Why don't you ask me what you want to know, and I'll work out if I have anything to tell you."

That seemed as good as it was going to be, and it promised to be better than nothing. That little voice in my head was at it again. This time counselling me to lead in gently – so I did. "I wanted to find out about Thomas' family. Did he have a wife; a family?"

"Aye, he was married. Bought the farm next door just before he married, and the two of them started doing the place up. His wife, Valerie, worked with him to make the old church into a home, and to help him get the farm up and running. Lovely couple; you couldn't ask for better neighbours."

He became silent. I let him dwell on his memories for a few moments before nudging him back to the here and now. "I believe they had a child, a daughter."

"Lucy… She was a beautiful little girl, and the apple of her parents' eyes. Her mother's death hit her hard – hit the both of them hard."

"Mrs Blaine, Valerie, died?" He gave a brief nod. "How old was Lucy at the time?"

"Oh, now you're asking. I'd say she was about ten years old, give or take a bit maybe. She was so brave. Such a young person and yet she seemed more worried about her father and how he was coping then with their own grief. I can't describe Lucy. She was special, one-of-a-kind. You'd have to know her to understand."

"What happened to the family after Valerie's death? How did Thomas and Lucy manage?"

"That pair were so close. He adored his daughter, and I think she idolised him. He did his best to bring her up on his own. But, a man on his own with a farm to run and every-thing else to take care of… It was too much for him. After a couple of years, he remarried. Took us all by surprise it did. People reckoned he made a mistake. What he needed was a housekeeper type person, but he went ahead and married the silly twit."

"Am I to understand the community didn't think much of the new wife?"

"You could say that. She didn't get on with people. That's not a crime, but there was something about her. I found her hard and a bit trashy-like. I've heard others describe her as cheap, but I don't know it that's an accurate description. Anyway, apart from all that, I don't think anyone in the community could forgive her for the way she treated that child."

"For the way she treated Lucy, you mean?"

"Argh, none of us really knew what went on, but it was plain to everyone, the girl was unhappy. It just about broke the hearts of anyone who knew the family to see young Lucy so miserable. To make matters worse, a few months after they married another child came along; a daughter. As I said, none of us really knew what was going on in that family, but it was fairly obvious the woman wanted rid of Lucy."

"That's a harsh assessment for outsiders to make. It might be that Lucy became a typical rebellious teenage girl."

"No, it was more than that. Any time the woman was with a group at some social gathering, she asked about good boarding schools in the area, and complained about the long days involved for local kids attending the nearest high school. No, she was doing her best to get rid of Lucy."

"If Lucy and her father were so close, I find it hard to believe he went along with sending her to boarding school. After she lost her mother, I imagined he'd be reluctant to be separated from Lucy."

"Look, I'm sorry, but I have an appointment to meet with my accountant in town this afternoon. I have to get going or I will be late. I don't doubt you have loads more questions, but they will have to wait for another time."

"That's okay. I don't want to hold you up. As you say, the rest of my questions can wait for another day."

"Thanks, but I will tell you this before you leave. Tom wasn't too keen. A couple of times, I heard him argue that other kids from around here managed the long days involved in attending high school, and Lucy was no different from the others. He said it a bit more forcefully than that. It was clear he didn't want Lucy to go away to school. But, in the end, that woman won. She got her own way. I don't remember ever seeing Lucy again after the day she boarded the train for boarding school. There she was, a slip of a girl, stony-faced like that boulder over there, but not a tear in sight. I think she was trying not to make a fuss to avoid upsetting her father. Anyway, as I said, I don't remember her ever coming back to Tanwood after that day."

"She didn't … not until I met her in Millhaven two days ago." He fought his response well, but I saw his jaw sag slightly. For the next few seconds, his hard, searching gaze, as he dealt with my bombshell, had me feeling a little uncomfortable … and I waited for whatever might come next. I needed to move things along, so I announced, "Okay Ned, I'll go now so you can be on your way. Here's my card. If you ever want to talk, give me a call or, if you're in town, drop by my office. If I'm there, I'll shout you a coffee."

Then, I was at my car. As I opened the door, he called after me. "I don't know how long I'll be tied up with the accountant, but it shouldn't be long. If there's time, I might call at your office."

"As I said, I'll shout you a coffee." Our meeting was over.

My head spun with information overload as I drove back to town. For a brief moment, I thought of returning to the coffee shop for lunch, but I didn't want to talk there anymore today. If I returned to the coffee shop, there would be questions about what happened after I left before. The only person I wanted further conversation with was Ned, and I hoped his accountant didn't detain him too long this afternoon.

The lunchtime rush was over by the time I arrived at my office building. There was little left to choose from, so I settled for an unexciting looking sandwich from the dregs of the deli's offerings and took it up to my office. With my mind so preoccupied, the sandwich and coffee could have been cardboard and pond water for all the attention I gave them. Then, it was time to commit to paper all I learnt this morning, but there was one thing I wanted to do first.

After a spot of not too complicated arithmetic, I arrived at a date. Lucy was now aged twenty-one and a half, or thereabouts. I brought up the online version of the local newspapers and flipped back to the approximate date of her birth. She didn't appear in the pages of baby photos published every week but, after a bit of scratching around in the 'Notices' pages, there it was. The birth of Lucy Adele Blain, daughter of Thomas and Valerie, was announced. Bugger! I had hoped it would give me Valerie's maiden name. So, more complicated arithmetic required to arrive at a date. It was only a guess, but I felt sure Lucy was conceived not too long after her parents were married.

From about nine months before Lucy's birth, I started working my way back through the copies week by week, as I searched for anything relating to the marriage of Thomas and Valerie. After searching the notices and social jottings pages back about eight months, my instinct kicked in.

It was possible the couple had been married for some time before Lucy came along, but somehow I didn't think so. Maybe I missed something on my way through. I went back through the papers towards Lucy's birth notice, slower and more meticulous this time. I let out a yelp. "There it is."

While it wasn't what I expected to find, it told me all I needed to know. There, in the Notices section, were three entries extending best wishes to Thomas Blaine and Valerie Telford being married on Saturday. The names of those sending the good wishes didn't mean anything to me. None of those had Blaine or Telford surnames, and one notice only had a string of given names attached to it.

"Telford eh…? What's that all about?" I asked my empty office. At some point during her short life, Lucy took her mother's maiden name. There has to be a story in that, and I don't doubt it has something to do with the ugly stepmother. Was Thomas involved, or was it of Lucy's own choosing. If it's the latter, then it probably happened sometime after she was eighteen and had attained her majority. Maybe she changed it soon after Thomas's death. Regardless, there's a story behind the name change, and I intend to ferret it out at my meeting with Lucy tomorrow.

The rest of the afternoon was to be spent updating my case file with the information gathered this morning. That plan changed, when Ned Edwards arrived carrying a box containing two mini cheesecakes. I slammed the coffee machine into action as soon he showed me what was in the box. A few minutes later, we were settled in my lounge chairs and enjoying coffee and cheese cake.

I couldn't help wonder if Ned would have come to my office this afternoon if I hadn't mentioned meeting Lucy in Millhaven two days ago. Perhaps I'm being sceptical, but I feel I received 'abridged' information this morning. It's true I gained a lot from Ned and, once he got going, he seemed happy to chat, but I felt I was being given 'selective' facts. Even when mentioning the second Mrs Blaine, he never once referred to her by name. I had no doubt he disapproved of everything about the woman. My gut told me there was something more.

It was clear Ned was keen to resume this morning's conversation. Before I was halfway through my cheesecake he asked, "Will you be seeing Lucy again? Is she still here in Millhaven?"

"Ye-es, we made tentative arrangements for another meeting after I looked into the matter of her father's death. It was a bit loose-ended, as I didn't know how long it might take me, or how difficult it would be to familiarise myself with the circumstances surrounding the death. I don't know if she plans spending time until our next meeting here in Millhaven or somewhere else."

My response disappointed him. It was right to be cautious in what I said. I suspected he might be angling to meet Lucy while she was here. That needs to be Lucy's decision, and not one engineered by Ned. Still, being vague about what Lucy was doing, allowed me to pose my next questions in a less direct manner.

"Ned, it occurs to me, the next time I talk to Lucy – whenever that is – she might ask questions about her father's old Kirk Michael Farm. Of course, she might not be interested. If she hasn't returned for so many years, perhaps she is not interested. Nevertheless, if she does ask about the property, what can I tell her. I'm not sure how she'll react if I describe the state of the place as I saw it today."

"You might be right. Maybe she no longer has any interest in anything to do with Tanwood. If she does, describing the place as it is today might break her heart. I couldn't stand the thought of it, not after all she's been through."

"So… Why is it in the state it's in? It looks completely abandoned. What's the story?"

"Well, it's a bit of a mystery to everyone at Tanwood. We don't know what happened or why, but the place is abandoned. It's been deserted for… Oh, it must be more than a couple of years now."

"What happened to the place after Thomas' death? I mean, immediately after his death. If it's been abandoned only for about two years, and Thomas has been dead for more than three years, what happened during the intervening period?"

"The short answer is, very little happened. That woman and her daughter stayed on all right, but nothing happened as far as the farm was concerned. It was let run down to nothing. And, I think, for a few months after Tom's death, she and the daughter were often away from the place. I don't know what was going on. I suppose it was more a case of just noticing no one was around; no one coming or going, and no lights on at night."

"I assume the farm was left to the wife, and she and her daughter continued to live there – albeit after a fashion –until the place was abandoned. I guess the next question is, what happened for them to abandon the place? Even if she wasn't deriving any income from the farm, at least they had a roof over their heads."

"…Probably had something to do with the lover. That might not be the case, but everyone thought so at the time."

"What's this about a lover? That sounds like it might have a major impact on the story."

"Argh, I don't know he's even worth discussing. He was hanging around even before Tom died. I don't know whether Tom thought anything was going on or not. Everybody else thought there was. Anyway, if Tom was concerned about it, he didn't do anything about the bloke – didn't try to get rid of him. The bloke just continued to be here. Then, when Tom was found dead, it was only natural, the bloke was seen as a likely suspect. Everyone had him pegged as the culprit. Even the police thought he was guilty for quite a while but, in the end, no one was charged with the murder."

"I don't know what to think. The wife and/or the lover must have very thick hides for him to move in and live in Tom's house so soon after the murder. They must have been aware how the community felt about him. You said earlier today she didn't get on well with anyone. So, she was already unpopular with the community. Still, I suppose it was better than having no one running the farm. What happened after he moved in?"

"That's a laugh. …Him, do something about running the farm! All I ever saw him do was maybe cut a bit of grass every now and then. All the stock was gone. No crops were planted. The farm wasn't bringing in any income. I don't know what they survived on. Maybe Tom left her a pile of cash. I don't know but, if you think about it, there is a bit of a mystery involved … and I don't just mean the mystery surrounding Tom's death."

"Yeah, we aren't short on mystery. Just as the police were, I think we are a bit short on evidence; evidence to help make sense of at least some of the mystery. Did the lover have a job? Maybe they were living off his income."

"If he had a job, he would have to work. Work appeared to be something he was allergic to – or at least not something he was fond of. There was some story doing the rounds about his working at one of the mines. He was supposed to be on one of those funny rosters where they work so many days and then have the next so many days off. That was before he moved into Tom's house. After that, I never saw anything to suggest he was gainfully employed. I did wonder whether the story about working at a mine was just that: a story. A story put about by the pair of them as a cover for the amount of time he spent hanging around in Tanwood."

"It's plain your opinion of the man hasn't mellowed with time. Think back to the time when you first noticed no one around at the farm any longer." Ned appeared to give it some thought before nodding to indicate he had located the appropriate memory. "Did anything happen just prior to that? I mean, was there any incident which might have caused them to leave – perhaps a run-in with a neighbour, or someone else in the community?"

"Nothing occurred that I'm aware of and, if something like that happened, we all would hear about it."

He was right. That's one of the hallmarks of small rural communities: everyone knows everything about everybody. "Do we know the contents of Tom's will?" Ned gave me an indignant look. I knew he was about to protest the question, so I jumped in to explain before he did. "What I'm asking is whether the farm was left to his wife?"

"No idea, I'm sorry. My late wife and I were witnesses when Tom signed his will, but we didn't see its contents. It would have been improper for us to know what was in it."

My phone rang causing a temporary lull in proceedings. It was Ben Richards to tell me he would pick up something to bring for dinner tonight. I checked the time. It was after five o'clock already. Ned saw me check the time, and bounded up out of his chair. As soon as Ben's call ended, Ned picked up our coffee mugs and carried them across to my kitchenette.

"I didn't realise it was so late. I had better be on my way," he said. I assured him I kept my own hours and the time didn't matter. "Not to you perhaps," he replied, "but I have animals to feed when I get home, and I would prefer to do it while some daylight remains."

As I walked Ned to the door, we agreed we would keep in touch and, should he remember anything significant in the meantime, he would call me. Then he was gone, and I had a heap more information to add to my case file before going home to dinner with Ben.

Chapter 5

In my city office early this morning tidying up my Blaine case notes before meeting Lucy Telford at nine o'clock. Nine o'clock came and went. Lucy didn't. Her no-show worried me. I had her pegged as someone with the manners to call if she didn't intend keeping an appointment. Tried telling myself there were plenty of reasons why she didn't make the meeting, but I didn't manage to convince myself about any of them.

Still half confident I would hear from her, I continued with my research. By lunchtime, I'd run out of interest. Much of the stuff I looked at this morning went over old ground. So, I wasted another half a day researching something which might never become a case. Frustration and anger levels were rising.

After a long, leisurely lunch with today's newspaper, I spent time dealing with yesterday's emails and messages. There were no potential new exciting cases in any of them. Three o'clock saw me with nothing of any consequence to be going on with. I toyed with the idea of going home, but decided to have a coffee before I left. Why rush home to deal with overdue domestic chores when I can put my feet up on the desk and enjoy a coffee instead?

As I stood beside the coffee machine waiting for it to finish doing its thing, Lucy Telford occupied my mind. How much did she know about her father's death? How much did she know about what life was like on the family farm during all those years she was away from the place? If the answer to any of that is *not much,* anything I tell her might be treading on sensitive ground.

My first task, therefore, needs to be establishing what she knows and how authentic it might be. Did father and daughter maintain contact during Lucy's absence from Tanwood? Somehow, I doubted it. If the new wife was so anti-Lucy, it's unlikely she would condone continued contact between Thomas and his daughter. A rogue idea slid in from left field; one of those 'what-if' lightbulb moments.

What if Thomas set up an arrangement with the local postmistress for certain mail addressed to him to be kept back for personal collection rather than having it delivered to the farm with everything else? It is possible Thomas wrote secret letters to Lucy, posting them whenever he happened to visit the store. Nah, that doesn't gel. If that were the case, the moment letters from Thomas stopped arriving, Lucy would know something was amiss at home. But, she told me some time elapsed after Thomas' death before she knew about it.

"Why am I wasting my time even thinking about this?" I asked aloud as I put my coffee down on the desk. I am determined not to waste any more time on this 'case' until, and unless, I hear from Lucy. I was beginning to kick myself about not collecting better contact details from her, and not having spent time explaining my pricing structure to her. If her lack of contact continues, I told myself, I will be sending her an invoice for the work done so far on her behalf.

With coffee drunk and mug rinsed, I picked up my bag and started for the door. That's when the phone rang. After a moment of indecision about whether to answer it or not, I returned to the desk and snatched up the phone.

"Miss Whittington, this is Lucy – Lucy Telford. I'm so sorry about missing my appointment this morning but, when I went to my car, it wouldn't start. It turns out it was something more technical than a flat battery. At first, the mechanic suggested the battery was the problem, and they'd have me on the road again within a half-hour. If that were the case, I would still have made the appointment on time. When the car still wouldn't start, they looked for something else. They've just finished fixing the thing. I know it's too late to come to see you today and tomorrow is the weekend. I wouldn't expect you to work on the weekend, but I do want to see you. Please, may I have another appointment?"

On my part, scepticism reigned supreme. My initial temptation was to refuse another appointment. Common sense kicked in and, while I didn't entirely believe her story, there was still a good deal of the afternoon left. "It's possible for me to be in my office until six o'clock this evening. If you come now, I could see you this afternoon."

"Oh, I didn't say, did I? I'm not in Millhaven. The thought of hanging around Millhaven for a few days with nothing to do left me cold. So, I decided to spend the time at the new beach resort place on the north coast. I could leave here now, but I wouldn't be in Millhaven until after five o'clock at the earliest. Do you still want me to come this evening?"

"No, that's not the best option for either of us. Let's leave it until nine o'clock on Monday morning. I don't know how long our meeting might last but I don't want it curtailed by time constraints. How does Monday suit you?"

"Thank you, thank you. It suits me fine. I'll see you then."

Tempted as I was to threaten to send an invoice if she reneged on the appointment, I decided to make nice instead and didn't mention it. The way things worked out today, it looks as though I will have a weekend to myself. With no ongoing cases, and not being able to do much more on the Blaine murder until I speak to Lucy, it should be a leisurely weekend. Feeling pleased with the situation, I again picked up my bag, and made it out of the office without further hindrance.

As I turned onto my driveway, Emily called. "I tried your office but you've finished early today. If you're home tonight, could I call round to catch up on what's happened with the Blaine case?"

"Come over and have dinner. I've no idea what we'll be having. I haven't heard from Ben today, so I don't know if he's coming or what's on the menu. I've just arrived home, so come over when you're ready." About half an hour later Emily walked in carrying a bottle of wine and a shopping bag loaded with various nibbles to sustain us until dinnertime. We took our drinks out onto the deck to watch the sunset.

"Now, come on, don't keep me in suspense. What have you found out about Thomas Blaine's murder? The more I think about it the more intrigued I become. I wouldn't mind taking a couple of days off to work on this one with you. It promises to be interesting."

"I'm not sure it's even a case yet. I have been gathering background information, but Lucy didn't appear for her nine o'clock appointment this morning. She called just before I left the office this afternoon and I gave her a new appointment for Monday morning. I have hit a brick wall. Without more details or clues from Lucy, there isn't much more I can do. It's frustrating to think I can't do anything over the weekend, but that seems how it will be."

"Did you get a chance to ask Ben about looking at the police investigation files?"

"No, there hasn't been an opportunity to broach the subject."

"If he comes for dinner tonight, I think we should try to engineer an opportunity. It could be as simple as my asking you how your murder investigation is going. That should be enough to stir his curiosity but, if it's not, we could make sure the resultant conversation is sufficiently obtuse to give us what we want."

About an hour later, the question of whether Ben was coming to dinner was answered. He arrived carrying something large in a plastic shopping bag. "Work took me down to the fishermen's mooring area this afternoon. I've only just left there. I hope you haven't prepared anything for dinner. They were unloading the catch and I couldn't resist this fellow. I thought we might bake him whole. What do you think?" He unwrapped his parcel and, beaming with pride, held up an enormous fish.

"We could bake it on the barbecue," I suggested. "There's more than enough of it to feed the three of us. Let's start it cooking or we will be waiting all night to eat it."

Several leaves from the neighbour's banana tree hanging over the fence were sacrificed in the interests of our Epicurean delight. With all of us involved, in no time the fish was stuffed, wrapped in the banana leaves, slapped on the grill and the hood closed. "We should test it after about half an hour. That might be long enough to bake a fish its size."

Emily and I prepared a salad and set it aside in readiness. Then, accompanied by a selection of nibbles, we all adjourned to the deck again. At the first lull in conversation, Emily dropped me a wink, before initiating our plan. "So, Sonny, how is your new murder investigation going? From the little I know, it sounded like it would be a full-on job."

Ben didn't comment, so I played along. "Not a lot to tell so far. Progress is slow, mainly due to a lack of evidence. I'm sure I would have gained worthwhile information if my scheduled interview for today had happened. Still, I have another interview scheduled for Monday. I might have a better handle on things after that."

Our gambit was paying off. We had Ben's attention, but he wasn't yet at the point of asking questions. Emily stoked the 'fire'. "I don't know how you will go with this one. I suppose we can only wait and see how it goes."

"What's this murder case you're investigating?" We had hooked our man. "Where did it happen? I haven't heard of any murders around here lately. Did it happen in Millhaven?"

"Hmm … More or less," I murmured thoughtfully, "in the Millhaven environs."

"Are you telling me there's been a murder and I don't know anything about it? I'm sure I don't have officers investigating any incident of that nature at the moment. So, how can it be that I don't know about it?"

"Well, I don't know whether you knew about it or not, but I'm inclined to think you probably don't know about it."

"Oh, that's very helpful. Now, would you like to try translating what that means, like who was murdered, when and where?"

"It happened up the valley at Tanwood. Thomas Blaine was murdered at home, but evidence is scarce."

"Yes, okay, but Tanwood is in my area, and I haven't heard about it. When did it occur?" Ben's tone was becoming sharp. I was exasperating him, and I was enjoying it too much to stop.

"Oh dear, well, I'm not really sure of the time or date … As far as I can make out, it was near enough to three and a half years ago." I leaned in close to him to deliver this 'important' information and put on my most solemn face.

Whether it was my performance or Ben's reaction that caused it, I'm not sure, but Emily dissolved into a fit of the giggles. Ben had a few words to say, none of which bear repeating. Then, after a quick check on the fish and flipping it over onto its other side, he asked for all the details of the murder. That didn't take long. After all, how much had I learned so far? But, in the interests of advancing our cause, I made frequent mention of a police investigation at the time, and speculated on their level of frustration at its not ending in a prosecution. Eventually our ploy paid off.

"I don't know anything about this case. Of course, I wouldn't, would I? I wasn't stationed here at the time it occurred. Nevertheless, I'm now curious about it. I think I might dig out the files tomorrow. If we have a cold case on the books, it wouldn't hurt for me to take a look at it."

"I can understand how frustrating it must have been for the investigating officers. I'm feeling more than a bit that way myself. I've a whole weekend ahead of me and I can't do anything more until I speak to my client again. I'm hoping whatever she can tell me allows me to progress my case.

In the meantime, it looks as though I'm going to have a wasted weekend." I knew I was laying it on a bit thick, but I was desperate to persuade Ben to offer – or for me to be in a position to ask for – a look at the police files.

There's only so much groundwork, so much prodding and prompting, can be done before it becomes overdone and wrecks everything. Concerned I had reached that point, I backed off. Ben also made no further comment, but I could almost hear his mind working at full speed as he went to check on the fish. Our dinner was ready. All the usual faffing about involved in dishing up food and settling down to eat took precedence over everything else.

Ben was quiet throughout the meal. A couple of times Emily glanced over at me and raised her eyebrows in question. She shared my concern at Ben's apparent withdrawal. As Emily and I cleared the table and carried everything back to the kitchen, I put my concern into words. "Ben is a touch too quiet. I hope I didn't 'overcook' our strategy to give me access to those police files."

"I don't think so. I admit, he did take a bit of prodding. But I think – or at least, I hope – he's quiet because his mind is preoccupied with what you told him about the case. We'll see how he goes over coffee. Perhaps we should play it the same way; stay quiet and see if he notices."

"Okay, that sounds like the way to go. We'll both say nothing while having coffee. Let's see if he asks what's wrong."

Heavy dew and a definite chill drifted in on the night air while Emily and I cleared away after dinner. We were still loading the dishwasher when Ben strolled in and announced, "It's becoming too bloody uncomfortable out there. I suggest we have coffee in the lounge. Does anyone else feel like a port with their coffee?" Both Emily and I raised our hands. "Good; I'll take the bottle and glasses through with me. You won't be much longer in here will you?"

A couple of minutes later, we were settled in our usual chairs in the lounge room with mugs of coffee and glasses of port beside us. Ben remained uncommunicative, preferring instead to stare at some indeterminate spot on the carpet. In the ensuing several minutes, Emily and I exchanged a couple of looks, but we stuck to our game plan. Neither of us spoke, but I was beginning to doubt its effectiveness. Ben didn't show any sign of having noticed the lack of conversation.

During our silent interlude, mugs and glasses were emptied. I had enough of playing that game. If conversation didn't resume, the others could leave. There were plenty of other things I could be doing instead of sitting here like someone half comatose. In a bid to bring things to a head, I bounced up out of my chair. "Anyone want a refill; more coffee or port?"

Emily uncurled her legs and stretched them. "No thanks. I think I'll head home. There's not much on TV these nights but, whatever I can find, will be better than sitting here in this morgue."

"Eh … It's still early. What you mean by that anyway?" Ben demanded and then continued before anyone could answer. "What's gotten into you tonight, Emily? It's not like you to make such a comment."

"Well Ben, it's your vow of silence, or whatever has made you lose the power of speech that's the problem." As she delivered her barb, Emily made a show of picking up her mug and glass and flouncing off to the kitchen.

Ben's stunned look when he turned to me was almost comical. "What got into her? Why is she comparing our company to that of a morgue?"

"I'm inclined to agree with her. It's a bit like sitting in a morgue. All through dinner, and while we've been in here, you've hardly said two words. We've tried respecting your need for silence, but both of us are over it. I understand why Emily wants to go home. Ben, I'm happy for you to sit there in silence for as long as you like but, as soon as Emily leaves,

I'm going to find something else to fill in the rest of my evening ... Something more productive than sitting here in deafening silence."

"Oh…"

"Is that all you have to say? No explanation...? If you find us so boring, perhaps you should go home too."

"I never said I found you boring. I don't know what you both are on about. Okay, maybe I haven't said much, but it's not because I found your company boring. I've been thinking. For God's sake, sit down, Emily, and stop carrying on like a prima donna. If you want to blame someone for what's happened, then blame Sonny. It's her fault."

"What? How can it be *my fault?* What did I do?"

"If you hadn't told me about your current case, and alerted me to the fact I had a more than three years old cold case, I wouldn't have spent the evening thinking about it. Now, how about the two of you stop acting like a pair of sulky four-year-olds and tell me what you know about this murder Sonny is investigating?"

Emily resumed her seat. I took the hint. "This could develop into a long conversation. Maybe we need fresh coffee to help it flow." I marched to the kitchen and stirred the coffee machine to life again. As I settled back into my chair, Ben refilled our glasses. With the interruption dealt with, Ben was in a more talkative mood.

"Sonny, the thing intriguing me about your new case is why someone became interested in what happened so long after the event. To be blunt, I'm surprised you've taken on a case with such little prospect of a successful outcome. If the police investigation didn't result in a prosecution, after so much time has elapsed, what are your chances of achieving a different outcome? Anyway, what have you discovered so far?"

"To correct you on a couple of points, the person is not my client; not yet anyway. But, I suspect after our next meeting, she will be."

In anticipation, Ben and Emily perched on the front of their seats as I sorted out in my mind how to answer the inevitable barrage of questions to come.

Chapter 6

Ben cleared his throat and the question and answer session began. I knew he would launch into a raft of questions after the little I told him. So far, this case was unlike how I usually work, so I jumped in before he could ask his first question.

"The reason I didn't accept the case at the outset was because I knew nothing about the murder. I think I was overseas when it happened. Yes, it was strange to have someone interested in the crime after so long, especially when they knew the police investigation drew a blank. So many things were hard to understand. I delayed accepting the case until I familiarised myself with crime, and was in a position to judge whether I wanted to take on the investigation or not. That occupied most of my last three days without bringing me any closer to understanding what happened."

"You must be losing your touch," Ben quipped. "Where have you looked?"

"Media coverage seemed the best place to begin, so Emily and I searched everything we could find. It wasn't the most enlightening exercise."

"I agree," Emily said. "We found a bit of stuff. Not as much as I expected. I imagined a murder up the valley would keep at least the local media busy for ages. It wasn't like that. There was so little, we wondered if the police imposed a media blackout or embargoed the story."

Ben shook his head and gave Emily a dismissive look. Then he turned to me. I knew he expected me to refute Emily's comments. "Emily is right, Ben. There wasn't the level of coverage I expected. More surprising perhaps was the lack of details in any there was: a man, alone at his place of residence at Tanwood at the time, was shot and the police were investigating. Every mention of the crime we found carried the same basic story. You see why we thought there was a clamp down imposed on the media?"

"I doubt there would be and, if there were, it's likely only the locals complied. My experience is the interstate media isn't averse to reporting more details than they are supposed to in such situations. Their approach seems to be, if it didn't happen in their backyard, no one would care what they reported. So, apart from that, what have you found?"

"Not a lot… When I drew a blank with the media coverage, I decided to drive to Tanwood."

"What did you hope to gain there? Don't tell me you were going to listen to gossip and rumour. You must be desperate."

"No, that's not why I visited Tanwood, but you shouldn't discount local sources. The gossip and rumours developed by locals about happenings in their community usually have a grain of truth – some reflection of fact – as their basis. It's a case of going through all you collect to sort out what's worthwhile. Often, it is possible to glean enough from you hear to point you in the right direction for the next stage of your research."

"If you didn't go there to collect yarns about what happened, why did you drive all that way?"

"I hadn't seen Tanwood in at least ten years. I wanted to get a feel for the place and its community, and I hoped to see the site of the crime. Sometimes you pick up vibes –maybe it's the look of the location – which suggest a line of enquiry."

"…And did the spirits suggest anything to you?"

"If continue like this, I won't discuss it with you. What's it going to be?"

"Argh, I'm sorry. Just ignore me. I'm feeling a bit… Can we start again? Please tell me what you've managed to uncover."

"Okay … Truce … So far, my efforts were on researching the backgrounds of the people involved. There's no better way of finding out about the people, and all their inherent idiosyncrasies, than to ask the locals who knew them. One local helped me by drawing me a map to the crime scene. I found the place. It's an old church converted to a residence more than twenty years ago."

"How did the present residents react to your poking about their property?"

"It wasn't an issue. Nobody was there. I wouldn't mind a look inside the place. From the little I saw of it, I think it became quite a nice home. Nobody was home, but I did chat to a neighbour. I'm hoping to talk further to him in the coming days. As we'd just met, I didn't press him about the murder itself, focusing instead on the people who were his neighbours and what they were like. Exploring that angle further is likely to produce useful information."

"Useful how…?" Emily said. "I'm sorry, Sonny, but I don't see how discussing people's personalities might help solve a crime … unless … Oh, wait a minute… Such an approach might work if it uncovered something suggesting a possible motive for the crime. So, after talking to the locals, who do you now fancy as the murderer?"

"No one… I still don't have details of how the man was murdered, or the evidence discovered by police. Worse still, I doubt my potential client knows more than I do about it. I suspect anything worth knowing about the crime is locked up in those police files. And that's another good reason why I'm undecided about taking the case. Without at least as much as is in those police files, I have no hope of providing the client with the outcome she requires."

"And you hate not being able to solve a case," Ben murmured. "I can relate to that feeling. I don't know how hard it will be to ferret out those files, but I intend looking for them tomorrow. Will you be around for the weekend?" I nodded. "Good. If I find the files, I'll give you a call. Maybe two fresh pairs of eyes might see something others didn't, but I wouldn't bet on it."

Emily dropped me a wink before announcing she felt tired and, as she had an early start at work tomorrow, she needed an early night. Ben said he too might try to catch up on some sleep. It wasn't quite ten o'clock when I found myself alone.

For a few moments, I thought I might spend a couple of hours in my office. Then I remembered my research had hit a brick wall. I too opted for an early night. My last thoughts were about those police files Ben would look for tomorrow – and how his comments suggested I would be allowed to examine them.

*****

With nothing better to do today, I threw myself into domestic chores. Over the past couple of months, new cases were overwhelming. Dealing with them all in a timely manner meant working long hours. I wasn't complaining. That's how I like it to be. The unfortunate downside is the domestic aspect of life is overlooked. I had a mountain of laundry begging for attention. At night, I kept the lights in the living area dimmed so the dust covering everything wasn't so obvious.

By lunchtime, the pursuit of domestic purity had lost its appeal. The weekend newspaper on the breakfast bar kept sending me 'come-hither' calls. I hadn't even stopped for coffee this morning. To hell with all this 'cleanliness is next to godliness' nonsense. I'm starving, and I'm sure there is stuff in the newspaper requiring my attention.

With the newspaper tucked under my arm, I took my sandwich and coffee through to the lounge room. Curled up in my chair with the paper, I settled in for what I hoped would be an indulgent couple of hours of blissful solitude. That's when the call came.

"You are not in your city office, so I assume you are not working today. Do you feel like driving into town?"

Ben had my attention. His wanting me to drive into my city office meant only one thing: he had found the Blaine murder investigation files. "I'll jump in my car right now. Should I go to my office, or do you want to meet elsewhere?"

He assured me my office would be fine. I grabbed my bag, checked its contents, and dashed out to my car. My pulse raced all the way. As I sat at the last set of lights before turning onto my street, a sobering thought occurred to me. Maybe I was getting my hopes up in vain. If the police couldn't find enough evidence for a prosecution, there might not be much useful in the files.

I consoled myself with the thought they should at least provide a detailed picture of what occurred at Tanwood. Over the last couple of days, I developed doubts about how much more information Lucy might be able to provide. She wasn't here at the time of the murder and hadn't been back to the district until a few days ago. How could she gain an insight into, and gather details of, what happened? She couldn't.

Unless a Tanwood local with insider knowledge of the incident at Kirk Michael provided information – someone like Ned Edwards – Lucy's only source would be the same media details as I accessed. If the latter is the case, it's unlikely Lucy can provide much, if anything, to progress my case. As I let myself into the building and ran up the stairs, all my hopes were pinned on those police files I assumed Ben was bringing to my office.

Five minutes later, I was filling the coffee machine when he called to say he was on his way. I presented him with a coffee as soon as he arrived. Then, we took our places at my desk and he dumped a stack of files on one end of it. After a couple of sips of coffee, Ben took charge.

"Right, this is how I thought we might do this. We each take a file and go through it, making notes of any salient points as we go. Then, before starting on another file, we compare notes. How does that sound?"

"Sounds okay, but there is one thing I'm not sure about. What I consider a salient point might not interest you. Details I'm hoping to extract from these files might differ from those you are looking for."

"What are you on about? We are both trying to figure out why Thomas Blaine was murdered and by whom, aren't we?" I shrugged and nodded. "Right; then the same information is of interest to both of us. Now, shall we stop wasting time and get on with it? Just make a note of anything and everything that grabs your attention. Are we right to go now?"

There was no point in arguing. My only response was to grab the top file and slap it on the desk in front of me. I had to admit there was merit in his suggested approach. Without further ado, I pulled my pad closer, placed my pencil on it in readiness, and read the first document in the file.

Time meant nothing. The contents of the file were fascinating, while perhaps not as helpful as I hoped. Nevertheless, I was lost in the world of crime scene investigation as I worked my way through the file page by page. I was disappointed the folder contained no photos but, thinking about it later, it made sense. The aspects of the case covered by the documents in this file require no photographs. Having read the last document, I closed the folder and set it to one side … and reached for the next file from the stack.

"Hang on a minute. That's not how this is supposed to work. We are to compare notes when we've completed a folder, and before we start a new one. Give me two seconds to complete this last document. Then we will compare notes."

I glanced at the clock. It took me nearly two hours to finish that one file. How long will it take to work our way through the whole stack? I interrupted Ben's reading of his last document. "Shall I make us a coffee while you finish that file?"

"Good idea; you don't happen to have something to go with it do you?"

"Like what for instance?"

"Oh, I don't know. A biscuit, or piece of cake, might be nice."

"Chance would be a fine thing. I don't run to such extravagances. But, I agree. Something with our coffee would be nice."

That was all the encouragement Ben needed. "Okay you get on with the coffee while I dash to that little shop next door. Hopefully they'll still have something worth eating at this hour on Saturday afternoon."

The small lemon meringue tarts he brought back went down well and were just the sustenance needed to keep us going. Comparing notes at the end of each folder took longer than I expected, but was worth every minute of it. It was almost six o'clock when we called a halt to proceedings. Ben suggested he could duck out for something for us to have for dinner if I wanted to work on after we had eaten. After some discussion, it was clear neither of us wanted to work on tonight. We agreed to regroup at my house at about 7.30 for pasta. The files and the pile of photocopies I accumulated over the afternoon were locked in my safe for the night.

Ben perched on a stool at the breakfast bar while I finished putting together our fettucine carbonara. What little conversation we had was stilted. We were halfway through dinner – and a glass or two of wine – before conversation again flowed freely, but without one mention of the files we worked on this afternoon. We agreed to pick up from where we left off with the files at eight o'clock tomorrow morning. It was a little after nine o'clock when I waved Ben off before grabbing a coffee on my way through the kitchen to my office.

For the next two hours I typed and organised this afternoon's notes before falling into bed a bit short of midnight.

*****

This morning seemed to arrive much sooner than I preferred, but there was no time to protest about it. I needed to be at my office in town before eight o'clock to let Ben in when he arrived. On my way into the city, I assessed how valuable or otherwise the work we did yesterday might be towards progressing my investigation. I had no clear opinion by the time I reached my office. Wait until you know the whole story, I told myself as I climbed the stairs. Yesterday's files contained a lot of interesting stuff, but I wasn't sure any of it provided clear indication of the direction in which to take my investigation.

Both Ben and I heaved a sigh of relief and slumped back in our chairs as we closed the last of the folders. After being hard at it all morning but, if our last session of discussing our notes didn't drag on too long, we might be finished with the police files by lunchtime. In the event, it was just after one o'clock by the time we had everything wrapped up and Ben was on his way back to the police precinct to return the files to from whence they came.

While returning my office to normal, I debated whether to work on for a while or go home. As I dried and put the coffee mugs back in the cupboard, I decided. I was going home to do nothing for the rest of the day. At least, that was my intention when I left my office, and it remained so when I arrived home ... but that changed while eating a sandwich and attempting to read the weekend paper out on the deck. With Lucy coming to see me at nine o'clock tomorrow morning, I needed to know more about her father's murder by then.

A massive amount of information accumulated over the weekend needed collating before it told a coherent story. So much for the weekend paper…! I plonked the newspaper and my plate on the breakfast bar as I trudged through the kitchen to my office. Working on the files over the two days left me brain-dead, so it was back to the kitchen for coffee to help stimulate my brain before attacking the task in hand.

The remainder of the afternoon was lost in a haze of words and sheets of paper. I was thankful nobody called and nobody came to dinner. By the time I wandered out to the kitchen at about eight o'clock, I had collated the information in my case file into one – albeit brief – crime timeline. While I felt better informed about Thomas Blaine's death, I was no wiser about how it happened.

As I lay in bed willing sleep to come to keep me company, Lucy and my meeting with her in the morning occupied my mind. If, as I now thought might be the case, Lucy knew few details of what happened to her father or, more importantly, subsequent happenings at Kirk Michael Farm, my conversation with her might need to be considerate and gentle.

Chapter 7

Over breakfast, I scanned m Thomas Blaine murder timeline created from information in the police files. It was a series of facts rather than a story. Being brief, it didn't take long to read. My breakfast doesn't take long either, and I was soon another vehicle among the early morning traffic heading into the city.

After filling the coffee machine in readiness, my first task was to sit and think about how to handle my meeting with Lucy. The top page of the folder on my desk was my new timeline. As I read it again, questions screamed at me from every line. I scribbled them as close to their respective facts as possible wherever I could. There was nothing more I could do. I checked the time. It was a couple of minutes before nine o'clock.

"Two minutes of anxious waiting to see if Lucy shows up today," I told the universe. I had no sooner uttered the statement than there was a knock on my door. I managed not to heave a sigh of relief as the door opened a little and Lucy stuck her head around it.

"Is it all right for me to come in?" She looked nervous. Maybe it was a good sign.

"Come in, and take a seat at the desk with me. Would you like a coffee?" The usual few minutes of activity followed as coffee was made and we settled ourselves at my desk before beginning today's serious business.

"Before anything else, I need to ask you whether you still wish to engage me to investigate your father's death."

"Yes. Yes, nothing's happened to change my mind. I wouldn't be here today if I didn't want you to take the case, but you said you weren't sure you would take it. You wanted to look into it first. Can you give me an answer now?"

"I believe I can, but it comes with provisos. I admit to being intrigued by the case, and I am willing to investigate your father's death on your behalf. In view of the unsuccessful outcome of the police investigation, I need to warn you there is a distinct possibility my efforts might not result in any different outcome. My investigation might not provide you with the outcome – the information – you want. So, if you wish me to proceed with the investigation, it must be on the clear understanding it's possible you might be disappointed by the results."

Lucy studied her clenched hands for a moment before answering. "I hear what you're telling me. There is nothing new in that. I half expect there will be no answers to any of the questions I have about my father's murder. Anything you find, no matter how small the detail, probably will be more than I know now, and might help me come to terms with what happened. So, will you take the case? If you're concerned about money, don't be. I can pay whatever it costs."

"I will take the case, but I can't give you even an approximation of what it might cost. You will be updated as the case progresses, in terms of the information discovered and approximate costs incurred to that point. You may end the investigation at your discretion."

With the formalities completed and an agreement in place for me to investigate Thomas Blaine's death – or murder, I set about discovering how much Lucy knew about the events at Kirk Michael Farm approximately three and a half years ago.

"You told me you were overseas at the time and that it was sometime later before you knew about it. Tell me about where you were and what you are doing when it happened."

"This is going to sound ridiculous, but it might help explain why I have to know more about it. After I graduated from high school, I took a gap year and went overseas. I don't know if I had a definite plan when I left Australia. I think, if there was a plan, it was to travel through Europe and the UK, picking up work wherever I could and doing whatever was available. That's why I was overseas when it happened."

"Did you come home at the end of the school year and hang around over Christmas before heading overseas?"

"No. I didn't come back here at all. Year 12 ends quite early, and then there was the formal and a couple of other parties for our student cohort before we all went our separate ways. I stayed with my friend's family for that time before heading overseas. By the end of November, I was in Europe and about to embark on my big adventure. I spoke to Dad on Christmas Day, and then there was no further contact for a while."

No doubt it was a difficult time for her. It was evident in her face, her voice, and in the tears welling up in her eyes. But, Lucy is one strong woman. Those tears never came. As I was about to reach for a box of tissues, I saw her swallow hard a couple of times and take a couple of deep breaths. She appeared to regain control, but I allowed her a few seconds before resuming the questioning.

"Was there anything different or unusual about the call on Christmas Day? Did you call him or was it the other way around?"

"All our calls were unusual. To anyone else, that's how they would seem. He always called me. It had to be that way. Dad was in the paddock checking on the stock when he call me on Christmas Day. To avoid trouble at home, it had to remain our secret. So, we had an arrangement. He would call on my birthday and at Christmas, and also on his birthday and on Father's Day."

"*He* would call *you* on *his* birthday and Father's Day...? Why was it that way?"

"As I said, our calls had to be kept secret. His wife should not know they happened. It meant I couldn't call him on those special days. He had to call me so I could wish him a happy birthday or whatever. Even for my birthday, he would have to wait until he was in the paddock somewhere, or there was no one at home, before he could call me. There would have been hell to pay if she knew about the calls."

It took all my self-control not to comment. I needed to be professional, not emotional. "I see; so there was nothing about his call at Christmas to suggest anything was wrong, or he was upset, or concerned about anything?"

"No, there was nothing like that. It was a lovely call, and maybe a bit longer than usual. We just chatted. I suppose a lot of it was taken up with his questions about where I was, where I had been, and what I was doing. Thinking back on it now, it must've been so hard for him. He wanted to know every little detail. I think he wanted to be there with me. But, I didn't pick that up at the time, and there was no indication something might be wrong. Are you suggesting something was happening then, which might have led to his death?"

"I'm sorry. I didn't intend to give you that impression. I'm not aware anything associated with his subsequent death was happening at that time. This meeting, as much as anything else, is about finding out what you know. Some questions I ask might seem a little odd. Please humour me and answer them as best you can."

"Okay, I'll do my best, but I'm afraid you won't find out much from me. I don't know anything. What I do know might amount to no more than one sentence on your notepad. So, ask away and let's see where it takes us."

"From what I've managed to establish so far, Thomas Blaine died either on the night of the last day of January or in the early morning of the first of February. You were overseas for about two months by then. Can you recall where you were at that time?"

"Not exactly; I spent the first few weeks in France before crossing into Italy. I don't know where I was on those precise dates, but it might have been around Naples. Is where I was important?"

"I'm not sure at this stage, but probably not. You told me it was sometime later before you knew of your father's death. I would have expected his wife, or someone close, to contact you as soon it happened. After all, if your father called you from time to time, your phone number would have been available for someone to call you."

"That wasn't the case. There was a phone at the house of course; a landline. Dad never called me on that phone. The risk was, she would find out. He had a secret mobile phone. I don't know where he kept it or how he managed to keep it a secret. But, unless they found the phone after his death, they didn't have my number and wouldn't be able to call me."

"Do you think the fact nobody called you indicates his secret phone wasn't found?"

Lucy shrugged. "I don't know. Even if she did know about the phone, or found it after he died, I doubt she would call me. That was her spiteful way you see. She would take great delight in keeping it from me – particularly if she knew we spoke occasionally."

It seems Ned Edwards wasn't exaggerating when he talked about the rough time Lucy had at home after the second wife arrived. Her words today go a long way to confirming Ned's assessment of the situation, and explaining why Lucy never returned home after she left for boarding school. Don't become emotional, I counselled myself, just ask the next question.

"When and how did you find out about your father's death?"

"Now, that's something I do remember. It was the last day of September; yeah, 30 September. I met a bloke in Switzerland, and a bit later we were working at the same hotel in Germany. We developed a relationship while there, and then travelled together afterwards. As soon as we arrived in England on 28 September, we went straight up to Edinburgh so Roddy could spend his birthday on 30 September with his family there. I received the letter on Roddy's birthday."

Again, Lucy looked as though she needed a few moments alone with her thoughts. I waited before asking my next question, as it was likely to further stir up the poor woman's emotions.

"The terrible news it contained, and coming so long after the event, must have put a dampener on the birthday celebrations."

"Yes, and no; it was a big day. Roddy had three older sisters, all married and all had children. They all turned up to welcome him home, so the house was full of parents and siblings, and nieces and nephews. I was coming down with a cold. By the time I reached Edinburgh, it was a full-blown dose of the flu. The letter arrived about mid-morning, and coincided with one of the kids falling off a bike and injuring himself. It wasn't serious – just grazes and bruises – but the performance he put on commanded everyone's attention. It gave me the opportunity to read the letter in private. When the fuss died down, I said I wasn't feeling well and, not wanting to pass on the flu to everyone else, I was going to my room for the rest of the day."

"The letter turning up on his birthday must not have impressed Roddy."

"I didn't tell him about it. Oh, he saw the letter arrive and noticed it was from Australia but, with everything else happening around him, he didn't think about it until the next day. That's when I told him Dad died. He went into a bit of a flap about making bookings for me on the first available flight home … until I told him it happened eight months ago. He still thought I should go home … but, he didn't know what home was like. The next day, I left Roddy with his family and travelled to London on my own. I needed to be alone to sort myself out, and not have to be polite to a swarm of people around me."

"Was Roddy okay with your taking off like that? He and his family must have been concerned for you."

"I made him promise not to tell the family; insisted it was my private affair and not to be shared with everyone else. Yeah, he was concerned and angry, until I sat him down and explained a few things. He was angry it took so long for anyone to tell me about it. But, he saw the envelope and how it had been on-forwarded so many times before it reached me at Edinburgh. At the time, I didn't tell him the letter had been floating around only for about six weeks before I received it."

"Tell me about the letter. I assume you still have it?" She dropped her eyes to her hands clasped together in her lap and nodded. "Who sent the letter, and what did it say?"

"It was from Jessie. It didn't say much. I mean, it wasn't a long letter, but it said enough."

"Is Jessie your stepmother?"

"God, no; Jessie runs a store and the Post Office at Tanwood. She was a good mate of my father's. They had an arrangement. From the moment I went off to boarding school, Dad and I wrote to each other – usually every week. My letters never went to the farm with the rest of the mail. Jessie held them at the post office until Dad came and collected them personally. When he wrote to me, he had to wait until he went to the store for something before he could post my letter."

"Yes, I've met Jessie. She struck me as one of the good guys, so I'm not surprised she was involved in keeping your correspondence secret."

"Dad often took me to the store with him when I was little. Jessie always managed to sneak me a sweet when dad wasn't looking. Anyway, getting back to the story… When my letters to Dad kept arriving after he died, Jessie knew something was wrong. Then, when I wasn't at the funeral, she began to suspect I didn't know what had happened. It took a while to decide to take matters into her own hands. She sent her letter to the address I had on my last letter to Dad. After that, the on-forwarding worked efficiently until it reached our last address in Europe. It was fortunate someone we were friendly with there remembered we were going to Edinburgh for Roddy's birthday. The place where we'd been working took a punt and sent it on to Roddy's home address."

"So, what did the letter say? Did she give you much information?"

"No, not much … I felt the letter was a bit tentative. As though she wasn't sure she was doing the right thing in writing to me. It was apologetic all the way through; apologising for writing in the first place, for leaving it so long, for telling me something I probably already knew and opening up old wounds again."

"Please tell me what you remember was in the letter."

"She told me Dad had died *at the end of January* – no precise date given. There was mention of a police investigation, that it wasn't determined how my father died, so nobody was arrested. I think she said it was now an 'open case', or maybe she called it a 'cold case'. Whatever her words were, they told me the police investigation had ended with nobody arrested. The only other thing she told me was that his funeral was in April – again, no date given. The last little bit of the letter contained more apologies for what she hoped I wouldn't consider an intrusion into my private life."

"Did you continue corresponding with Jessie?"

"I did send a note back to her thanking her for being so thoughtful, and confirming her letter was the first I'd heard of what happened. I also told her I was moving around and it would be almost impossible for mail to find me in future. At the time, I hoped it would tell her I didn't want to establish regular correspondence with her. It seems she understood the message as intended. I only ever received the one letter from Jessie. I could bring in her letter if you want to see it."

"No, I don't *need* to see the letter but, if you think of it the next time you are in town, I wouldn't mind a look at it."

Pleased with the way the morning had progressed, I was about to suggest we take a coffee break when Lucy's phone played some strange tune. She dragged it out of her bag and took one quick look at it. "I'm sorry. Would you excuse for a moment please? I do need to take this call."

"Go ahead. I'll make us fresh coffees."

Lucy rushed out the door as I headed for the coffee machine. I hadn't progressed much further with the coffee when Lucy reappeared looking a bit flustered.

"Is everything all right, Lucy? Was it upsetting news?"

"What? Oh, no; nothing like that, but I do have to go. I could come back later if you want me to."

"I certainly do need you to come back. I know it has taken us half the morning, but we still have a long way to go. Now, if you need to deal with whatever this emergency is, then do so, but I do want you to come back. If, for whatever reason, you can't come back, please let me know so we can schedule another meeting for as soon as possible."

"Yes, of course I will. I am sorry about this, but I do have to go now."

Disgusted, I returned my attention to the coffee mugs on the bench as she rushed out the door. I slammed one mug back in cupboard, made my own coffee, and went to sit in one of the lounge chairs. "She might have said something about the nature of her emergency so I had some idea of whether she was likely to return today," I snarled aloud.

By the time I had drunk my coffee – one slow sip after another – most of my anger had dissipated. Lucy Telford was fast becoming one of my least favourite clients... and there is a distinct possibility my account will reflect it.

Chapter 8

In a bid to show some productivity for the remainder of the morning following Lucy's hasty departure, I wrote up my notes from this morning's meeting and added them to my case file. Then I strolled along the street to my favourite little bistro for lunch. I told myself I was pushing my luck. It probably was packed and I wouldn't find a table. I was wrong. There was a small table against the plate glass front of the place which provided an uninterrupted view of the street.

A calorie and cholesterol loaded calzone accompanied by a salad and washed down with a chai latte went a long way to restoring my outlook on life … and clients. As I was settling my account on the way out, my phone chirped for attention. It was Lucy. I ignored it and let it ring out. Convinced she would leave a message, I waited for the phone to tell me one had arrived. Nothing happened. This is not the way to treat a client, I reminded myself, and flicked through my contacts to Lucy's name.

"Hi Lucy, apologies; it seems I missed your call."

"I called to see if you wanted to continue our meeting from this morning. I've sorted everything out now. I can come back if you want."

In what felt like record time, Lucy again was sitting opposite me at my desk. I still felt none too kindly disposed towards her, and she probably sensed it.

"I'm sorry about dashing out this morning. When the mechanic got my car going again on Friday, he told me quite a bit was wrong with it. He said it would give me heaps of grief in the near future, expensive grief. It was an old clunker I bought soon after arriving back in Australia. Stuck here in Millhaven with nothing to do all weekend, I looked at new cars and found a model I like and in the colour I wanted. But, it was the last one they had. Making it even more appealing was the model run-out price and a minimum trade-in deal offering more than my rust bucket was worth. I told the salesman I wanted to think about it over the weekend. I couldn't do anything anyway as the banks were closed. The call I received this morning was the salesman telling me someone else was sniffing around the car. I wanted that car, so I had to act then. I am now the owner of a brand new – reliable – car. They are doing the pre-delivery stuff on it now so I can pick it up tomorrow."

"If you could afford a new car, why did you buy a used car in the first place?"

"I wasn't planning on staying long before returning to England. The trip home was to sort out my trust fund. Once I was twenty-one, under the terms of the fund, control of the fund reverted to me. But it hadn't and, as it turns out, the trustees weren't too keen for it to happen. When it became obvious I would be here longer than expected, I needed transport. I just wanted something a bit better than a bicycle. …Bad move, buying the car I did, I know."

"So, now you have a brand new car. Does it mean you plan on sticking around a bit longer before returning to England?"

"…Not sure, but I don't think I'll be going back any time soon. I might take my new car out on the highways and byways to see a bit of Australia first."

"What about Roddy, what's he think about all this?"

"Roddy…? It has nothing to do with Roddy. He hasn't been a part of my life for a while. We lived in a share house with other students while we were at university. Roddy had a great time at university – at significant cost to his studies. Late in his second year, he pulled out, just before they chucked him out, and went home to work in the family business. I haven't seen or heard from him since. I am no longer romantically encumbered."

"Okay, so after you explore Australia, then what? What will you do when you are back in the UK?"

"With every passing day, I'm more inclined to think I'll stay here. Oh, I don't mean in Millhaven; maybe somewhere down south. There are farms down there producing lots of interesting things these days: macadamias, olives, truffles, wine, and there are excellent cheesemakers. I'd love to be a part of that scene."

"It sounds like your roots are calling you back to a life on the land. What did you study at university? Are you going to throw that away?"

"No, and I still work in my chosen field. I studied IT and have five clients I still work for, even while I am here. It's lightweight stuff I do for them – maintain their websites or keep their Facebook pages updated, that sort of thing – but it brought in a bit of cash while I was at university, as it does now."

"So, if you find a farm you like while you are touring the countryside, will you give up all those years of university to grow … turnips or something?"

"No, I could still do some IT work as well as growing something, but not turnips."

'Uhmm … do you have a copy of your father's will?"

"Funny you should ask, I was just thinking about that. My solicitor in Brisbane was going to get a copy and send it to me. It hasn't arrived and I haven't heard a word from him. Do you think it's important?"

"Maybe… Have you seen copies of your mother's or your grandmother's wills?" Lucy shook her head and looked a bit confused by my question. "It might be worth a call to your solicitor to ask if he obtained a copy of your father's will. If he has, we might ask him to email it."

"Okay, I'll give him a call now."

While Lucy remained seated at my desk to make the call, I opted to take advantage of the break to make us fresh coffee.

The snatches of the one-sided conversation I heard above the coffee machine told me nothing, but they didn't sound encouraging. When I returned to the desk, her face tended to confirm my assessment. "Why so glum, what's gone wrong? Did you speak to your solicitor?"

"I spoke to his secretary or whatever she is. No copy of the will has been received, and she doesn't think he applied for one. It seems, the day after I was last in his office, he was involved in a major traffic accident on his way to work. He has just come out of a coma, and is likely to remain in hospital for some time. She asked if I wanted to talk to one of the other solicitors, or what I wanted to do. I don't know any of the others and, I was so taken aback by the news, I said not to worry about it. Is it so important we have a copy of the will?"

"I'll answer that in a moment. First, tell me about your trust fund. How was it set up, and what was to happen with it?"

"My Grandmother Telford set it up when I was born. I'm the only grandchild of an only child, you see. Over the years she made regular payments. I don't know too much about it. After my grandfather died, she inherited everything: a huge farm and several businesses. Later, she sold the farm, keeping just kept the small parcel of land containing her home she had surveyed off from the rest of the farm. So, I think she was a wealthy woman. While sorting out all the stuff to do with the trust fund, I discovered that, on Grandma's death, a large dollop of cash went into the trust fund. I understand it was a bequest in her will."

"Did she still have the other businesses at the time of her death?"

"I don't know, but perhaps she did. The other thing we discovered while sorting out the trust fund was to do with my mother. It was only about twelve months after Grandma died when Mum first became ill. She fought it for a terrible year or so before she died. The trust fund records show that, a few months after her death, another large bucket of cash was paid into the trust fund. Then, about six months after Dad died, another significant amount went into the trust fund. You don't need to be a genius to work out I'm not exactly short of cash at the moment."

"I didn't ask about the wills to see how much cash you had. But, I think it might help us understand what was going on, if we obtain copies of all three of those wills. Do you know if your family used local solicitors?"

The question was unexpected, and she took a while to think about it. I had to remember she was still young when she left home never to return. Children so young don't know much about their parents' legal dealings. Nevertheless, after dredging her memory banks, she remembered the name of someone she thought was their solicitor, and remembered his visiting the farm after her mother became ill.

"That firm of solicitors still has a practice in town, and the man you mentioned remains part of it. We could enquire if they hold copies of the wills. If they do, we should be able to obtain a copy of each of them from the solicitors' office. Failing that, we could take a walk to the courthouse to order them or, alternatively, we could order them online."

"What difference does it make where the copies come from?"

"The only difference might be how long we have to wait for them to arrive. Let's give it a try and see how we go. There might be one problem. Wherever we go, it's likely they will demand to see documentation which proves who you are, and your connection to those estates we're asking about."

"I have everything in this bag I carry around. I had hoped for time today to do something about the car. Before I left this morning, I loaded everything into my bag in case I ran into trouble proving who I was at the bank."

About half an hour after I called the solicitor's office, they rang back. They retained the relevant documents amongst their security files. Copies would be ready for collection after ten o'clock tomorrow. I updated Lucy on the situation and told her to make sure she brought all her documentation with her again tomorrow in case we needed it when we went to collect the copies.

There wasn't much else we could do this afternoon, but we both had unfinished mugs of coffee sitting in front of us. It gave us a chance to chat while we finished them. I decided to ask a question which resided in the back of my mind since my visit to Tanwood. "Have you taken a drive up the valley since you've been back in the area?"

"No, and I won't be. There's nothing for me there now, and I don't want to be seen up there. It's too complicated. I don't want to talk about it; too hard to put into words. Returning to Millhaven was hard for me."

"I understand how you feel, but I thought you might like to thank Jessie for letting you know about your father's death. And, I wondered if you might like to say hello to Ned Edwards while you were here."

She shook her head, and murmured, "No. No, I don't think so."

There wasn't much else to say and our mugs were empty. Lucy was keen to leave, and I was happy to see her go. It took almost the whole day to be a bit better informed than I was yesterday, but I wasn't sure how much information I collected today. I felt I knew a little more about Lucy and her family, but there remained much I didn't know or understand. As I showed her to the door, I told myself tomorrow was another day, and maybe those copies of the wills would clarify more of Lucy's background.

It was almost seven o'clock when Ben Richards' call distracted me. As soon as Lucy left my office, I wrote up the next lot of notes for my case file, and then spent the rest of the time trying to get the story of her life straight in my head.

"Were you planning to go home for dinner tonight, or are you working on in your office instead?" Ben asked.

"I hadn't thought about it, and didn't realise what the time was. Hmm … I think I'll just put things away here and go home. Are you coming over to eat tonight?"

"Yes, now I know you will be home. I'll pick up something to bring for dinner. See you in about an hour's time." An hour gave me time to get home and shower so I was at least half intelligent again by the time Ben arrived.

The piece of roast pork Ben brought was an excellent choice. He relaxed with a cold drink while I prepared the vegetables to accompany it. Then, our conversation touched on nothing of significance until we finished dinner. While we cleared the table, he decided it was time to talk shop. "Have you given any thought to the Thomas Blaine murder? Weren't you going to talk to the daughter today?"

"She managed to take up most of my day. In spite of it, I'm not sure the murder investigation has progressed much. I suppose I'm developing a picture of what life in the Blaine household was like for young Lucy. I don't know what it was like after she left and throughout the subsequent period up until the time of the murder. I can't help thinking what happened during that period of time might be critical to understanding what led to his murder. I don't imagine you've had time to devote any thought to the work we did yesterday."

"It's been in the back of mind all day and, when I found some time late this afternoon, I went back to those files and our notes. I don't know what I was looking for, but I had a feeling we missed something. If you feel up to it tonight, perhaps we could take another look."

"If you had asked me earlier, I would have said no, but my shower revived me. Now I wouldn't mind another look at them. The thing bugging me is the lack of evidence – no, the lack of *detail in* those files. Everything about the investigation appeared too superficial for a murder investigation. That's not meant as a criticism of the officers involved. I think it says something about me, and how I didn't know what I was looking for. Perhaps, now I know more about the family relationships, things might jump out at me if I went through the files again."

"Good; I brought the files with me in case you felt up to it. I wondered whether the way we went about it yesterday might be part of the problem. If we look at the files again, I suggest we don't use the same approach. Instead of working on separate files as we did yesterday, we could study each file together, and discuss it as we worked through it. What do you think?"

"Okay, but do you have any ideas about what we should look for?"

"Not really… It's a case of looking for anything, however obscure, which might provide insight into what happened at Kirk Michael Farm that night."

While Ben fetched the files from his car, I cleared a table in my office and put coffee on to brew to help sustain us through what I suspected would develop into a late night. A few minutes later we were seated at the table with the stack of files at one end, and each of us with a writing pad at the ready.

I thought the first file Ben would select would be the same one as we started with yesterday: the top folder of the stack. He had other ideas. Tonight he selected one from towards the bottom. As we scanned each page of the folder and commented on its contents, something struck me. "I still can't get my head around the scenario in place at Kirk Michael Farm on the night of the murder. It had rained for days, and then a severe storm came in that night. Records of subsequent police interviews don't include those of Mrs Blaine and her daughter."

"I noticed that too. Perhaps they couldn't contribute anything to the investigation. In another file, there is mention of Mrs Blaine and her daughter not being at home on the night in question. If you stop to think about it, if they were, there might have been different outcome. Maybe they would have prevented Thomas' death … or, perhaps all three of the Blaine family might have been murdered."

"Okay, I accept that. But, I can't help feeling their absence was convenient. What do we know about the situation?"

"Another file makes mention of the woman and her daughter having gone into town for a few days. It doesn't shed any light on why or when they went."

At a little after eleven o'clock, Ben received a call. It brought our night to an abrupt end. "Duty calls," he quipped as he gathered up all his files. "My leading detective thinks I might be interested in their current crime scene. Gotta go…"

"Doesn't happen to have anything to do with the Thomas Blaine murder, does it?" The sarcasm in my voice was stronger than intended. On his way out, Ben shot me a disparaging look over his shoulder.

After waving him off, it took me no time to fall into bed. Sleep was not in a hurry to arrive. Thinking up possible scenarios for why Mrs Blaine and her daughter were not at home on the night Thomas was murdered occupied my mind well into the wee hours of the morning. In amongst it all, I found myself wondering about Ben's interest in his precinct's cold case. Did he know something I didn't now driving him to scrutinise the police files? I wasn't going to question his motivation, but it was out of keeping with what I considered 'normal' for Ben.

Chapter 9

In my office early again this morning for no particular reason, I occupied myself with basic administrative chores. My mind insisted on focusing on the Blaine murder case, leaving me little headspace for anything else. I decided to wait until nine o'clock to hear from the solicitor's office. If I hadn't, I would call to enquire when the copies of the wills would be ready.

A few minutes before nine o'clock, they called. The copies were ready. As soon as the call ended, I keyed Lucy's number. Her phone was playing its tune as she walked into my office. 'You must be psychic. I called to see when you might be here to accompany me to the solicitor's office. Do you have all your documentation in case they need you to prove who you are before they hand them over?"

"Yes, I brought the folder with me. Let's go." No time wasted; we crossed the street and walked the two blocks to the solicitor's office.

A secretary came to meet us. She carried a large manila envelope and requested proof of identity before handing it over. It seems she simply followed the required procedures, giving Lucy's documentation no more than a cursory glance before handing over the bulky envelope. I thought it best to ask the question before leaving. "Are copies of all three wills in the envelope?"

The young woman looked perplexed for a few moments before snatching back the envelope, marching across to an empty desk, and dumping the envelope's contents onto the desk. I watched her shake her head as she checked the photocopies. "No, I'm sorry. There are copies of only two wills, those of Thomas Blaine and Mrs Valerie Blaine. Was there supposed to be a third will?"

I knew it. This was proving too easy to end well. "Yes. We also asked for a copy Mrs Maree Telford's will."

"Did anyone check if we held a copy of the particular will?"

"I believe so. I asked if copies of all three wills were held here, and I was assured they were. Does only two of the ones requested having been copied indicate the third will isn't held here?"

"Please, take a seat for a moment while I look into the matter."

She clacked away on a keyboard while we sat in uncomfortable chairs in the reception area. When she returned to speak to us, there was a triumphant air about her. "Mrs Telford's will was much earlier than the other two. Someone searched for it yesterday, but it was overlooked later when they did the photocopying. I could pull the document and copy it for you by tomorrow or, perhaps, by later today."

"Thank you, but that would be most inconvenient. We are prepared to wait here while you do whatever is necessary to produce the copy for us now. But, we are not inclined to leave without the other copy."

For a brief moment, she stood nonplussed by my refusal. Then, adopting a condescending tone, she began explaining why it was not possible for her to photocopy the required document while we waited. I cut her off mid-sentence. "If you are too busy at the moment, perhaps someone else might take care of the matter for you. If it's a problem, I could have a quick word with my solicitor, Mr McGregor. I'm sure he could arrange for the photocopying to be done without upsetting the continued operation of the place too much while we wait."

No further argument required. About twenty minutes later, a second bulky enveloped was slapped down on the counter in front of us. I paid for the photocopying and we left the solicitors' office, our relationship with the young woman in tatters.

On our way back to my office, Lucy ducked into the bakers while I went on ahead to brew fresh coffee. By mutual agreement, we would 'fuel-up' before tackling whatever the three wills had to share. We dispatched the sweet treats and coffee in record-breaking time before, applying logical thought to the process, we started with Maree Telford's will, and worked forward chronologically from there.

I went straight to the inventory page … and let out a low whistle. "Your grandmother was one wealthy woman. If you extrapolate some of these values to today's money, she was 'rolling in it' as they say. At first glance, it was surprising how few pages comprised the will, but we soon realised why. The document opened with the usual paragraph about the person being of sound mind and all that other stuff, before providing the details we were interested in. As expected, there was a lengthy paragraph relating to the significant cash bequest to be added to Lucy's trust fund. No surprises there.

Then there were two paragraphs relating to bequests to Maree Telford's only daughter, Valerie Blaine. The first of these dealt with all of Maree's existing business interests and real property, while the second paragraph bequeathed any residual cash to Valerie. It was enough to send me back to the inventory page to determine exactly what Valerie inherited.

In spite of the considerable amount of cash deposited in Lucy's trust fund, a couple of hundred thousand dollars remained for Valerie. Both Lucy and I sat in silence for a minute or so while digesting the information.

"I had no idea," Lucy murmured. "I had no idea Grandma had so much cash. Some of it would be from the sale of the farm. I remember when she had her big house and several acres surrounding it surveyed off from the rest of the farm. Both Mum and Grandma were sad to see the farm go, but Mum explained how it was best now Grandpa was gone and Grandma was getting too old to manage the workers she employed to run it. My memories of that time don't include anything about the actual sale. It was a big farm; about the size of three of today's average sized farms. The sale would have brought in a pile of cash."

Those business interests Maree owned, or was a shareholder in, interested me. It appeared they intrigued Lucy as well. "Sonny, do you know any of these businesses? Are they located in this area, or somewhere else?"

Two of the businesses I recognised, but in name only. Another two, I had never heard of, and the name of one of those suggested it was not local. In addition, there were a couple of businesses in which Maree had been a major shareholder. I recognised them as large state-wide enterprises with their headquarters in Brisbane. A trawl of the internet showed all the businesses mentioned continued to operate. I opted to leave establishing ownership or major shareholders in each of them until later, in favour of continuing extracting information from the wills.

Lucy again asked if I knew anything about any of the businesses mentioned. "I've never had anything to do with any of them. Both the local ones have substantial premises in the old industrial area near the harbour. They have been around for quite a while and seem relatively prosperous. Before we start digging into their operations, I suggest we deal with the other two wills. After all, your mother might have disposed of the business interests she inherited from your grandmother."

As Lucy again scrutinised the inventory page, I realised there was another page after the inventory. We hadn't scanned it bcause I didn't realise it was there. Charged with static electricity from the photocopying, the two pages, clung together.

"Ooh, that is interesting," I murmured. "Look, Lucy. This last page isn't part of the original will, but is something like a codicil attached at some time."

"It looks like a letter … to my mother."

"Yes, it is, and I can see why it was done this way."

"Well, I don't understand. If Grandma wanted to send a letter to my mother, that's exactly what she would do. If she was at the stage where she couldn't take care of it herself, she could have her solicitors send it for her. After all, it looks as though they produced the document. Why didn't they just send it to Mum? If you understand why it was done this way, maybe you should explain it to me."

"I think it has something to do with what you can and can't say in a will. Here's an example of that. If your grandmother bequeathed something to your mother, your grandmother couldn't then dictate what must happen to that 'thing' on your mother's death. Once it is bequeathed to your mother, your mother owns it and, like everything else she owned, she could do whatever she liked with it – both while she was alive and on her death."

"Ok-ay, I think I understand, but let's see if I do. In the case of those businesses Grandma left Mum, she could not stipulate in her will that, when my mother died, what was to happen to those businesses. Is that correct?"

"That's exactly what I was talking about and, if you read that letter, you will see most of it does refer to those businesses. It would be inappropriate for Maree Telford to stipulate in her will how her daughter could use the income from those businesses. But, in this separate letter, she can suggest how her daughter might use some of that income ... And that's exactly what she has done."

"The letter suggests my mother consider any surplus income received from those businesses – surplus to her requirements, that is – be paid into my trust fund. So, the contents of this letter are not enforceable under the terms of the will, as they are only a suggestion. Even the suggestion doesn't tie my mother down by quantifying how much should be paid into my trust fund. In reality, the letter creates an emotional obligation, rather than a legal one, and is one my mother might ignore if she so chose. Does that about sum it up?"

"From my understanding of it, that's what it seeks to do. I don't know how your mother reacted to the letter, or what she did about the suggestion."

"While I don't know how she went about it, I think she did comply. I need to check the trust fund records to be sure. When my solicitor and I went through everything with the trustees at the time of the handover, I noticed there were some small deposits which stood out as different from all the others. I intended looking into those deposits, but haven't done so."

"Your mother died not long after your grandmother's death. It follows that she did not have income from those businesses for long before she died and, therefore, there would not be many deposits during that period – if any – of surplus income. I would be interested to know what you find when you do check out those unusual deposits."

"Is there anything else we need to look at in Grandmother's will? I still haven't got my head around everything on the inventory list, but that's something I can do in my own time. Right now, for me, the most significant thing about Grandma's will is her apparent wealth."

"There is that. One other aspect of the will has me intrigued. The only people mentioned in it are you and your mother. Did you have any other relatives from your mother's side of the family?"

"No, none that I know of. I've always understood my mother was an only child, although I don't remember ever being told that."

"It's not something to worry about now. If you have nothing else you wish to bring up regarding Maree Telford's will, let's move on to your mother's will."

In spite of knowing Valerie Blaine died not long after her mother, I was surprised at how soon after it was. It seems Valerie first became ill about twelve months after her mother died. That was the start of a two-year long battle before she died. This meant there was only a period of about three years during which Valerie had opportunity to send her 'surplus income' to Lucy's trust fund. Valerie's will was another eye-opener.

After the usual opening gambit about being of sound mind etcetera, her will mentioned only the two people who meant the world to her: her husband and her daughter. Again, the amount of cash involved in bequests was staggering. Lucy noticed it too.

"I skimmed the two pages. The one thing to stand out is the amount of cash involved in Mum's bequests. See here; she left Dad a walloping amount of cash, as well as whatever else she had. Then, when you look over here, it's hard to believe she still had so much money left to leave to me."

"Yeah, I had noticed. Let's start at the beginning of the bequests and work through it. This first bit deals with what she bequeathed to your father. Apart from the significant amount of cash, it appears she still had most of the business interests her mother left her. From what I can see from the inventory list, one of the companies in which she was a major shareholder has disappeared, and another small local company also is no longer on the list."

"She must've used quite a bit of Grandma's money. The amount of cash Mum left is a bit reduced from the amount she received from Grandma. I wonder what she did with it."

"We have to remember that, while she might have spent quite a bit of money on whatever it was, at the same time, she was receiving income from those businesses. It's not possible for us to determine how much money was spent as we don't have any of her bank statements or transaction reports to work with. I suppose it is possible some of her money went into the farm. Perhaps it was spent on creating a comfortable home, or maybe on paying off the debt incurred in purchasing the farm in the first place. Again, as we don't have those financial records, it's impossible to determine where the money went."

"The farm is mentioned in those paragraphs relating to Dad's bequests. I don't understand the ownership of the farm, but it seems Mum had some part ownership in the place until she died. Then, because of the nature of that ownership, the place reverted to Dad. I don't understand it. It was Dad's farm. He owned it before he married Mum; probably even before he met her."

"To me, it looks like it was a case of joint ownership. The original ownership of the farm might have been in just your father's name but, if your mother invested her money in establishing the place, it's possible the situation was changed to joint ownership. In cases of joint ownership, when one party dies, ownership of the whole of the property reverts automatically to the other party. The words included in your mother's will were unnecessary, but serve to confirm that situation. They might have been included to avoid any possible confusion or challenge to ownership after her death."

"Mum added another massive bucket of money to my trust fund. The figure makes me feel guilty she left so much to me and less than half as much to Dad. Why didn't she leave it all to Dad? He wouldn't waste it, and he would make sure I was well looked after. She knew he would look after me."

"I don't think either of us will ever know your mother's thinking at the time she made her will. But, I'm confident she was not motivated by doubts about your father or his future relationship with you."

"You're right, but it's frustrating knowing so much of what happened and not the whole story. Even a letter to my father, like the one Grandma left for Mum, would help me understand her thinking."

Being a bit short on the answers Lucy craved, I opted to refrain from comment, and returned my attention to the inventory page of Valerie's will. At the time of her death, she remained a wealthy woman, and one determined to ensure her daughter's future was well taken care of after she was gone.

With no more surprises, and not one further skerrick of information to extract from the document, we laid Valerie Blaine's will aside and turned our attention to the last photocopied document.

Thomas Blaine's will contained just as few pages as the previous two documents we examined. From the outset, it was apparent his focus was on providing a sound future for Lucy. In fact, I found his will surprising in how little mention was made of the second Mrs Blaine and his daughter from that marriage. Lucy picked up on it as well.

"There's the next big inflow of cash to my trust fund. It's even more than the amount Mum left to Dad. Were my family printing money, or did they have a money tree I didn't know about somewhere in the backyard that?"

"You might be forgiven for thinking that. As much as I hate to remind you, it's another one of those situations where we have little hope of understanding the thinking behind it, or the prevailing circumstances. The date your father made this will was some time after your mother's death … and after he remarried and there was another child. All sorts of things could have happened in the ensuing years before his death, but it seems he preserved the cash your mother bequeathed him with you in mind."

"I can't imagine she was happy with the contents of this will. She would not have wanted all that cash to go to me."

"By 'she', I assume you mean your father's second wife?" Lucy shrugged and nodded. "Perhaps she didn't know what was in the will; might not have known a will had been made. It was not uncommon for the contents of a will to remain secret until it was read after the person's death. Still, I agree, she would not have been happy if she knew. And, she would not have been happy if the first she knew of it was after your father's death."

"She would be most unhappy I would think."

The vindictive smirk on Lucy's face as she spoke concerned me a little. It was clear I needed to know more about how the family functioned after Thomas' second marriage. Perhaps I need to organise another lengthy chat with Ned Edwards, and soon.

"Sonny, the only place giving us the actual dollars available for distribution is the inventory page. The will itself talks in percentages. It states what percentage of the available cash was to be bequeathed to each person. In the other two wills, specific amounts of money were mentioned. Why would this one be different? Why doesn't Dad's will say how many dollars were to be paid into my trust fund rather than nominating a percentage?"

"It's a fair bet he didn't plan on dying so young…"

"…Or being murdered."

"True; when he made his will, I'm sure he assumed it would remain dormant in his solicitor's files for a long time to come. He could have no idea what his cash reserves might be at any future time. His only alternative was to talk in terms of percentages of his cash reserves. But, if you notice, he makes it clear one hundred percent of one bank account is to go to your trust fund, along with a percentage of his other cash. I believe the bank account, of which you received a hundred percent, held the money your mother left to him in her will. To me, it suggests he always intended her money should be yours."

Tears welled up and she struggled to control them. There wasn't much else to be gleaned from the three documents, and it had been an emotional time for her. I asked Lucy for permission to copy the three wills for my files. When she agreed, I explained my photocopier was not a super-fast, high volume machine, and it might take me a while to copy them.

"Would you mind leaving them with me overnight? You could collect them in the morning, or I could bring them to you at wherever you are staying."

While it was obvious she was reluctant, she agreed to collect them in the morning. There wasn't much more to discuss, and it was just as well. Lucy became less talkative after we finished with the wills. In a bid to ease the emotional turmoil I sensed in her, I asked her about life in a share house in Oxford. She chatted about it for a couple of minutes. Afterwards, she looked more settled, although still tense. I figured she had a lot more 'unwinding' to do, and brought our meeting to a speedy conclusion. "Have you something to do in Millhaven for the next couple of days?"

"I'll find something to fill in my time."

"Good; I'll see you tomorrow to collect these documents. I'll need to look into a few things before our next meeting. I'll keep you informed of anything interesting. I'll call when I am ready for another meeting."

Lucy didn't argue, but looked dejected as she let herself out of my office.

Chapter 10

It was lunchtime when Lucy left. I wanted to sit and think about what I learnt this morning. Had it advanced my investigation? My initial reaction was *probably not ...* or, maybe, not much.

I had few scribbled notes to show for our scrutiny of the three wills. Adopting this morning's approach, I began reading the wills again, this time making a note of every fact each contained. About an hour later, my stomach rumbled. "Okay, okay, food...," I murmured. "Food, then sort out Thomas' will."

"What the...?" I exclaimed as I stepped out of the building and onto a very wet pavement. This morning was bright and sunny. Where did this drizzle come from? Judging by the state of the pavement, it had been windy enough to blow the rain in against the shopfronts. A fine mist continued to coat the pavement. It helped me decide what I wanted for lunch. I had thought to go further along the street to my favourite deli and treat myself. Instead, I ducked nextdoor to the coffee shop and bought a chicken and salad roll.

About twenty minutes later, with lunch dispatched, I was ready to tackle Thomas Blaine's will. Similar to the other two, Thomas' will was brief and succinct. The slim document comprised the two pages of the actual will plus the inventory sheet produced as part of the probate process. So, why was I procrastinating? I knew the answer. "Get on with it," I snarled aloud.

With more than a hint of trepidation, I ran my finger down the first page, adding to the few brief notes I made earlier as I did so. Then it was 'crunch' time. It was time to deal with the second page ... the page we did not discussed earlier. While

Lucy and I were discussing the paragraph dealing with her cash bequest, I flicked through to look at the inventory sheet. It gave me nothing more than a glimpse of the second page. Words which jumped off that page at me as I flicked past suggested a cautious approach.

This morning's exercise was an emotional rollercoaster ride for Lucy. Although I didn't know the details of the single long paragraph on the second page of Thomas' will, I knew it dealt with his second wife and their daughter, and Kirk Michael Farm. My trepidation was about how I might break the bad news gently to Lucy.

While I didn't know how Lucy might react to the paragraph, I suspected it would be upsetting, and more than she could deal with today. Hence, the reason for keeping the documents overnight: to allow me privately to examine that page before sharing it with Lucy. And, it would allow Lucy time to adjust to everything learnt this morning before having to deal with more emotional baggage. No point in hesitating any longer, I turned to the second page of Thomas Blaine's will and began reading.

"Well, well, well… that's not what I expected," I told my empty office. I read the long paragraph again before pausing to consider its implications. I was right about the page dealing with the future of Thomas' second wife and their daughter, but my assumption about what it said was way off the mark. This might not be so difficult to discuss with Lucy after all.

He did not bequeath the farm to his second wife, Rita Blaine (nee Cotter). Instead, his will simply made provision for some indefinite period into the future for the woman and her daughter. Rita Blaine and her daughter, Sarah, could continue to live on the farm and derive an income from it until such time as Rita remarried, or she abandoned the farm to live elsewhere. There was a catch to the arrangement.

The farm, and everything on it, was left to Lucy. The provision for Rita and Sarah to continue living there only applied for as long as Lucy allowed it to occur … or Rita remarried or abandoned the farm. If Lucy remained ignorant of the contents of Thomas' will, it would be possible for Rita to continue living there indefinitely … unless she remarried or left the farm ... and only if Lucy knew about it.

On my brief visit, I assessed Kirk Michael Farm as abandoned. From my interpretation of the terms of the will, Lucy now had clear title to the farm and could do whatever she liked with the property without fear of repercussions from her stepmother. How would Lucy react to that information? So far, any mention of the farm brought a neutral response from her. Perhaps, over the years, she reconciled herself to the loss of everything she once held dear.

It's possible, once her father died, she considered her ties to the area, her home, her childhood and everything it encompassed, gone forever. She struck me as being made of stern stuff. Maybe the hard lessons of life made her that way to help her survive. Nevertheless, she is in for a shock. How she deals with it, and how I can help with that process, are important now. Tomorrow seemed soon enough to begin dealing with the matter.

Finding it all difficult to take in, I sat for a few minutes in a semi-stunned state. While staring into space, I allowed the various facts extracted from the wills to churn around in my mind. I realised I needed to know about Rita Blaine and her daughter, and about their relationship with Thomas. Argh, I knew Rita and Thomas were married, but that's not enough. I needed the local gossip about the family; all the dirt on how the community saw things in the Blaine household. Now, who is most likely to give me the most accurate assessment of all things Blaine?

Ned Edwards, while being cautious in his earlier comments, was the most promising candidate for a question-and-answer session. Then, if needed, I could follow up with another chat to Jessie in the Tanwood coffee shop. I keyed in the mobile number Ned was somewhat reluctant to give me when I first met him. He was a while answering.

"I'm sorry. I was driving and had to find somewhere to pull over to answer your call. It's Sonny, isn't it? What can I do for you?"

"Yes, it's Sonny. Ned, I wondered if you might be coming into town in the next day or so."

"I'm in town now … and I'm not having a good day of it so far."

That didn't bode well for my request, but I went ahead and asked anyway. "I was going to invite you to my office for a chat. The invite comes with a bribe of coffee and cake. But, if you're busy and can't spare me the time, I can understand."

"I can spare you as much time as you like. I came into town today to have a tyre repaired and to pick up a part for my big tractor. They assured me the part would be here yesterday. I put off coming to collect it until today in case it was delayed, or arrived late yesterday. Now it looks like I have two options: go home and come back tomorrow, or overnight in town."

"Have you decided which option to adopt?"

"Yeah, I'm going to treat myself to a night in a motel."

"Good; well, if you have the time now, the offer of a chat over coffee and cake still stands. How does that fit with you?"

"I'll be there in about fifteen minutes. Tell me again where to find your office."

After giving him directions, I dashed nextdoor to the bakery. By the time Ned arrived, fresh coffee was brewing and an impressive strawberries and cream-filled sponge cake waited to be attacked. A few minutes after he arrived, Ned and I, accompanied by our coffees and large slices of cake, were seated in my ancient lounge chairs. He opened the serious conversation we were to have.

"I assume you are still working for Lucy Blaine." I nodded. No further response seemed necessary. "And, I take it our chat is to be about events at Tanwood all those years ago." Again, I nodded, and led into the conversation I needed to have.

"After searching family wills for possible motives to give me clues as to who might have been involved, all I have for my trouble is confusion. When I spoke to you previously, I think you were careful about what you didn't tell me; focused on maintaining a proper decorum when speaking about the dead. I'd like you to rethink your position. I am trying to help Lucy find the answers she wants. I need your help to do that."

Ned squirmed in his chair, and studied his half empty coffee mug before answering. "The poor girl deserves to know. She received the rough end of the deal all the way along. It's the least I can do if it helps her come to terms a bit with everything. What do you want to know? Mind now, some of what I tell you is what I think, not what I know, but I'll indicate which it is."

"It seems to me, the rot set in once Thomas remarried. I sense his new wife, Rita, was a different person from Lucy's mother, Valerie. What can you tell me about her? I appreciate they might be only your observations, but it will help."

"To put it bluntly, she was a wrong 'un; not pleasant and somehow sort of … cheap. I think I told you she didn't get on with anyone around Tanwood. Thought they were beneath her, and spoke to them that way. She couldn't even get along with our lovely young schoolteacher. It must have made it tough for Lucy. Lucy was the school's star pupil, and there was her stepmother giving the teacher a hard time and accusing her of not doing her job properly. More or less told the teacher it was her fault Lucy was dumb because she hadn't taught her anything. That little girl was not dumb. Lucy was bright; clever beyond her years."

"If Thomas and Lucy were so close, bringing in a stepmother was bound to create some tension. Was Rita a local before the marriage?"

"Not a local; no. Not as I would call her anyway. She had been around the area for a year or so. I think she was camped somewhere up the top end of the valley, and we only saw her in Tanwood on occasions."

"Camped…? What, in a tent or caravan, or something?"

"Eh? Oh, no. By 'camped', I mean she was living with a bloke who lived in a shack on one of the big properties up there. I don't think he worked on the place. I heard he often was away for days at a time. They weren't married or anything, just 'shacked-up' as they say."

"How did she and Thomas meet? You said she wasn't a regular in this area."

"Even before his wife, Valerie, died, Thomas used to pick up the odd bit of work on some of the big properties along the valley. He continued to do so after Valerie's death, so it's likely he met Rita when he worked up there, either before or after Valerie's death."

"It must've been a tricky situation if they started a relationship while she was living with another man. It doesn't fit the picture I was building up of Thomas. Still, I suppose he was a man, and driven by human urges."

"Oh, I don't think anything underhanded went on. I think it was not too long after Valerie died, Rita moved to Tanwood. She was on her own then, and I don't think she wasted too much time approaching Thomas about the possibility of becoming his housekeeper. I don't remember the exact timing, but it was about twelve months after Valerie's passing when Rita started working for Thomas. She came out to the farm two or three days a week to do the usual domestic chores and cooked meals for them while she was there."

"So, it sounds like it developed into something more. Thomas and Rita must have gotten on okay for him to marry her."

"Rumour around town was that they didn't get on so well; often quarrelled. I can't comment on the truth of it. We lived next door, but I never saw or heard anything to suggest a volatile relationship. But, there were days when Thomas was not himself; withdrawn and you could sense anger in him. Still, life's like that isn't it? We all have good days and bad. Things couldn't have been too bad. He did marry her – eventually. Young Lucy was growing up and would soon develop into a young woman. Thomas couldn't run the farm and take care of Lucy as well as he felt he should. I think he believed Lucy needed a woman around at that time of her life."

"I think I worked out Lucy was about ten years old when her mother died. It wasn't long after, when Rita started working for Thomas."

"Yes, I think Lucy was about ten. Then Rita came on the scene as a housekeeper when Lucy was about eleven, or maybe a bit older. The housekeeper job lasted about twelve months or maybe a little bit longer before she and Thomas married. No time after that, a baby arrived on the scene. It was no secret Rita wasn't too happy about Lucy being there. Oh, she was as nice enough to Lucy before the wedding but, once she and Thomas married, it was obvious to everyone Rita wanted Lucy gone."

"I suppose it's not unnatural for her to want her baby to take over pride of place in the household. Lucy's being about to start high school provided Rita with a means of removing her stepdaughter from the home during term time."

"Rita worked hard at persuading Thomas sending Lucy away to school was the best thing he could do for her education. She made it sound like it was about doing the best for Lucy. Everyone who heard the story knew it was a load of rubbish. She wanted Lucy out of the house; wanted her daughter to be the focus of attention."

"Well, it seems she achieved it."

"Yes – and no. Lucy went off to boarding school okay – and never came back to Tanwood. I suppose it was a victory for Rita. Sending Lucy away worked better for her than she expected, but it didn't result in all she wanted. Thomas never took to the new baby as he did with Lucy. I don't think things were too good at home."

"What makes you think that about the Blaine household? Did Thomas comment on it at some time?"

"No, there was nothing like that, and he wouldn't. Thomas was too much of a gentleman to discuss personal matters outside the home. People noticed the situation though. No one ever saw the couple together. Argh, they lived together on the farm all right, but they never went anywhere together. Rita came into Millhaven a lot. I don't know what for, but Thomas never accompanied her."

"Maybe she was one of those who prefer to shop in bigger centres. Some people just like to shop. They don't necessarily buy anything every time they go shopping. I think the appeal is wandering through the different shops."

"Do you like this shopping thing?"

"Me…? No. I hate shopping – even for necessities like food. But, not everyone is like me. Perhaps Rita was a city girl, and Millhaven was the closest thing to normal for her if she was missing her roots. Anyway, going into Millhaven a tad too often by local standards, doesn't mean something was wrong with the marriage."

"No, but his sleeping in the cottage does…" Ned's smug look was priceless.

"Why was that tiny cottage built behind the church?"

"In its heyday, the minister used this church as his base from which to service the entire valley's parishioners' needs. He had to live somewhere, so they built him a 'residence' – the two-roomed cottage behind the church. When first built, it's primitive 'facilities' consisted of a few sheets of corrugated iron tacked around four big trees out the back. He had to carry buckets of water out there for a bath. It must have been freezing out there in winter. After a minister was no longer stationed here, the church sold the property to Thomas."

"Does the name, Kirk Michael Farm, have anything to do with the place's original use?"

"Yes, it was St Michael's, the parish church for the area."

"So, the cottage was the home of the incumbent cleric and wasn't used after the place was sold?"

"The cottage wasn't used again until Thomas took to sleeping out there."

"Aah, yes, I see. That does tend to suggest trouble on the home front. I don't expect you know much about it, but do you have any idea when the 'altered' sleeping arrangement began?"

"He was out in the cottage around the time the baby was born. I feel he was out there before then."

"Are you suggesting the new baby created stress on the relationship? If Thomas moved out to the cottage soon after the baby was born, it might be because Rita wasn't coping well. Maybe she had postnatal depression; was hard to live with. Perhaps that created the rift between them."

"Hmm, maybe… The community had a different slant on the situation. They all seemed to know something was wrong, and they blamed the arrival of the baby. But, scuttlebutt at the time wasn't about Rita not coping. It was about the baby … and *whose* baby it was!"

"Eh…? That would be pure speculation. It must have been a quiet time in the valley and they had to find something to talk about. Maybe people gossiped about it because the marriage appeared to start falling apart around the time the baby arrived."

"If you were of a generous disposition, you might think so, but a couple of factors supported their speculation. Firstly, it was one of those shorter-than-nine-months pregnancies.

People in the area made much of the fact. After the birth, Rita went to great pains to tell everyone how the baby's arrival, so far ahead of time, caught her and Thomas by surprise and ill-prepared."

"So, people thought *she doth protest too much*... You said there were a couple of things. What else gave credence to such speculation?"

"To begin with, people were inclined to humour the 'shortened pregnancy' story. Then, when they saw the baby, any doubts they had disappeared. Both Thomas and Rita were olive-skinned with black hair and dark eyes – like Lucy. People had trouble believing the couple produced a fair-skinned, blue-eyed child with a startling mop of red hair."

"Oh dear, the gods were not in Rita's corner, were they? I can see how the community might react as they did. Do you think Thomas shared their doubts, and that's what drove him out to the cottage?"

Ned shrugged and appeared to ponder the question for a few moments. Before he could reply, my phone rang. I answered it, intending to organise to call back later, but it didn't happen that way. The call about a possible new case only lasted about two minutes. Nevertheless, it also broke the thread of my interview with Ned. By the time the call ended, it was obvious Ned had 'switched off' interview mode.

I checked the time and was surprised to see it was 5:30PM. "Goodness, Ned; look at the time. I'm sorry I've kept you so late."

"I didn't have anything else to do. I'm staying in town tonight, so it helped me fill in time."

"Since you are staying in town, how about letting me take you to dinner?" After a feeble protest, he agreed. "Great ... what would you like to eat?"

I expected him to say 'steak', but I was wrong. It seems he eats plenty of steak, and other prime beef, at home. We finally agreed on seafood. I hoped a last minute reservation was possible at the best seafood place I knew at the marina. I trusted my luck and proceeded as though confident it would be. "Okay Ned, I'll pick you up at seven o'clock for dinner."

As soon as he was out the door, I called the restaurant and booked a table, and then made a quick call to Ben to tell him I wouldn't be at home this evening. He assumed I would be working on a case. In a way, I suppose I was, so I let him think so. I looked at the pages of scribbled notes made during Ned's visit but couldn't bring myself to make a start on writing them up properly. Instead, I settled for another coffee and a long time staring at nothing in particular, while allowing my mind to digest some of what Ned told me, and to fill in time until I needed to freshen up before collecting Ned.

Chapter 11

Never having ventured as far as the marina, he was greatly taken with everything about the place. The arrival of the seafood platter with both hot and cold morsels included for two amazed him. I held back a little to allow Ned to indulge in the crustaceans, fish and oysters served up in several different ways. Dinner was a success, and I managed to avoid any talk of the Thomas Blaine case all night.

On my way to drop Ned back at his motel, I asked what time tomorrow he would be able to collect the part he was waiting for.

"They tell me the parcels arrive between nine and ten o'clock. I told them I would there at ten o'clock and I expected my part to be waiting for me. I need to get back to my animals at home and can't be hanging around in Millhaven for too long."

"As you have a couple of hours to fill in tomorrow morning, I will be in my office by eight o'clock if you would like to drop in for a coffee and to fill in a bit of time. By ten o'clock, we might be ready to attack that cake again before you collect your part. If you have nothing better to do, the invitation is there."

He didn't accept or reject the offer but, as he climbed out of the car he said, "Thanks for dinner, I did enjoy it. Goodnight; see you in the morning." I understood I should be in my office as promised by eight o'clock.

It wasn't until I was almost home the consequences of what I did tonight dawned on me. I believed Ned accepted my invitation to join me in my office tomorrow morning. The invite was to continue today's interview. We were at the part about the new baby, and I wanted to know more about that.

My problem is, Lucy is likely to arrive at my office tomorrow while Ned is there. Under different circumstances, the two of them meeting again wouldn't be a bad thing, but Lucy didn't want anyone to know she was in Millhaven and didn't want to see anyone from Tanwood.

"Perhaps it won't be a bad thing for them to encounter one another," I murmured as I tried to convince myself. "No doubt Lucy will think I set it up intentionally." It might impact on whether she continues as a client or not. Nevertheless, such a meeting might be just the thing to shake loose memories and stories I might not otherwise hear, and that could be useful.

*****

Well before eight o'clock this morning, I was aware of more than a hint of trepidation as I bustled about my office filling the coffee machine and setting out mugs and spoons. This morning could be wonderful, or it could turn into a complete disaster. I didn't have long to wait to find out.

Ned arrived a couple of minutes before eight o'clock and was surprised to find me there. "I know you said eight o'clock, but I didn't expect you here at this time. From my experience, city folk don't come to life until nine o'clock." I let his observation go by without reply.

When settled once more in the lounge chairs with our coffees, I confessed. "As much as I enjoy your company, Ned, I admit I also wanted to know more about the Blaine's red-headed baby who had the Tanwood community abuzz after her birth. It is possible for two swarthy coloured people to have a fair red-haired child if there was something in either of their backgrounds to cause it. Maybe it was something that surfaced from a couple of generations ago."

"Or maybe not... I agree it might be possible but, in this case, there's a more obvious reason. *The child wasn't Thomas Blaine's.* It didn't matter how much Rita preached her five-month-pregnancy to the locals, none of them was so gullible as to believe it."

"Okay, so what was the alternative source of the child's colouring?"

"Lyle Rogan…!"

"At the risk of sounding dense, that tells me nothing, Ned. It might help if you accept I know nothing of any of this and explain it accordingly."

"Well, I think I told you, before she met Thomas, Rita was living with a bloke on a property further up the valley. The bloke was Lyle Rogan. He and Thomas – and Rita – met when the property owner hired Thomas to help out with some work on his property. Later, when Rita became Thomas' housekeeper for a few hours every week, Thomas' 'old friend' Lyle Rogan started dropping by." I raised my eyebrows in mock surprise, and Ned continued. "Of course, his visits were to catch up with Thomas, not to see Rita," He added with his tongue firmly planted in his cheek.

"There wouldn't be much opportunity for any extramarital activity with Thomas there as well."

"Rita was always going off somewhere, into town, to the Tanwood store – and she was even seen further up the valley on a regular basis."

"It would be reasonable to assume she visited Rogan on the days she didn't work at Thomas' place."

"True … but nothing in the story changed after Rita and Thomas were married. And, on occasions when Thomas picked up a bit of casual work on surrounding properties, and Rita was home on her own, Rogan still managed to visit the farm."

"The question begging to be asked is: what was Lyle Rogan's colouring?"

"Identical to the baby's … and, from day one, the likeness to her father was obvious to everyone, or so they all said."

"…Including Thomas?"

"Yeah, I'm sure he was aware. That's when things fell apart for him. For a while after the baby was born, Rogan no longer visited the farm, although Rita often travelled up the valley with the baby. Thomas continued sleeping in the cottage."

"Did you see Rogan's likeness in the child?"

"Me…? No, can't say I did, but I was never much good at that sort of thing. My wife said she thought she could see some similarity."

"I'm with you on this one, Ned. I've so often heard people claiming a new born baby resembles someone or other. When I look, all I can see is a baby who looks like – a baby. They have to grow up a bit before I start to see any resemblances in them."

"I exasperated my wife by telling her the same thing when she told me about the likeness she could see in the baby. They all banged on about the child's red hair being a dead give-away. I couldn't see it myself. Rogan's hair was that real dark red – not far from a brown sort of colour. The child was really fair with gingery hair, more burnished copper-coloured."

"Oh well, it seems neither of us mastered the art of assessing babies' looks. But tell me, why did Thomas and Rita stay together if it was so obvious what had happened? If Thomas had figured out the truth – and I doubt he was a complete fool – I can't imagine why he didn't kick her out."

"That's another of life's mysteries. Rita always claimed it was Thomas' child. She even made up some story about how the child took after one of her grandparents or great grandparents, or someone like that in her family tree. None of us believed it. But, maybe Thomas harboured some doubts about the child, and felt he couldn't throw them out in case Rita's story was true."

"What became of Lyle Rogan? Is he still hanging around up the valley?"

"No, not him … he's long gone now, but he was there for a couple of years after Thomas' death."

I glanced at the clock. It was 9:15AM. My face must have betrayed my surprise. Ned noticed. "Is something wrong? I should be going. I've taken up too much of your time. I'm sure you have a lot to do; clients to see."

"No, Ned. I was surprised to see how time had slipped away. Would you like a fresh coffee … and I could bring out what's left of the cake we had yesterday." Before he could answer, someone else entered my office.

Some months ago, my office space was modified. It always worried me someone could barge in while I was with a client. I needed to provide a degree of privacy for anyone who came to see me. To that end, a friend, who had become the agent for a fancy screen arrangement installed one as a demonstration model. It was free and there for me to assess and promote. Made of some fabric-like material, it ran between a track on the ceiling and a matching track on the floor. By pressing a button on the remote on my desk, I could bring the two halves of the screen out from the wall to create a small semi-circular reception area just inside the door. It operated a bit like those racks you see in a drycleaner's. While my system is a bit more sophisticated – and perhaps aesthetic – it works on much the same principle.

When there is no one with me, the two halves of the screen are snug back against the wall and out of the way, giving me one open space to work in. It took me awhile to remember I had to close the screen whenever I had a client with me, but now I do it without thinking. And, that's how Ned and I, in our lounge chairs, were invisible to the person now waiting in the little reception area. The identity of that person wasn't a mystery. I doubted it was anyone other than Lucy Telford.

This is when I discover how Lucy reacts to finding Ned here. No point in procrastinating, I had to go to Lucy. "I'm sorry, Ned, I heard someone come in. Would you excuse me for a moment please?"

"I'll leave you to it. Like I said before, I've taken up too much of your time already." He made a move to stand up.

"No Ned. Stay where you are while I see who this is. You are helping me investigate a case. There is nothing more important to me. If you could spare me a little more time, please stay." He shrugged and settled back into his chair as I climbed out of mine.

A quick tap on the foot pedal and the two halves of the screen slid about a metre apart creating a small doorway into my office area. Lucy, swivelling her head from side to side, a confused look plastered across her face, stood on the other side of that doorway. She had never encountered the screen before; hadn't even noticed it tucked back against the wall.

"I've come to collect those copies of the wills. I can wait outside – or come back later – if you're busy."

"No, now is fine." I beckoned her in. "Come on through. Would you like a coffee? I'm afraid I have to 'fess up to having created something of a *faux pas* this morning. On a spur of the moment thing last night, I invited someone to have early morning coffee with me. I hope you don't mind. In fact, I'd like you to say hello to him." I saw reluctance manifest. She gave a slight shake of her head. "You don' have to stay and chat. Just say hello and then go if you want to."

"I didn't want anyone knowing I was back in town."

"Your secret will be safe with this one – if you tell him that's how you feel." She heaved a dramatic sigh of resignation, which I ignored, and led her around to the corner with the lounge chairs. "I doubt any introductions are necessary … I'll make fresh coffee while you two re-acquaint."

"Uncle Ned…" Lucy was first to react. Incredulity was writ large in her voice. "Why are you here with Sonny? What's happened?" Now there was genuine concern.

"Nothing has happened. I was just chatting to Sonny. I can't tell you how good it is to see you again after all this time. You forget people grow up while you're not watching, and you sure have done plenty of that since I last saw you." So far so good; both voices sounded relaxed now.

Lucy hadn't bolted for the door, so I felt it safe enough to assume three for coffee and cake. After cutting yesterday's cake into hefty slices, I dug out three small plates and plastic forks. Thank goodness there weren't any more of us. There were only three plates. I shuttled the coffees and cake to the lounge area in a couple of trips before carrying over a chair from my desk so I could join the others. A short silence prevailed until I was settled and Lucy reignited conversation.

"How is Aunt Norma? I've thought about the two of you so often."

"I lost Norma – two years ago last week. No, don't look like that. It was quick, but unexpected. That made it all the more of a shock I suppose … coming like that without warning. Still, she didn't suffer, and that's a good thing. She never stopped talking about you, and wondering where you were and what you were doing. We kept a look-out for you after your father died; half expected you might come home, you see."

"Uncle Ned…"

"Now you're all grown up, I think we can drop the 'uncle' tag. It was nice when a little girl called us uncle and aunt, but it doesn't feel so great when a beautiful young woman calls me that. Let's make it just Ned, shall we? Now, what were you about to say before I interrupted you?"

"I was going to say it was a good six months later before I knew Dad had died. It was only thanks to a letter from Jessie at the Tanwood store that I found out at all."

News of Norma Edwards' death hit Lucy hard. But, it initiated a wander down memory lane for Ned and Lucy as they revisited memories of shared past good times. I zoned out as their conversation flowed on, keeping only half an ear open in case something of relevance to the case came up. After about fifteen minutes, I gathered up the plates to take them to the kitchenette and to refill the coffee machine while I was there.

As I bent to pick up Lucy's plate, she asked Ned, "So, are you still on the farm now Norma is gone?"

"Yeah, where else would I be?"

"What about our old place – Kirk Michael Farm – is it still there?"

This was dangerous territory the conversation strayed into. I hadn't told Lucy about the state of the old farm, or that it was abandoned. I intended to do that today – until I met Ned yesterday. Norma's death was enough bad news for one day, and I wanted to be the one to break the news about the farm to her. Having picked up her plate, and standing slightly behind her, I shook my head at Ned. He picked up on my signal and responded beautifully.

"Yes, it's still there. Like everything else at Tanwood, life goes on and nothing much changes. Sometimes that's a good thing, and sometimes it's not."

Time slipped by almost unnoticed. It was after ten o'clock … and past when Ned planned to pick up his part before heading home. I was torn between reminding him about his plan for this morning, or letting the pair of them reignite what had once been very close relationship. A phone call from a potential client delayed taking any action on the matter for a few minutes. I tidied up the notes I took during the call before heading back to my guests.

As I approached the two of them, Lucy reminded me. "I thought you were going to make us fresh coffee." She gave me an impish grin. It was a most pleasant thing I'd seen in days. Her time with Ned seemed to work miracles on her outlook on life. Her conversation was animated, and she looked so bright and alert. Ned would have to remember for himself the part he was supposed to collect this morning. I wasn't going to remind him and risk ruining the transformation his time with Lucy brought about.

For some time, conversation focused on people they knew at Tanwood and other parts of the valley. Lucy was catching up on who was still there, had left the area, or died, or married. None of it meant much to me as I knew nothing of the names being bandied about. Not much before twelve o'clock, I began wondering about lunch. Should I bring something back to the office for the three of us, or suggest we go out to eat somewhere. In spite of the change in Lucy, I remained unsure how she would feel about the suggestion of having lunch in one of the eateries close to my office. Wondering about it was never going to solve the dilemma, so I asked the question.

"There's a nice little bistro in the arcade further down the block from here. Should I try booking a table for the three of us for lunch … or, if you would prefer, for the two of you to eat alone?"

Ned's response was immediate. "It would be lovely for the three of us to have lunch together, don't you think, Lucy?"

She hesitated. "Uhmm … Ye-es, I suppose that would be nice – if Sonny can spare the time."

Never one to let a chance go by, I reassured them not only was I available, but I was keen to introduce the pair of them to my favourite little bistro. After the usual faffing about rinsing coffee mugs and cake plates, I locked the door behind us and led the way to our luncheon venue.

A pleasant hour and a half later, Ned remembered the part he was supposed to collect this morning. He was torn between needing to get back to the farm and wanting to spend more time with Lucy. She picked up on his indecision.

"No, Ned, you must get back to the farm. You've animals to attend to and probably a myriad of other things you should have done today. It's been wonderful to just sit and chat to you, but you do have to go. I understand."

"Are you going to be in town for long? I mean, I hope this is not the only time I'm going to have with you before you disappear again. There is so much I want to ask you about:

where you've been, what you've done, what your plans are for the future. Please tell me you're not going to disappear again before I spend more time with you. Come up and visit me at the farm. Bring Sonny too if she wants to come."

Ah, there was that reluctance returning. "Uhmm … Maybe… I'll think about it. And, it will depend on what else I have to do while I'm in town." Ned persisted and she responded. "It's not that I don't want to come, Ned. It's more about not wanting to have to deal with people up there, not wanting to have to deal with what happened at Kirk Michael. I will think about it, but I won't make any promises. I don't want to disappoint you."

I risked adding my few words to the decision-making process. "A trip to Tanwood would provide an opportunity for a quiet visit to the coffee shop to thank Jessie personally for letting you know what happened."

"That's true. Perhaps I will try to visit, but still no promises mind."

Having achieved all he could hope to, Ned took his leave. Lucy and I remained at our table for a little longer. The staff started glaring at us. "I think they're about to chuck us out."

After a few moments back in my office, she decided she wanted to spend the rest of the afternoon alone with her thoughts. I suggested dinner. She declined. We agreed not meet the next day. I wanted to undertake more research into Thomas Blaine's death before I met with Lucy again, and I felt she had a myriad of emotions to deal with after today. Before discussing the condition of Kirk Michael Farm with her, allowing her a day to settle down seemed like a good idea.

As I walked Lucy to the door, I apologised again for surprising her with Ned this morning, and reiterated how his presence was inadvertent and not by design.

"I understand how it came about," she said quietly. "As it turned out, it wasn't a problem." I wasn't convinced it was the truth.

Then, the smile she gave me as she said goodbye reassured me no damage had been done. On thinking about it later, I felt a degree of satisfaction in my assessment of today as ending well for both Lucy and her neighbour, Ned Edwards.

Chapter 12

The phone call came as I sent my last email before closing up for the day. "Sonny, it's me, Lucy. Apologies for disturbing you again today, but I left the copies of the wills behind. I should have put them in my bag as soon as you gave them to me. Instead, I remember putting them down on something while I scratched around in my bag for my car key. Please tell me they are still there somewhere … and I haven't left them somewhere else."

I cast my eyes wildly around my miniscule domain. The missing envelope was nowhere obvious. My heart went into jungle-rhythm mode at the thought of such private documents being mislaid in some public place. Then I spotted the envelope. It triggered clear recall of the events leading to its being left behind. Lucy went to the lounge area to collect her bag. She had the envelope in her hand. Needing both hands free to scrabble around in her enormous bag for her car key, she put the envelope down on the chair recently occupied by Ned ... where it remained safe and sound.

"Phew, thank goodness for that. I won't worry about it now, but will it be okay for me to come by for it in the morning?"

"Yeah, any time after nine o'clock would be fine. See you early tomorrow then."

My drive home was a blur, my mind preoccupied with analysing everything about today. So much so, my mobile startled me as I turned onto my driveway. It was Emily.

"Do you think you could put up with an extra one for dinner tonight? I haven't seen you for a couple of days, and I'm in need of some intelligent and stimulating conversation."

"You're most welcome. I don't know what is on the menu or who will be here, but come on over. Nothing from Ben today, so I don't know whether he is coming or not."

Less than a minute after Emily's call ended, Ben called. "Are you home tonight or working?" I told him I was at home. "Good; I'll be there about seven o'clock with something for dinner."

"Fantastic; I don't have my head on straight enough to cook for us tonight. Oh, by the way, there will be three for dinner. Emily is joining us. She is bringing wine."

A long, hot shower followed by a stinging cold reviver had me feeling almost human by the time the others arrived, but not enough to bring me properly to life. Maybe I was coming down with something. A long day of interviews never left me feeling this way before. My head felt shrouded in dense fog, and everything I tried to do felt like I was trying to swim through treacle. I did manage to steam some greens to go with the roast chicken, roast vegetables, and gravy Ben brought.

While I fussed about preparing dinner, Ben and Emily held an in-depth discussion about some new forensic technique. It seems Emily was excited to try it. Their enthusiasm for the topic allowed me to be a bystander. My contribution to the conversation was no more than a one- or two-word answer to the occasional question in my direction.

Dinner improved my outlook to some extent. By then, the others noticed my virtual withdrawal. Emily broached the subject as we cleared away the table. "Would you rather I hadn't come tonight?"

"No, of course not, I'm pleased you're here. If you weren't, Ben would have been talking to himself all night." He wandered into the kitchen in time to catch our exchange.

"You don't seem yourself. Are you all right?"

"Ye-es … Well, no … Oh, I don't know. Somehow today has left me flat."

"Maybe Emily and I should to leave you in peace to have an early night."

"No, don't do that. I'm sure I'll come good as the night goes on."

Emily shot Ben a glance before she asked, "Has it something to do with your current case? Do you want to talk about it, or is it something you might discuss only with Ben?"

"I don't know what my problem is tonight. I spent three parts of today talking to people about the case. Maybe I'm like this because I didn't produce much to progress it. From the outset, the conversations I had were intended to gather background information, and they did. So, why it left me despondent is a mystery."

"Is this a new case, or the one you were working on last time I spoke to you?" Ben asked.

"It's the same one: the Thomas Blaine murder. I doubt it's progressed at all since we discussed it, however long ago that was." Ben was nodding as though he understood my frustration. Nevertheless, he had more questions to ask.

"Did this quest for background information have any upside to it?"

"I'm not sure. I suppose bringing Lucy and Ned Edwards together after such a long time apart might develop into something good. That remains to be seen. It depends on what Lucy does next; whether she follows up on his invitation to visit him."

"What background stuff did you pick up? Perhaps you just need a chance to analyse what was discussed. Maybe sharing with us their topics and any salient points which came out of the discussions might help you to pick up something overlooked at the time." Emily had a point, so I revisited the conversations from both yesterday afternoon and today. I was about to embark on a rundown of the topics when Ben added his comment.

"Emily, that's a sound suggestion. Sonny, unless there's something you feel is too sensitive to discuss, just start at the beginning and let's see where it takes us. If you brought your notes home, get them and use them to jog your memory." It all made good sense. I was out of my chair and on the way to my office when Ben finished speaking.

With my folder open in my lap, I began what I suspected might develop into a long session. "Okay, the discussion started yesterday afternoon when Ned Edwards came to my office. We spent the rest of the afternoon together, and then I picked him up and took him to dinner last night." I went on to explain how I invited Ned for coffee this morning, having forgotten Lucy was coming to collect some documents, and hence the two of them were in my office at the same time.

Ben, leaning forward with his forearms resting on his thighs, was obviously eager to hear what we discussed. "So, what came out of yesterday's discussions with Ned?"

"We talked about Thomas Blaine's second marriage and the birth of a daughter early in the marriage. Without going into too much detail – I'm still a bit confused by it anyway – it might be summed up as a sordid love triangle. Added to any other thoughts on the matter, the paternity of the child gave the community something more to speculate about. To make matters worse, for many of the locals, the child's colouring tended to confirm their doubts about her being Thomas Blaine's child." Ben was unmoved by this information, but Emily's eyes lit up.

"Was Thomas aware it? He needed to be pretty dumb not to work out something was amiss, when the child's colouring tended to suggest he wasn't responsible. …Maybe I should have waited for the next chapter of the story before I asked the question."

Ben added his thoughts. "Whether Thomas was aware and, if he was, how he dealt with it is something only Thomas could tell us. As he is long since gone, we can only draw assumptions from what became apparent to outsiders at the time, that is, the stuff of rumour and speculation. Do we have any indications worth mentioning?"

"It appears, soon after the child was born, the Blaine marriage fell apart. At least, it seemed the basis for Thomas' decision to sleep in the cottage for some period of time afterwards. I think he still frequented the house in an otherwise normal manner, just chose not to sleep in the house."

"Do we know anything of the third party in this drama? Was he still on the scene at the time of Thomas' murder?" Emily seemed deep in thought as she posed her questions.

My précis of Ned's comments was brief and to the point regarding Lyle Rogan's regular appearance at Kirk Michael Farm, and the community's labelling him as the third member of the triangle. "Regardless of whatever his involvement was while Thomas was alive, as the last man standing, so to speak, in the end, he won the 'prize' when the players were reduced to two."

Emily gave a brief nod of satisfaction. "Yep, he was guilty. I don't think there's much room for doubt and, by the sound of it, the community didn't think so either. I know you're going to tell me I'm jumping to conclusions. So, having discussed the matter at length with Ned, what is your take on the situation at that time?"

"I suspect people have been hanged on less evidence. It seems the bloke in question was a part of the woman's life before, during and after her marriage to Thomas Blaine. I am trying to keep an open mind, but it's a struggle."

Ben entered the discussion. "Am I right in assuming Lyle Rogan is the third person in the triangle you referred to, and he is the man the community believed fathered the child?" I nodded. "That does explain a couple of things. For a while during their investigation, the police had Rogan as their prime suspect. Then, for no apparent reason, he disappeared from their list of 'persons of interest'. I found nothing in the file to indicate why they eliminated him from their inquiry."

After being in apparent hibernation all evening, my synapses jolted back to life. Something Ben said woke them. What had he said to stir them to life? It was about the police eliminating Lyle Rogan as a person of interest. Ah hah, that does beg questions. "Ben, at what stage of their investigation did the police decide Rogan was no longer a suspect?"

"Eh…? What do you mean?"

"Was it in the early stages, or later in their investigation?"

"Off the top of my head, I'm not sure, but I think it was towards the end. Why…? Is when it happened important?"

"Possibly… I know you don't have the file in front of you, but do you remember the line of inquiries they were following at the time?"

"Geez, you don't expect much, do you? Let me think for a minute." Somehow I managed to bite my tongue while he stared off into the distance. Then I watched him give a slight nod before turning to me. "Yeah, I think it was during the latter stages of their investigation. They were interviewing locals at the time. Of course, they did that at the outset, but then went back to re-interview some of them. Something must have triggered that, but I don't remember anything in the file to suggest what it was."

"Do you remember anything significant in the statement they took from Rita Blaine?"

"I remember it was brief, but anything of significance…? No, I don't think so. She wasn't at home when it happened. She and her daughter were staying in Millhaven for a few days. They went into town because of something to do with the daughter. I don't remember the details."

My line of questioning and Ben's responses sparked Emily's interest. "It was convenient she wasn't home at the time. I wouldn't mind knowing about the issue with the daughter which so conveniently had them away from the farm at the relevant time. Do we know anything about it?"

Emily's question caught me off guard. "Hang on a moment while I check my notes. I knew they were away from home, but I don't remember ever hearing the reason why." A quick flick through my notes from my discussions with Ned produced zilch. "No, I don't have any clues about it." But, I made a hasty note to find out.

"Sonny, what are you doing?" Emily demanded. "Have you remembered something? I can just about hear your mind whirling from over here."

With my mind churning at high speed, I doodled along the top of a page of my notes to help my thought processes. It wasn't until Emily called my name and asked her question again, that I realised she had spoken to me. "Sorry, Emily, I was trying to sort something out." …And I had done so.

"Ben, here's a hypothetical for you: When the police went back to re-interview the locals, maybe those locals shared their assumptions about the relationship between Rita Blaine and Lyle Rogan with the cops. If that were the case, is it possible the police assumed Rogan was in town with Rita Blaine and her daughter at the time of the murder?

"I suppose anything is possible, but it is only a hypothesis. We have no evidence to support it."

"I like your line of thinking, Sonny," Emily said. "Do we know anything about the Blaine duo's trip to town – when they left home, how long they stayed in town, where they stayed, anything at all?"

"Unless there is something in Ben's files, there are no firm details."

"I'm beginning to understand why you were so glum earlier this evening," Ben said. "How many days have we spent looking into this cold case, and how much have we to show for it? …Not much at all."

"Are any of the officers who worked the case still attached to the local precinct?" I asked the question in spite of common sense suggesting Ben would have talked to them before this if there were.

"That's one of the odd things about the case file. The names of only two officers appear on any of the paperwork. One was the officer in charge of the investigation and the other was a senior constable. There must have been more than those two involved, but there is no evidence of it. Neither of the officers mentioned is still here. From what I've determined so far, the young bloke resigned soon after the case to return home to run the family's property when his father became ill. About twelve months later, he was killed when the helicopter he was using for mustering crashed."

"What about the senior officer, is he still around?"

"He is no longer a serving member. It seems he took early retirement almost two years ago. He is supposed to have moved to live with, or close to, his daughter, but nobody knows whether here in Millhaven or somewhere else. There's suggestion health prompted the early retirement. Again, it's not clear whether it was his or his daughter's health was the concern. I am working on tracking him down. So far, indications are he moved to the Ralston area."

"It would be pointless asking Pete Messell to talk to him. Pete isn't familiar with the case. And, it would be inappropriate for me to drive down to have a chat with him. So, that leaves the ball in your court. I don't suppose you happen to be going to Ralston anytime soon?"

"As it so happens, I might have a quick trip coming up in the next week or so. If I do locate him, I won't make any arrangements until I know the exact dates I will be there."

"In your efforts to locate people, you haven't come across the whereabouts of Rita Blaine and Rogan, have you?"

"No. Should I have looked for them? I didn't know they were missing. I know you mentioned the farm was abandoned, but I didn't realise they disappeared."

"Yeah, they disappeared. Consensus is they are no longer living anywhere in the valley. If they were still around, I'm sure they wouldn't have abandoned the farm. While neither of them was energetic enough to do anything on the place, at least it was a rent-free roof over their heads. I'm inclined to think something precipitated their disappearing act. If only I knew what it was…"

Emily climbed out of her chair and collected the coffee mugs. She had been quiet for some time. On her way to the kitchen to make fresh coffee, she asked over her shoulder, "Doesn't the old bloke you've been talking to know anything – have any clues – about what was going on at the time?"

"I suspect not. I'm confident he would have shared it with me by now if he knew anything. Nevertheless, I'm half inclined to take another trip to Tanwood tomorrow. It will depend on how things go with Lucy tomorrow morning."

Ben sat up and looked interested. "Any particular reason for the trip … or is it just a case of wanting to escape from the office for a while?"

"If I wanted to escape, I'd stay home and catch-up on some housework." That brought raucous laughter from the other two. I ignored it. "No, I've put together a list of direct questions to ask Ned, and maybe I'll put some of them to a couple of other local identities as well."

As we sipped our fresh coffees and glasses of port, Emily suggested, "I don't suppose there is much I can contribute to this investigation … unless there is evidence collected from the crime scene you would like me to take a look at, Ben. Today's advances in forensics might pick up something missed before."

"It's an option worth exploring. I hadn't thought about it, but it is worth a try. I'm not sure what evidence was collected but, as it remains a cold case, all evidence should still be held. I'll check it out tomorrow and let you know. It might need to be done covertly. I'm not sure why, but I'm keeping my interest in the case under wraps."

With the coffee and port dispatched, my guests made noises about departing. I didn't discourage them, and my actions probably suggested I would be happy to see the back of them tonight. I wanted to write up notes from tonight and tidy up my list of questions for Ned.

Alone or otherwise, I would be driving to Tanwood tomorrow.

Chapter 13

After spending the drive into the city this morning trying to figure out how best to tell Lucy about the condition of Kirk Michael Farm, nothing was resolved by the time I flopped down behind my desk. I had half an hour to decide as I was sure Lucy would be at my door at nine o'clock.

I was wrong. She arrived ten minutes early. With the envelope containing the wills centred on my desk, I made my usual offer of coffee. We took our coffees and the envelope over to the lounge corner of my domain. "I'll drink this and then be on my way," Lucy said as we settled into our chairs. "I don't want to hold you up. I've taken up too much of your time over the last few days."

"You're not holding me up. I wanted to chat to you anyway so, if you can stay for a while, we can relax into it."

"I've nothing happening in my life today. What did you want to talk about? I mean, what in particular about the case did you want to talk about?"

"First things first, have you thought about accepting Ned's invitation to visit him at home?"

"Yes, I did think about it, but haven't decided yet. I might go up north for a few days. When I come back, I'll see how I feel about a trip up the valley. That was something I wanted to ask you about this morning. Will it be okay if I'm not around for a few days?"

"That depends on the outcome of our discussions this morning. Perhaps we should start and see where it takes us."

Upending the envelope, I tipped the copies of the wills onto the coffee table. I pushed Maree and Valerie Telford's wills to one side, leaving Thomas Blaine's holding pride of place in front of us. Lucy reached to for those I pushed aside.

"No, leave those. I want to talk to you about your father's will."

"I thought we did that. It's a slim document, so there's not much to talk about." There was something in her tone. I couldn't decide whether she was being defiant or dismissive.

"Yes, we looked at it, along with the others. And yes, your father's will is a slim document, which didn't take us long to discuss…" Lucy went to interrupt. This time I detected a definite defiant look about her. I rushed on before she could speak. "But we did not examine the entire document." She looked taken aback.

"I…don't…know … what you mean."

Time to break through whatever nonsense was going on in her head; maybe a blunt approach will do it. "You did not read the final page of the will. The key point of which, is that you now own Kirk Michael Farm … and have done so since probate of your father's will."

She sat silent, staring at me, her face devoid of expression. The only change I noticed was her jaw had dropped and her lips had parted slightly. I let her digest my bombshell in silence. For a few moments she studied her hands firmly clasped in her lap. Then there was a gentle shake of her head before she looked up at me. Her eyes pleaded.

"Now, if you feel so inclined, let's look at that last page of Thomas' will." I snatched up the will and folded it over to expose the final page. "Perhaps you should read it for yourself, before we discuss it."

Her hand trembled slightly as she reached for the document. The silence between us stretched on as I watched her read the page at least twice. Then, with the document lying on her lap, she sat staring at it for a long minute before she spoke.

"Yeah … okay … so I own the farm. What a laugh that is. She had nothing – absolutely nothing – when they married. And now, *that woman* has more rights, more ownership, than I do. The will is a joke, and a poor joke at my expense."

"Yes, there are those provisos, but…"

"That's the point. Those provisos give her virtual ownership of the place. Argh, I know she can't sell it or anything like that, but he basically gave it to her. Under the terms of the will, I can't throw her off the place. And, she's never going to leave of her own choosing. Why would she. She came with nothing, and now she has a home and income from the farm for as long as she complies with the terms of the will. No, she's never going to leave. She would make sure she never gave me the satisfaction."

"You're wrong. The will says you can ask her to leave but, unless you do, the other provisos apply. If her status changed and she was no longer compliant with the terms that allow her to remain there, what would you do?"

"What…? I'm not sure what you mean by 'what would I do'.

"Okay, if the situation changed … she was gone and the farm was yours, what would you do about it? Would you sell or lease it out? Would you return to live there? You could work the place yourself, or lease it out to someone else to farm it."

"I hadn't thought about it. Why would I? She's never going to leave. She will make sure I don't get my hands on the place."

"Lucy, I understand how you must feel, how bitter you must be towards the woman, but your comments tell me you retain a strong attachment to the farm. Perhaps it wouldn't be a wasted exercise to think about what you might do if circumstances changed. No, don't argue that it's never going to happen. Neither of us has a crystal ball to tell what the future might bring. But, in your case, it wouldn't hurt to have some ideas about how you might progress if the place was yours again."

She made a couple of attempts to argue before lapsing into silence again. This time it was a brooding silence, and I wondered whether my direct approach had done more harm than good. I remained undecided about informing her of the farm's present condition, but I was leaning towards not mentioning it. I wanted her to discover it for herself – preferably when we went to visit Ned. That thought reminded me to revisit the subject of visiting Ned.

"While I can't make you do anything you don't want to do, I encourage you to take a drive up the valley. What you do when we finish here is up to you, but I intend driving to Tanwood to visit Ned. I would appreciate some company, but the choice is yours."

Lucy sat staring at the coffee table for a few moments. Then, she heaved a sigh, and read the last page of her father's will again before sliding all three wills back into their envelope. Her eyes met mine for a couple of moments before she spoke.

"Okay, I'll come with you. If I own the place, I suppose I should check the condition it's in. When do you want to go?"

"What's wrong with now? I'll call Ned to let him know we're coming. We'll pick up something to take for morning tea first. Where is your car parked?"

"I walked here this morning, so I don't have to worry about a parking fine."

A few minutes later, we loaded an impressive chocolate cake and a hot cooked chook into the car and headed out of the city. Lucy remained quiet until we were beyond the inner suburbs. Then, she seemed to become aware of the landscape flying past her window, and a running commentary began. She noticed things that weren't there when she was a child, how the suburban sprawl stretched out further beyond the city, how traffic had increased, and she commented on the condition of the paddocks of cane as we approached valley.

Once we started up the valley, she fell silent again. I chanced a couple of glances in her direction. They told me she was a bundle of emotions. It wasn't surprising. She hadn't been back to this part of the world for a long time. I felt my stomach tightening. Had I done the right thing? What if it proved too traumatic for her? As the lead ball developed in the pit of my stomach, I tried convincing myself she had to face reality sometime, and it was as well she did it with support around her.

As we approached Tanwood, I noticed her sit upright and clasp the shoulder strap of her seatbelt with both hands. Lucy was so tightly coiled, anything could happen. The next few minutes before we reached Ned's place could prove tricky. By the time we turned onto the road leading past the farm, Lucy wasn't the only one in the car so uptight.

We were about halfway up Ned's driveway when Lucy realised where we were. "This is Ned's farm. That means our farm – my farm – is over there." She waved her arm across in front of me to indicate the farm next door. "That can't be right. We must have driven past it, but I didn't see it. Are you sure this is Ned's farm?"

I ignored the question. We were almost at the house and Ned stood on the verandah waiting for us. He waved as I drove the last short distance through his yard to pull up beside his front steps. Then he danced down the steps and rushed around to fling open Lucy's door. "Welcome, welcome; I'm so glad you could make it. Come up onto the verandah. I've put the kettle on."

"Oh, Ned, nothing's changed. It's just as I remember it from all those years ago. The only thing missing is Norma. How you must miss her. You were so close. I never saw one of you without the other being close by."

While Ned led Lucy by the arm up onto the verandah, I trailed along behind carrying the cake and the chook. There followed the usual faffing about while coffee was made and cake dished out. Then, for the next few minutes, Ned and Lucy revisited memories they both held precious for so many years. I waited for the first appropriate lull in their reminiscing before initiating the conversation I wanted to have. When it presented, I decided on the round-about route, as opposed to diving straight into discussing Kirk Michael Farm.

"Ned, have you always had cattle? I notice you have some cropping happening as well."

"Yep, always had cattle but, a few years ago now, we turned our herd into a stud. It was a good move too; done well it has. And, there has always been cropping as well. What we grow varies according to the season."

"Where are they putting the animals on the farm nextdoor?" I noticed Lucy didn't refer to the farm in a personal way, choosing instead to call it 'nextdoor. "The stock used to be in those paddocks along the fence line. Now, it doesn't look as though those paddocks have seen stock forever. They are full of long grass and weeds."

"There is no stock on the farm these days, hasn't been for some time." Ned looked uncomfortable sharing the information.

"What about crops? When I look across to the farm, I don't see any areas under crops."

"No; no cropping going on either."

The conversation had headed exactly where I wanted. I hoped by mentioning Ned's cattle, it would cause Lucy to ask questions about stock –or absence thereof – on the Blaine farm. It worked. It aroused Lucy's curiosity about the farm. I gave Ned a hard look to grab his attention. Then, after flicking my eyes between him and Lucy a couple of times, I jerked my head over towards Blaine's farm. Top marks to Ned, he worked out what I was suggesting.

"Well, my girl, why don't we go over so you can have a look around for yourself to see what's happening over there?"

"No. No, I don't want to go near the place. I don't want to see her."

"She is not there."

"With my luck, she'll come home while I'm there. No, I don't want to see the place. I've lived without it as part of my life for too many years now to damage the shell I've built around of my memories."

"Ned, I have to tell you, Lucy didn't know where we were until we were about halfway up your driveway. She didn't recognise the farm when we drove past it."

"I'm sorry about that. After I brought that tractor part home yesterday, I was busy all afternoon getting the machine going again, so I didn't have time to do anything. This morning I was busy first thing, but I intended to go over and mow the place in case you decided to come up this way. I didn't get a chance to do it before you arrived."

"You shouldn't be mowing the farm next door. It's not for you to worry about what the place looks like. Then again, it seems no one else is too worried about it either. When I think back on how neat and tidy Dad kept the place, it's heartbreaking to see it the way it is now."

I felt it was time to intervene. "The heartache is worse because you haven't come to terms with it, and it will continue to gnaw at you until you do. Your only way to do that is to go and look at the place. Ned and I will come with you. We will be there with you if you need support. Come on, get up off that chair and let's go. We can take my car."

"No need to drive, Sonny, we can walk across. That track over there leads to a gate in the fence. I think Sonny is right, Lucy. Come on, let's go and have a look at the place."

With Ned in the lead and me tacked on the end, we made our way single file to the gate in the boundary fence, and then onto a rough, partly overgrown track towards what was once Lucy's home. She didn't go straight to the house, choosing instead to wander willy-nilly around the place. As she walked around the machinery shed, I called out to her.

"Ned and I are going to make ourselves comfortable on that big log under the tree. Take your time, have a good look around, but we will be here if you need us." I shoved Ned towards the log.

"Do you think she will be all right on her own? It's a lot for her to take in and it's bound to be upsetting."

"Relax, Ned. She's a tough young woman. She's had to be. Yes, it will be upsetting … until she realises what the situation is here. Once that happens, it will be easier for her. But, she has to come to terms with it herself. It will not be helpful if we keep trying to ease the situation for her. All we can do is to be here if she needs us."

While I was speaking, I noticed Lucy was circling the house and trying to peer in the downstairs windows. Ned noticed it too. "It'll do her no good trying to look in those windows. The house is dark inside and there's such a thick coating of dust on the windows, she won't be able see anything."

After a couple of circuits of the house, she went and stood a few metres out from the front door. I wasn't sure what to make of it. She just stood there looking at the house. Then, after a minute or so and as if she'd made up her mind, she marched up to the front door and tried the knob – with predictable result. There was no surprise. The door was locked.

Lucy tried the knob a couple of times more before accepting the door wasn't going to open. She took a couple of steps back and just stood there, her disappointment clear from where we sat. Ned heaved himself up off the log and strolled towards her. I saw him slide his hand into his pocket, the same pocket he surreptitiously slid something into before we left his house. Staying some distance behind him, I followed as he made his way to Lucy.

In a quiet voice, I heard him ask, "Did you want to go inside?"

She shrugged. "It's not meant to be. The place is locked. I don't suppose I should go in there anyway."

"Nonsense; you might find this useful." I watched as he withdrew his hand from his pocket and held it out, palm upwards, towards her. She looked down at his hand and let out a squeak.

"A key…! Where did you find a key? Is it for this door?" Ned nodded.

"I've always held the spare key to this place, just as your father held one to mine. And yes, it opens this door – if you want it to."

"Does she know about this arrangement?"

"If you are referring to Rita, then no, I'm confident she didn't. Anyway, she would never have come to me for help if she had a problem."

"Why not? You're her nearest neighbour and she knew how you and Dad used to help each other."

"She didn't like me. It didn't bother me. I didn't have much time for her either, so it wasn't a problem." Ned's comment struck a chord with Lucy. I watched a wicked grin slide across her face.

Ned kept his hand with the key cradled in its palm extended to Lucy. She looked uncertain; sceptical even. When she continued to hesitate, Ned lowered his hand, stepped up to the front door and inserted the key in the lock. Without unlocking the door, but while blocking access to it, he turned to face her.

"It's your decision. You can go inside, or you can stay out here and not find out what you want to know. What's it to be?"

"I want to go inside … I need to go inside."

"I'll open the door for you. Will you be all right by yourself? One, or both of us, will come in with you if you would prefer to have someone with you."

"No. Thanks, but this is something I need to do by myself. Don't go away though, and yell out if you see her coming back."

"She is not coming back. Go in and do whatever you need to do. Don't hurry. Take all the time you want. We will be out here if you need us. Just shout and we'll be there."

Ned stepped aside. Lucy stepped up to the door. I watched her rest her hand on the door knob for a couple of moments before turning the key and easing the door open. Ned came back to stand with me. I felt something akin to what I image a mother feels when she drops off her child for its first day at school: a writhing turmoil of nervousness and pride.

"Relax, Sonny. You know she has the strength to do this. It is the only way she ever will deal with her demons. Shall we resume our seats on yonder not-so-comfortable log?"

He was right. There was nothing for it but to sit and wait it out, but I knew every minute she was in the house alone would feel like an hour.

Chapter 14

Suspecting we might be perched on our log for some time, it made sense to capitalise on my time alone with Ned. Not wanting to read from my list, I had to rely on memory for the list of questions I wanted to ask him.

"Ned, I have questions, and most of them I want to deal with while out of Lucy's hearing. I'm concerned finding the farm in the state it is might have significant adverse impact on her without my adding to it by dredging up information which could cause additional emotional distress."

"All that makes sense, so what do you want to know? Mind you, I'm not saying I will have the answers you're looking for."

"I suppose the issue nagging me most is the convenience of Rita and her daughter being in town at the time of the murder. When did they leave the farm?"

"There is a bit of confusion about that. It won't surprise you to know I didn't discuss the matter with Rita, so I don't have the facts. There were two versions floating around the community. One had the pair leaving the farm for town the day before the murder, while the other one insisted they went into town on the day of the murder. I can't vouch for either of those 'facts'."

"Maybe so, but I suspect you have a preference for one of the versions."

"Not a preference as such; it's more a case of applying common sense. Late in the afternoon of the day before the murder, I'm sure – almost sure – I saw the girl emptying Thomas' rain gauge. Rain was so heavy and constant, rain gauges overflowed if you didn't check on them a couple of times during the day. If you weren't interested in how much had fallen, it didn't matter if the gauge overflowed. Most farmers keep records and want to know.

Anyway, it was late when I went for one last check on the stock before it became too dark to see. I checked over the fence on Thomas' stock while I was there, and noticed he had put out supplemental feed for them. It was then I reckon I saw her emptying Thomas' rain gauge."

"Did you tell the police what you saw?"

"Nah, they didn't ask me, and I couldn't swear to it. I could be remembering something from a couple of days before the murder. It's one of the problems with getting old, not being confident about your memory."

"While you might feel that way, I would put my money on the veracity of your memory. For this discussion, let's assume they left for town on the day of the murder, leaving Thomas alone at the farm. According to all accounts, it was a thoroughly unpleasant night when the murder occurred. For me, that begs two questions. Who knew Thomas would be home alone? And who would want to be out skulking around on such a filthy night?

"My response to your first question is 'hardly anyone'. I'm nextdoor, and keep a bit of an eye over the fence, but even I didn't know. Up this way, the houses aren't close to the road. They are built back from the road and up on higher ground above flood level."

"Okay, so it's possible no one knew, unless she told someone of her intentions beforehand. What do you think?"

"Seems a reasonable assumption to me… It leads me to think about your second question, and produces one of my own. If she told someone they were going to stay in town, and that 'someone' was prepared to go and do the deed on such a filthy night, then was it all part of a grand plan?

"That's the same question the little voice in my head is asking. Such a plan is so horrendous, it's difficult to consider.

If we do consider it, who would she be in league with who would be prepared to carry out the deed?"

"…And why? I mean, what would the killer get out of murdering Thomas?"

"Whoa, hang about, Ned. The way this is supposed to work is for you to answer my questions, and not for you to pose more questions for me to contemplate. But, Ned, I think you just raised the question that is the crux of this whole case. Who benefited from Thomas's death – either directly or indirectly? Is there anyone you can think of?"

"Hmm, when you put it like that, yeah, someone does come to mind."

"…Lyle Rogan maybe?"

"Might he be a tad too obvious though? From the outset, the whole community had him tagged as the killer. Even the police had him in their sights for a while, but they must have found something to change their mind."

"Are you saying you don't think Rogan is to blame?"

"Not at all, all I'm saying is, the community always saw him as the bad guy. The rumours had him hanging around Blaine farm because he was having an affair with Rita behind Thomas' back – remember, they liked Thomas and couldn't stand Rita. Then, when the baby came along, of course Rogan was the father, just look at its colouring. And, when he moved in with Rita, the community saw it as confirmation of all they suspected."

"I see your point. It's too easy to pin everything on him. So, let's think about it. Who else might benefit from Thomas' demise? The next person on the community's suspect list would be Rita. It doesn't matter that she reputedly was in town and couldn't have done it. What are your thoughts on Rita as a suspect?"

"Nah, she was in town. I don't buy her as the guilty party."

"She did benefit though. She was left some money, and was able to stay on at the farm and derive an income from it.

Although she wasn't here, might another person have done it for her? She could pay someone else to kill him."

"What… like a hitman? …Up here in Tanwood? … You've been watching too many gangster movies." Ned was silent for a few heartbeats before continuing. "Still, I have to agree. Thomas' death tidied up her life for her. She gained from his will, but also was free to resume her live-in relationship with Rogan."

"In the same way, Rogan benefitted too from no impediment to his moving in with Rita and sharing his daughter's life – if he was her father."

"Do we know how Rita went to town? Did she have her own car or was there just the one car on the property?"

"When she first came to do a bit of housework for Thomas, she had an old rattletrap of a thing, nothing but rust holding it together. It disappeared once they were married. I don't know what happened to it. She couldn't sell it, except to a scrap dealer. Thomas had a big SUV and they both drove that."

"Let's test your memory. Here is the big question, Ned: was Thomas' SUV still at the farm after he died?"

"Oh yes, it was still here. She drove it everywhere. They shot through in it in the end. That's when it disappeared."

"Okay… For a brief moment, I wondered if they were helped go into town, but seems unlikely. So, I will scrap the idea and accept they drove into town in the family's car."

"I don't remember there ever being a question about that."

"Paint me a picture of what it was like here in the time immediately before Rita headed into town. I'm trying to understand why she felt it necessary to make the trip when the weather was supposed to be so bad."

"It was the wet season, and raining hard as it does at that time of the year. It felt like it had been raining for weeks, and looked as though it was going to continue coming down like that forever. The river always floods during the wet season. We can count on it happening a few times each year. Flooding cuts the road on both sides of Tanwood, leaving it isolated from the rest of the world for three of four days every time. That year, we had one small flood which came up and went down again overnight, but the rain continued and became heavier. We knew we were heading for a big flood."

"With flooding being a regular occurrence, I imagine the locals stock up and are well prepared to cope with being isolated. By the time Rita evacuated into town, she had been living here for some years and used to coping with the situation. …Or did she always disappear into town when flooding was imminent?"

"I hadn't noticed it happen before. There were other big ones during the years she lived here. The funny thing is, she never felt the need to evacuate during any of the floods after Thomas was gone." Ned gave an emphatic nod after his last comment. He was right. It was worth noting.

"So, that brings us back to why the threat of this flood was different? Why, on this occasion, did Rita and her child escape to town until the risk of flooding was over?"

"I've heard tell the child has a health problem. I'm not sure what, but I think it was something like asthma, but with additional complications. Whatever it was, Rita didn't want to be cut off from town in the event the child had some sort of health event. She drove into town before the road was cut by floodwater. It was that night – I'm sure it was that night – Thomas was killed. Floodwater cut the road sometime in the early morning."

"Rita's actions were not unreasonable if the child's health issues were such as could become life-threatening if medical assistance wasn't readily available. While I'm trying to view the event from a logical perspective, the convenience of her absence still nags me. You told me you found Thomas' body."

"That's right. I knew something was wrong, but I didn't want to interfere. All the day after he was killed, I kept an eye out for him. It was still raining, but I expected to see him attending to his animals, or checking other things on the property. I told Norma I was a bit worried about the situation next door. She said to leave it until the next day. If I didn't see him around by lunchtime, I should go over to see if everything was all right. The next day, I couldn't wait until lunchtime. A bit after ten o'clock, I came across to this house. As I approached the front door, I was cursing myself for not having grabbed the spare key before I left home. I didn't need it. The front door wasn't locked."

One glance at Ned and I knew he'd taken himself off, reliving that fateful morning. I gave him a few moments before resuming the conversation. "You said you knew something was wrong. Why was that? What aroused your concerns about what was happening next door?"

"The first thing was, I hadn't seen Thomas around. It wasn't like him. But there was something else. When it's cold and wet like that, the grass is full of water and doesn't have enough nutrients for the stock. We give them supplemental feeding to maintain their condition and survive. Thomas fed his cows on the morning Rita left for town. He should have fed them again the next morning, but he didn't … and he didn't feed them at all that day. It wasn't like Thomas. He was a good farmer. He cared for his animals. The following day, when he still hadn't fed the stock, and I still hadn't seen him around, I knew something was wrong."

"Did it occur to you that he might have gone into town with Rita and the child?"

"At that stage, I didn't know they went to town. So no, I didn't think Thomas had gone into town. Later when I learnt about Rita being away from the farm, I knew I'd seen Thomas out in the paddock after she left."

"So, on the day Rita went into town, nothing happened over here on Thomas' farm to concern you, and it wasn't until the next day you started feeling uneasy about the situation?" Ned nodded and I continued. "Tell me about that day. Did anything unusual happen? You said you saw Thomas around outside. What was he doing?"

"It was still pelting down rain. There wasn't dry bit of ground anywhere, and it was cold. Norma kept the combustion stove going all day to keep the house warm and dry. As I told you, when I went down to tend my stock, Thomas was putting out feed for his animals. I went down to my stock again in the afternoon. Thomas was out in his paddock too.

A cow had calved sometime during the day, but things had gone wrong and the calf was dead. The mother was in a bit of a mess, and her condition combined with the state of the paddock and the weather, meant she had to be put down. Thomas took care of it and then moved the stock into the next paddock, leaving just the two carcasses where they were. His intention would be to come back and deal with them later, preferably when there was a break in the weather. That dead cow and her calf still lying there in the sodden paddock for more than twenty-four hours was a good indication something was not right at Kirk Michael Farm."

"Thomas didn't have a good day, did he? When you said Thomas took care of the cow, I assumed he shot her. Is that correct?"

"Yeah … It's unpleasant, but it's what you have to do sometimes. When an animal can't be saved, the best thing is to put it out of its misery. I saw Thomas put her down. I was in my paddock on the other side of the fence line the time. He would be a bit upset about it, but it wasn't the first time he had to do it, and any upset you feel at the time doesn't last long. You know it's necessary, and you know you've done the best thing for the animal."

"Let's move forward to when you came here to the house. You cursed yourself for not bringing the spare key, but found the front door unlocked. Were you surprised the door was unlocked? If you thought Thomas was at home, why would you expect the door to be locked? I'm surprised you didn't try the cottage out the back first. After all, that place had sort of become Thomas' home away from home, so to speak."

"Thomas didn't avoid going into the house altogether. He spent a lot of time in the cottage and slept out there, but he still went into the house for meals, to shower, and that sort of thing. Most of the time, his visits to the house were brief. There was heavy rain that morning, and it was cold and dark. Lights were on in the house, but the cottage was in darkness. I didn't know whether I would encounter Rita or Thomas when the door opened. I knocked and called out. When there was no response, I opened the door a fraction, stuck my head in and called out again. That's when I saw Thomas."

"As much as I hate asking you to relive those terrible memories, until I know the full story of what happened here, I can't help Lucy to understand it either. If you can do it without upsetting yourself too much, please describe the scene you found here."

"If I'd walked around to the other side of the house, I wouldn't have had to come in to find what I did. The window around there was open. The rain was belting up against this side of the house, so it was common practice to leave a window partially open on the other side to allow in a bit of fresh air, particularly if you had a fire going in the fireplace. Thomas was lying there below the open window. I could see the bullet hole. He was dead."

"Ned, I'm aware Lucy has been roaming around inside there for some time. I want to make sure she is all right. Before we do, tell me what you did after finding Thomas. I think you said you called the police, is that correct?"

"Yes. I had my mobile phone with me. Norma insisted I carry it everywhere in case something happened to me when I was out in a paddock. I called the police and described what I'd found. Their immediate reaction was Thomas had committed suicide. I tried arguing with them but it got me nowhere. They couldn't come up the valley because the road remained flooded, so they told me to leave everything as it was and to lock the door. Twenty-four hours later, they arrived."

"Okay, let's leave it there and see what Lucy is up to."

"I don't know how this visit will affect her, and whether she is in there looking for something in particular or just revisiting memories. On the off chance she might decide to come up here, apart from mowing the place to make it a bit more presentable, I intended to look in the house. I haven't been inside since the others moved out, so I've no idea what condition it's in."

We stood and, before strolling over to the front steps, rubbed our backsides to encourage circulation into them after sitting on the hard log. As Ned reached for the door, I caught him by the arm to stop him. "Wait … before we go in. Ned, I'm no psychologist, but I think I would have difficulty living in the house where the man I was married to was found dead on the floor." Ned gave a nod of understanding. "Yet, it didn't appear to bother Rita. Nor was she concerned about what impact it might have on her daughter. Was Thomas' body still here when Rita returned?"

"No. When only a bit of water remained on the road, the police managed to get through. I think it was the following day, after taking photographs and whatever else they did, they removed the body. The place still hadn't been cleaned up though when Rita came back. They were keen to interview her and all that, but wouldn't let her back into the house. She kicked up a fuss, and demanded to know where she was supposed to live in the meantime. They were adamant the place was a crime scene and nobody was allowed to enter the house or its immediate surrounds."

"Where did they stay?"

Ned shrugged. "No idea; probably went further up the valley to stay with Lyle Rogan in his shack. It was a week or more before I saw them come back. The police still had a man on guard, and he sent them away again. It was another week after that when Rita and the child moved in again."

"Interesting… Come on let's see what Lucy is doing."

Chapter 15

The house was deathly quiet; no sign of Lucy. Then, a soft sound came from the upstairs bedroom area. "Lucy, is it all right if we come up?" I wanted to avoid startling her by bounding up the stairs unannounced.

"Yes, of course, come up. There are no ghosts up here."

Her choice of phrase surprised me. I looked over at Ned. He gave me another of his unfathomable shrugs. We climbed the stairs and found Lucy in the master bedroom rummaging through a wardrobe – still containing clothes. There might not be ghosts, but seeing those clothes still in the wardrobe was a bit eerie. They were men's clothes. …Could be Lyle Rogan's rejects, I told myself.

Lucy's rummaging seemed to have a purpose. "Are you searching for something specific, or just indulging in a random poke about?"

"Searching… I wanted to look in the office downstairs but it is locked. I don't know where Dad kept the key. He never locked the office – not until after they were married anyway. After that, he tended to keep it locked, but I've no idea where he hid the key. I had a bit of a nose around possible hiding places downstairs but came up empty. Then it occurred to me he might keep it up here in the pocket of one of his coats or something. No sign of a key, or anything else of interest, so far. Feel free to join in the search."

Are these her father's clothes, or is she assuming they are his because they are in what used to be his wardrobe? Should I risk suggesting they might be Lyle Rogan's clothes? Would it be insensitive at this juncture? While I struggled with the dilemma, out the corner of my eye, I saw Ned shake his head. Did he read my mind? Was he signalling me not to say anything?

While Lucy was speaking, he seemed lost in thought. I suppose his thoughts might have been unpleasant and he shook his head to rid himself of them. Regardless, I decided not to mention Lyle Rogan. Lucy may not be aware he moved in with Rita after Thomas' death. Ned shoved those thoughts aside when he spoke.

"I don't think your father kept the key up here. If he kept the office locked, it was for a good reason. He needed to feel confident no one might 'accidentally' find the key and access whatever he didn't want them to see. It's probable he didn't keep the key in the house at all."

"Are you suggesting it's hidden somewhere in the shed? I wonder why he found it necessary to lock it. I don't remember anything 'top secret' in there."

"Lucy, that's the important point. After you left, your father's life changed. I'm not privy to details of why it changed but, from all I've heard so far, there was a significant change. Perhaps we should be guided by Ned's superior knowledge of life on Kirk Michael Farm during your absence."

With obvious reluctance, she agreed. She planted her hands on her hips and turned to face Ned. "So, Ned, where do you think dad hid the office key?"

"If I were a betting man, I'd put my money on somewhere in the cottage out the back. Shall we adjourn to the cottage?" I risked a quick glance at my watch. Lucy noticed.

"Do you have somewhere else to be, Sonny? What is the time anyway?"

"No, I don't have any pressing commitments, but it is after twelve o'clock. Scouring the cottage for the missing key might take some time. Perhaps we should return to Ned's place for lunch before searching the cottage. How does that sound?" With unanimous support for my suggestion, we all trooped down stairs.

On our way across the ground floor to the front door, I stopped midstride. "Is that the door to the office?" The other two nodded in unison. "Did the police search the office?"

"I don't think so. When they told me to close up the place to keep everyone out until they arrived, I tried the office door. It was locked. After they arrived, nobody asked about a key for the office. The door hasn't been forced, so I'm guessing no one's been in there since then."

I took a closer look at the door. "It doesn't present too much of a challenge. If we can't find a key, we could try picking the lock. Then, if that fails, we could force the door." Ned responded first.

"Seems a shame, but I suppose it might be what has to be done."

"No… I don't want the door damaged. Yes, I do want to get in there, but there has to be a way to do it without damaging anything." Lucy's voice was shrill. Ned attempted to calm her down.

"It's okay, Lucy. We don't want to damage the door either. Let's have lunch and then look for the key. As a last resort, we could consider removing the door from its hinges. But, we're not going to think about it until after we've searched the cottage."

Discussion closed, Ned locked the front door behind us and we traipsed the rough and overgrown track to his home. We prepared a salad to go with the cooked chook we brought, and soon were gathered around the small table on the verandah to eat lunch.

Lucy seemed tense, although she insisted she was okay. Common sense said she couldn't be unaffected by her morning. I tried encouraging her to talk. It worked, but not as I expected. I was surprised she wasn't interested in discussing what she'd found in the house, but concentrated on talking to Ned about the general state of the farm. Nevertheless, the bottle of wine Ned opened to celebrate Lucy's return to Tanwood helped relax her.

While Ned explained the mysteries of farming to me, Lucy dozed in the squatters chair she had moved to after we finished eating. Ned and I moved to the opposite end of the verandah. There was unspoken agreement to allow Lucy to doze for as long as it lasted. We talked about nothing in particular in hushed tones until she woke with a start.

"Geez, was I asleep? How long…? What's the time? We should be over there looking for the key not wasting time here. You should have woken me." The rest of her indignant outburst was drowned out by our laughter. It was a few minutes after two o'clock when we were on our way back to Kirk Michael Farm.

This time we went straight to the cottage. It too was locked. Ned saved the day again by producing a key from one of his pockets. With a lift and a shove, the door was open and we were inside. "I have a vague memory of Dad and I being in here when I was quite young. It's the only time I was in here. In fact, I think it was the only time it was opened."

"Searching the place for a key shouldn't take too long," I suggested. "There's nothing much in here." We stood in the kitchen section of the cottage. To describe it as 'basic' would be an exaggeration. While Thomas might have spent time here, he never established it as a proper 'bachelor' pad. The scarred wooden small table and a matching chair bore the only evidence of use since the last cleric departed.

A big cast iron wood stove with a hot water reservoir on one side occupied the space Ned told us was the cottage's original open fireplace. After much complaint by the last minister about his primitive conditions, they purchased the stove, and the large stone chimney attached to the outside wall was demolished. The internal surfaces of the walls were unlined, leaving the noggins exposed. These still bore evidence of early occupants' use of them as handy shelves. At various places around the walls, candle wax still adorned the timbers.

We searched every inch of the room. Even ran our hands along every noggin in search of a key, but to no avail. It was unanimous. There was no key hidden anywhere in the kitchen.

That left the only other room in the cottage to search. A flimsy partition divided the bedroom from the kitchen. Sheeted on the kitchen side, it too was unlined on the bedroom side.

The bedroom looked more lived-in than the rest of the place. It contained an ancient single bed with an unappealing looking mattress. A packing case standing on its end next to the bed served as a bedside table. Someone – we assumed Thomas –strung a wire across one end of the room.

Several items of men's clothing on hangers occupied one end of the wire, while much of it was taken up by a couple of pairs of men's work trousers casually thrown over it. The partition's noggins held a few of Thomas' personal items; comb, razor, and a pair of nail clippers. The room made a poignant statement about the state of the Blaine marriage. I felt my heart go out to Thomas. If it affected me this way, what must it do to Lucy? I felt some degree of urgency for us to be out of there. "Come on, the day is fast away. I'm sure Ned has things to do on his property. Let's find that key if it's here."

Our search was quick but thorough – and produced nothing. A dejected looking trio, we gathered at the end of the bed to consider our options. "It seems I got it wrong," Ned said glumly. "We've proved the key is not here. I suppose we could try searching the shed."

"The shed…!" Lucy exclaimed in horror. "Searching in there would take forever, and we'd never find a key hidden in there. I do want to get into the office. Is the only option left to us to attack the door?" Ned nodded but didn't say anything.

A stray thought smashed in from left field, and the little voice in my head was screaming *check the bed.* I dropped to my knees beside the bed and started running my hand along the underside of the bed frame. Shuffling along on my knees as I went, I checked down one side and across the foot of the bed before turning the corner to check along the other side. As I came to the end of that side of the frame, I was beginning to feel guilty about my impetuous move giving the other two false hope. I told myself I should check along the bed head end of the frame while I was about it.

Halfway along the metal frame, my fingers found something. I dropped onto my back and rolled under the bed, wriggling myself into position to see what I'd found. There it was. … Well, there something was. Several pieces of tape secured a small lump to the inside surface of that part of the bed frame. Whoever put it there did not intend it should come off easily. My nails aren't long, but I managed to wreck one in trying to scratch up the end of the tape.

My behaviour excited my companions. I chose to ignore the questions they fired at me until I knew what I'd found. At last, I had enough of the tape free to grab hold of it and rip it from the frame. I dropped the sticky mass onto my palm. It lay there, sticky side up, with a key securely attached to the centre of it. For a few moments, I just stared at the key.

Once more Lucy demanded to know what I'd found. This time, I honoured her with an answer. "I might have saved us the trouble of vandalising the office door." Lucy let out a screech of excitement. Ned confined himself to murmuring his congratulations. While there was no guarantee this was the key to the office, as we made our way back to the house, I hoped my confidence wasn't misplaced.

We heard the lock spring back. A shout of 'yes' went up in unison. We were loud enough to be heard at the Tanwood coffee shop. Then, elation gave way to hesitancy. After waiting so long for the moment, I expected Lucy to push open the door and march in. She didn't. With the door half open, she stood outside with a hand resting on the knob. "I'm almost afraid to go in. It's the thought of what I might find in there. What can be so important – or so horrible – he needed to keep it locked and the key hidden?"

Ned stepped forward and patted her arm. "I'm sure the locked door wasn't meant to exclude you. For whatever reason, I'm sure your father intention was other people in this house shouldn't access the room. There will be nothing in there to hurt you. Maybe some of it will surprise you, even shock you, but nothing will physically hurt you."

"You're right, Ned. I'm just being silly. Nevertheless, will you and Sonny stay here with me please?"

"Of course; we will be out here. If anything in there bothers you just yell, and we'll charge in to rescue you. Ned, let's make ourselves comfortable in those chairs. This could develop into a long session."

The two lounge chairs we settled into were just inside the front door. While it was possible to see the office door from there, we couldn't see into the office. That suited me, as I felt Lucy needed privacy as well as time alone with whatever she found. My concern about taking up so much of Ned's time grew. From our earlier discussions, I knew he went down to check on his stock late every afternoon. It was fast approaching that time of day.

"Ned, if you need to slip away to do things over on your place, please feel free to go. I'll stay with Lucy. I won't let her stay too long today. In spite of her denial, I think today was a significant emotional strain for her. I would like her to relax a little back in Millhaven. I have no doubt she will be back here tomorrow, with or without me. If that is the case, and I am with her, we'll try not to disrupt your day as much as today."

"Of course you'll be back tomorrow. Even if Lucy wants to come back on her own, I know I'll see you again tomorrow. You don't have the whole story yet, and I don't need to be Einstein to know you still have a long list of questions. Yes, I will nip down to check on the stock, but I'll be back. In spite of what you think might be best, I'm sure the pair of you still will be here when I return."

After Ned left, I spent a few minutes examining my surroundings from the comfort of my lounge chair. I was at the front end of an open plan living area. The 'lounge room' end, immediately inside the front door, was a narrow strip across the building. Beyond that, the living area narrowed to about two-thirds the width of the building and comprised a dining area followed by the kitchen. Opposite the dining area, and occupying the other third of the width of the building, was the office. Along the same side of the building, next to the office and opposite the kitchen was another small room. Its door was closed, so I didn't know its purpose.

It was obvious a great deal of care and attention to detail went into turning the old church into a comfortable home. The refurbishment included installation of a mezzanine floor to house three bedrooms. I imagined the laundry and other facilities were located in the back part of the ground floor beyond the kitchen.

While assessing my surrounds, I realised there was no sound emanating from the office. Lucy had been in there for some time without making any noise. My stomach tightened. "Lucy, are you all right in there? You are being awfully quiet. Is everything okay?"

No reply worried me. I tiptoed across to the office door. Still no sounds coming from in the office, so I knocked gently. Still no response from Lucy had me bordering on panic. I flung open the door and rushed in. Lucy sat at her father's desk, papers strewn all over it. She wasn't reading any of it; just sitting staring at the mess.

"Are you all right," I asked again, more loudly than I intended. Startled, she almost fell from her chair.

"What…? Oh, Sonny … Apologies; I didn't hear you come in. Where's Ned?"

"He's gone to tend to his animals, but will be back when he is finished. What happened here?" I asked, gesturing at the chaos on the desk. "But, first, are you okay?"

"Am I okay…? Yes, why wouldn't I be?"

"You didn't look convincing when I came in. Now, tell me about all this mess?"

"Dad had this pile of paper clipped together in specific bundles and stacked in the middle of his desk. Beside them was a pile of file folders. It's as though he was doing his filing when … when it happened. I don't know how they got into this mess. I started going through them to see what they were. …And now they look like this. I don't know how it happened. I don't remember doing it."

"When I came in, you were just sitting staring. What was going on? Did you come across something upsetting?"

"No. Well, not really." She waved her arm across the mess on the desk. "This upset me. It made me realise how much I missed out on over all those years. …How I wasn't here for Dad when he needed me … and how meticulous he was in running this farm."

"Okay, so nothing specific; everything in general."

"Well, there is one thing upsetting me – the filing cabinet over there." She indicated the far cabinet of a bank of three.

"What's so special about it that upsets you?"

"It's locked. The other two aren't. They contain the files this pile of paper belongs in. Why did he need to keep the third one locked?"

"I doubt it contains top secret material of danger to the country if released … and it isn't as I imagined Pandora's Box might look."

"Sonny…!" The reprimand in her voice curtailed any further flippant comment.

"I'm sorry. Have you found a key for it, or do we need to embark on another key-hunt?"

"It doesn't require a key. It has a keypad, and requires entry of a code to open it. …And, no, I haven't found anything like a code."

"O-oh, that's a pity. Searching for a key might have proved much simpler than figuring out the code. I suppose the first thing to try is entering various birth dates, and other special events' dates like those of various anniversaries."

"I tried the birth dates I remember. Nothing happened. I don't know those of the other two people who lived here. Somehow, I don't think Dad would have used them."

She might be right about his not using their dates, I thought, but it just might be a comfortable option not to believe it. I didn't voice those thoughts. We had something more pressing to consider than opening the filing cabinet at such late time of the day.

"It's getting late. You have had a big day – in every way, including emotionally. Perhaps we should stop, and leave worrying about unlocking the filing cabinet until tomorrow. What do you think?"

"We can't come back tomorrow."

"Eh…? Do you have something else planned for tomorrow, something you can't change or cancel?"

"No, of course not; nothing is more important than this. We've been lucky to have this opportunity today. We can't expect to come marching in here again tomorrow to begin again from where we left off. More important than anything else, I don't want to see or meet that woman and her child ever again. I thought I had those feelings under control. They're not – not after today. All of it has come back to me, and been reinforced; all the memories, thoughts, feelings, everything from all those years ago."

"Good…" I saw a shocked look cross her face. "No, I don't mean it is good today has been upsetting for you. I meant it is good you've revisited all those things from the past. While you thought you had them locked away safely, in reality, they secretly have gnawed away at you the whole time. This is your opportunity to bring them out into the open and deal with them properly; to kill them once and for all."

It was then Ned returned. "We are going home," I announced, and gave Lucy a hard look to confirm it was not negotiable. "We will be back some time tomorrow morning, but we shouldn't need to disrupt your day again." I shot Ned a look and hoped he understood. He gave me a long blink in acknowledgement.

"That's a good plan. Come up to the house and have coffee with me as soon as you arrive to fortify you before you begin work for the day."

Chapter 16

The drive to Millhaven was notable for the stony silence emanating from the passenger seat. Lucy was not happy. I could not let the day end this way, although it meant the situation might become a lot worse before we cleared the air between us. It's possible I might not have a client by this evening.

"Lucy, silence doesn't solve the problem. We need to talk it through. When we are back in Millhaven, we should do that."

"I don't have time to sit around talking to you, and I'm not going to waste my time going back to your office with you. I've nothing to say to you."

"That is unfortunate, because I have quite a bit to say to you, and I think you need to hear it today."

"I don't want to hear it, but you need to hear this. You knew how important today was to me. How important to finish going through everything in Dad's office was to me, yet you decided we were going home. Today was my one chance to reclaim something of all those lost years with my father. So, no, I will not go back to your office with you."

"That's a good sign. I'm pleased to see you still have some spirit left after the gruelling day it has been. Here's a news flash: you don't have to come back to my office. You are a passenger in my car and, as long as I keep driving, you can't escape – not without damaging yourself. So, as my captive audience, you are going to hear what I have to say because, as sure as Hell, I intend telling you what you need to know."

She snarled and said something which I didn't hear properly. In a brilliant display of temper tantrum, she slapped her hand down on the dashboard in front of her. Then she reached for the door handle but hesitated long enough for me to acquaint her with a few salient facts.

"I can't stop you opening the door, but I gave you credit for more sense than that. If you do intend opening the door, I hope you have made a will. The Blaine estate is messy enough without your dying intestate to further complicate matters."

Out of the corner of my eye, I saw her shoot me a filthy look before slumping down in her seat. She didn't say anything, so I carried on.

"It is obvious you were quite distracted by everything about today. That's understandable. I don't think you noticed a significant fact about Kirk Michael Farm. Your comments when I suggested we head back to Millhaven, and moments ago here in this car, confirm it. I intended to do this differently, but your attitude means this is how I must acquaint you with the most important thing you missed during all your poking about today."

"Oh, I see. Now, I'm not observant, or not too bright, or both. So, maybe you should tell me about this earth-shattering thing I overlooked. If nothing else, it will make you feel better about having gotten it off your chest."

"Okay, here it is point blank. Deal with it as best you can. You could have stayed at the farm tonight. In fact, you could stay there forever. It is your farm. ...No, don't interrupt ... The fact you managed to overlook, in spite of all the hours you spent there poking about today, is that the farm is *abandoned.* And, it has been for almost two years. So, if you wish, you can pack your bags tonight and go back to the farm tomorrow to stay there for as long as you choose. Under the terms of your father's will, Rita could live there and derive income from the farm, only until such time as she remarried or abandoned the place. She abandoned the place two years ago. Is there anything about all that you don't understand or need clarified?"

Silence filled the car. I had said my piece and didn't have anything more to add. Lucy looked stunned as she dealt with the information. I allowed the silence to drift on, but slowed down a bit so it would take a little longer to reach Millhaven. For a minute or so, she sat slumped in her seat, bringing to mind the cliché about a rag doll. Then, hauling herself up in her seat, she sat rigid and straight, while clasping and unclasping her hands in her lap.

I didn't feel good about delivering the news the way I did, but I wanted her to know the truth today so she could plan accordingly … and I needed to clear the air between us. I hoped I still had a client when everything settled again. Thomas Blaine's murder was an intriguing case. It grabbed me from the outset. I would like to continue with the investigation.

"Will you come back there with me tomorrow – please? It will take me a while to get my head around everything, and I know I need to make a truckload of decisions."

"Hard as it might be, those decisions have to be yours, and yours alone. I planned to return to Tanwood tomorrow anyway, whether that was on my own, or with you. Unless you dismiss me from the case, I will continue to investigate your father's murder. Have you dismissed me from the case?"

"No, of course not; I want you to keep going … And I want to know everything that happened at Kirk Michael Farm during my absence. While I know I have to make the decisions, sometimes talking through situations with someone else helps see things more clearly. Somehow, I feel safe when you are around."

"That sounds good to me, but there is one thing: let me know if we are taking one or two cars tomorrow. There's something else you should remember too: Ned is there for you. He will help you and always look out for you. Don't keep him at arm's length. Whenever you need someone to talk to, Ned will be there."

"Ned and Norma always were there for me when I was growing up. They treated me like… like a special grandchild. Perhaps I filled a gap in their lives after the loss of their only child. I think we need only take one car tomorrow, so I'll meet you at your office. I'll let you know if I change my mind. What time do you want to leave?"

All ruffled feathers were smooth once more. An early departure tomorrow morning seemed a good idea. Another good idea was to depart from my house rather than my office. Lucy could drive to the house and leave her car there while we were away. I floated the idea with her and suggested we aim to leave my place by eight o'clock.

"I'll bring food," she announced. "…Enough for us and for Ned if he will join us."

Her idea had one major flaw. She had no means of keeping food cool – whereas I am well equipped for the job. She conceded it might be better if I took care of the food. For the rest of the trip into Millhaven, my thinking focused on what food to take tomorrow. There was some urgency to the decision making process as I needed to visit the supermarket on my way home this evening.

On returning to my office after dropping Lucy at her accommodation, I found three messages on my machine; one from Ben and two from Emily. Ben would be bringing something for dinner tonight but might not arrive until a bit after seven o'clock. The first one from Emily said she would be joining us for dinner at my house. Her second message told me there was a change of plan and she now would not be coming for dinner, but working late into the night instead.

Soon after arriving home loaded with food for tomorrow, I had a quiche in the oven. Cold quiche and salad for lunch might be nice and, if the oven in the old church still worked – or I used Ned's – I could reheat the quiche. Individual-sized lemon meringue tarts, a selection of cupcakes, and some Danish pastries all needed to go into containers in readiness for the morning. The salad for lunch would be a first-thing-tomorrow-morning job. By the time Ben arrived with a selection of Chinese take-away, tomorrow's catering was done, and I was starving.

Heavy dew saturated everything out on the deck, so we elected to eat inside. With an array of take-away containers open between us, we ate at my dining table. The levels in the containers reduced significantly before conversation intruded on our eating. This is how things were between Ben and I. We were so attuned, being together required no effort. That time all those years ago, when we were heading towards becoming more than good friends but didn't quite make it, didn't change the connection between us. When life threw us back together again in the course of our respective work, our strong friendship rekindled in an instant.

Ben opened the conversation. "What was your day like? Are you still working on the Thomas Blaine murder investigation?"

"A strange day overall I'd say. I'm still working on the Blaine case but it's progressing at the rate of about a mile-a-month. I'm no closer to unravelling what happened that night, but that's not to say it's been a waste of time. All I've managed to collect so far is a tragic story of unhappy lives."

"Isn't any of it proving useful? Why focus on background information?"

"I suppose I hoped to gain a picture of what life was like up there at the time, and possibly identify potential suspects. If that happens, I'll look for motives and/or gains. The main thing I'm trying to do is to ignore the police investigation. It would be too easy to assume their work was correct and relevant rather than following my own line of enquiry and running the risk of missing significant details."

"What source are you using for this background information you're gathering? How reliable or accurate is what you're collecting?"

"Most of what I know comes from Ned Edwards, the bloke living on the neighbouring property. He was close to Thomas, and to Lucy when she was younger, and was a long-time spectator of life on Blaine's farm. I took Lucy up there today and we spent the day with Ned. Lucy had a chance to poke around a bit in her old home. Although she doesn't realise it, the day took an emotional toll on her. We are going back tomorrow. I plan to leave Lucy do whatever she wants to in the house and on the farm, while I spend more time pumping Ned for information."

"You were creating a list of questions to put to him. How did that work out, or maybe I should ask if you've even gotten round to the list yet?"

"Have some faith; I am working through the list, but letting it take us wherever it goes. I suppose I still have a long way to go to get through it. The next thing I was going to tackle with Ned might be something already noted in the police file."

"I brought the file on the off chance we discussed the case." He fetched it from the car. Moments later the file was open on the table in readiness. "Now, what do you want me to check in this file?"

"I've heard it was some time after the police were involved with the murder before Rita and her daughter returned to the farm. It seems everyone knew she went into town before the road flooded, but nobody knew where she was staying in town. I thought it might be handy if the accommodation place confirmed they were there, when they arrived, and how long they stayed. I'm sure my thinking isn't original, and I'm sure the police also checked it."

"I have been through this file. While I didn't study it in great detail, I don't remember seeing any mention of where Rita and her daughter stayed while they were in town. Give me a moment while I go through it again."

While Ben went through the file, I took the opportunity to make coffee and pour a couple of glasses of port. As I placed them on the table, Ben looked up and asked, "Have you anything to go with that?"

"Like what…?"

"Oh, I don't know … Maybe crackers and cheese, or a biscuit would go down well." He continued checking his file, while I went to rustle up a plate of crackers and cheese. It could develop into a long night.

Half the snacks had disappeared by the time Ben finished with the file. After closing it, he looked at me for a few moments without speaking. I could almost hear his brain working at full speed. Not wanting to interrupt the process, I sat still and quiet until he spoke again.

"That is interesting. Now, why wouldn't they follow up that information? I suppose, it's possible they did. If so, the question is, why isn't it recorded in the file? I'm sorry, Sonny, but I can't help you. You're going to have to see what Ned knows. Maybe he can shed some light on where they stayed. Every time I look at this file, the worse my opinion becomes of the officers involved in the investigation."

"Have you had any luck tracking down the senior investigating officer?"

"I haven't had much time, but I think I've located the daughter and I now know when I'll be in Ralston again. I intended to try calling the daughter tomorrow. What's the time now? I suppose it's a bit late to call her at this hour. It just occurred to me she might work during the day. Maybe I'll try calling the number I have tomorrow and, if I don't do any good, I'll try again in the evening."

What I thought might develop into a late night came to something of an abrupt end. Ben became preoccupied with his own thoughts. He didn't share them with me, but I was convinced they were to do with the substandard police investigation of the murder. A bit after nine o'clock, he left.

Having been away from my city office all day, I felt compelled to check my emails before turning in for the night. By the time I sent off brochures and provided information in response to several enquiries, I was ready for bed.

*****

Out of bed this morning before the neighbourhood's resident rooster crowed, after typing up my case notes from yesterday, I packed the day's food supply and loaded it into my car ready for a quick getaway once Lucy arrived. We agreed she would be at my place by eight o'clock. She arrived a few minutes after half past seven. "I'm early, I hope you don't mind. When I couldn't sleep, I decided to see if you were okay with an earlier start to the day."

"It's fine. I'm ready to leave. Why couldn't you sleep? Was something from yesterday playing on your mind?" I knew the day had more impact than she was prepared to admit yesterday. It is good to know my instincts haven't deserted me.

"No, there wasn't a problem with yesterday … well, maybe there was a bit. That's not why I woke early and couldn't go back to sleep. I feel an excitement about returning to the farm today. Don't ask me to explain. I don't think I can. Maybe it was that talking-to you gave me on the way home. It made me realise my home is mine again. Sounds daft I know, but perhaps it is something like that."

Most of the morning traffic streamed into town, while little flowed out from the city centre. On our run up the valley to Tanwood, we encountered little to impede us. We went directly to talk to Ned on our arrival. He was with the animals in the paddock adjacent to Kirk Michael Farm.

"I just wanted to let you know we were here, Ned. I'm going to take Lucy over to the house. We have a stack of food in the car to sustain us through what looks like being another long day. If you have nothing better to do, come and join us."

"Thanks, but I don't want to be in the way."

"You won't be in the way, I promise you. I will be twiddling my fingers all day, so I would appreciate some company. Lucy tells me she will be busy with some serious 'poking about'. I'll be nothing more than a spectator. Besides, I still have plenty of questions for you."

"No doubt her first priority today will be that locked filing cabinet. Maybe I should come over now, and bring a few tools – the sort for breaking into locked filing cabinets."

"Climb in. I'll give you a lift back to the house."

After dropping Ned at his front door, I drove the rough track to the old church. I realised I didn't know Lucy's plans. We were almost at the end of the track when I asked the question. "What are your plans for today, apart from attacking the locked filing cabinet, that is?"

"Oh, I don't know. I'll just look around I suppose. Is there something in particular I should do while I'm here?"

That's what I was afraid of: no plan and no progress … and with nothing more achieved by the end of the day. We parked out front of the house, but I kept the motor running. Instead of us both scrambling out the moment we arrived, I told Lucy to remain in the car. "I'll allow you to attack the filing cabinet and do whatever else takes your fancy until morning tea time. After that, you need to have a plan to work to, and to help you make decisions about the future – your future and the future of this place. I'm a hard task-master, I won't let you get away with just faffing about all day."

At first there was a look of surprise, and then she giggled. "I knew I wanted you to come along for a reason. Come on, let's see if the fairies came and unlocked that cabinet overnight."

We hadn't progressed beyond the office door when Ned arrived. "I thought you would have that damned thing open by now. Instead, you've been sitting about yapping," he quipped. We both threw him a look, before the three of us marched into the office as soon as Lucy unlocked the door.

Ned's tools made such a clatter when he dropped them on the floor near the desk, it seemed to reverberate through the empty house for a few seconds. Lucy looked at the tools and gave him a wry grin. "Thanks for bringing them, but they are our option of last resort. I don't want to damage it if it can be helped. I feel sure Dad would have left a clue somewhere on how to unlock it."

On his way over to the cabinet, Ned stopped mid-stride and paused for a few heartbeats. "You know, Lucy, I think you're right. Maybe he did. When he hid the key to this office, he also hid the code. At least, I'm hoping that's what it is."

"What is…? What are you talking about?" Lucy squeaked in excitement. "Do you have the pin number to unlock it."

"No, you do, Lucy. You have it. It's on the key to this office. Have a look at it." She gave him a sceptical look and held the key out in the palm of her hand. "No, turn it over. There on the back of it, see the numbers scratched onto to key. I noticed them yesterday."

"Why didn't you say something then?"

"It didn't occur to me they might be the code to unlock this thing. I thought the numbers were to identify the key if you ever need to have another one cut. It still might be what they are, but let's find out shall we?"

I called the numbers and Lucy keyed them in. The locking rod made a resounding 'clang' as it dropped free. The cabinet was unlocked.

After exchanging looks, Ned and I headed for the door. "We are going to explore the possibility of boiling a kettle. Happy hunting…," I called as we left Lucy staring into the partially open top drawer of the cabinet.

Chapter 17

With no electricity or gas, boiling a kettle, short of lighting a campfire outside, was nigh on impossible. "I have to warn you, Ned, I will become unsociable if I have to go the whole day without another cup of coffee."

"We could go across to my place to eat and take breaks. Failing that, I have a camping stove and a small gas bottle I could fetch."

"There is another alternative, if we can find an axe. We could light that old wood stove in the cottage. It's been a while since its last possible use but it might be okay. Of course, apart from an axe, we also would need to find some wood to burn. It would be fun having it working again, and it might help the place feel more homely again for Lucy."

"Finding wood might not be a problem. There was a wood pile out back beyond the cottage. It means we should find an axe here somewhere."

"Let's see what we can find." As we passed the office door, I called out, "Lucy, Ned and I are going out to the cottage." I ignored the fact she didn't respond, and kept walking."

A thought occurred to me. "It might be worth checking the stove before we start chopping wood. It might not be fit for use." Our current direction took us past the cottage and out to the wood pile, so we detoured to the cottage's front door. When we were almost at the door, I thought of something else. "We left the cottage locked yesterday. I suppose Lucy still has…"

Ned withdrew his hand from his pocket. "No she doesn't. I locked the door as we were leaving and, through force of habit, shoved the key back in my pocket." By the time he finished speaking, the door was open.

"...Know anything about wood stoves?" I asked Ned.

"Not a thing apart from chopping wood for one a long time ago."

"My knowledge of them is historical as well. We had one in an old beach shack the family had when I was a kid. A lot of my learning to cook was done on one though. Let's hope familiarity kicks in today."

The stove looked okay. But, in truth, I wouldn't have recognised a problem if there were one. Ash remained on the grate, suggesting the stove was used since the last cleric departed. I shared my assumption with Ned.

"In the middle of winter, it gets a bit nippy up here. Thomas might have lit the stove to warm the place up after he came in from the paddocks in the evening. The stove heated water in the reservoir on the side of it so, by lighting it, Thomas gave himself a supply of hot water."

"Yes, I can see why he would light the stove. I remember, if a hardwood log managed to catch, it would smoulder all day so, at night, you came back to hot water and a warm bed."

Having agreed the stove appeared serviceable, our other bit of good news was finding an axe propped against the wall beside the stove. "We can't put it off any longer, Ned. Let's go and make the acquaintance of the wood pile."

Chopping wood was not something I expected to do today, nor was it something I had done in a long time. Still, it's probably a bit like riding a bike, I told myself. Once you've learned how to do it, you never forget how. There was no doubt in my mind, I would be doing the chopping. No matter how fit he looked, I could not stand by and watch an old man – one probably twice my age – swinging an axe.

In the end, there wasn't a problem. There was enough wood already split to keep the stove alight for several days. We gathered up several pieces, some chips and bits of bark, and tore up a handful of dead grass from near the wood pile. With the fire set on the grate, I reached for the packet of matches on a noggin just outside the stove recess – and prayed they would still light after so long.

My first couple of attempts were discouraging. The match heads had absorbed moisture and softened so they didn't strike properly. "I'll keep trying, Ned, but I'm beginning to think our efforts were in vain."

"Never let it be said, Lass. I used to be a Boy Scout you know. Aye, it was a long time ago, but you never forget lessons well-learned. Nah, don't take any notice of that rubbish. As a farmer I tend always to carry a lighter." He produced a bright red plastic model from his pocket and, within moments, a fire blazed on the grate. "Our next disappointment might be if the place fills with smoke because the chimney is blocked."

"Thanks for that, Ned. I already thought things were going too well." We had no need to worry. The fire kept burning, the draught was good, and I was soon on my way back to the kitchen to look for a kettle or something else in which to boil water for coffee.

With no kettle found, a saucepan was the next best option. I filled the small saucepan from the rainwater tank at the back of the main building and soon had it on the stove. It was early for morning tea, so I shoved the pot a bit off the heat to come to the boil slowly. It allowed me time to resume yesterday's conversation with Ned about Thomas Blaine's murder.

While I perched on the end of the table and swung my legs, Ned made himself as comfortable as possible on the rickety straight-backed wooden chair. "Ned, I have to admit I'm still intrigued by Rita's absence from the farm at the time Thomas was murdered. You said she took the child into town rather than risk being isolated by floodwaters if the child became ill. Do you know where she stayed while in town?"

"I heard she said they went into town for the sake of the child. I don't know if Thomas knew where they were staying. Nobody else did. The police couldn't find her. So, it wasn't until the floodwaters receded and she returned to the farm, she found out what happened here."

"So, even after she returned, nobody knew where she stayed?"

"Maybe the police did. They were the ones to break the news to her, and they interviewed her a couple of times afterwards. I've never heard anyone mention where they stayed while in town. Is it important to know where?"

"I'm not sure. If I were sceptical, I might say there was only Rita's word they spent those days in town. I don't know why, but it is strange the police couldn't locate her in town. Of course, we don't know what lengths they went to, but I imagine it was a high priority for the officers involved."

"Like so much about Rita, I don't know if she had friends. Maybe she had family members in Millhaven to stay with. After the way she couldn't make friends up here, I doubt she had friends anywhere. Apart from not knowing where she stayed, are you questioning whether she did go to town. I assure you, she wasn't here at the farm when Thomas was killed."

"No, I don't doubt she wasn't here, but I am wondering if she did go to town. Was the child sickly? Did she suffer frequent bouts of ill-health due to whatever was her condition? For example, did the child miss a lot of school because she was ill? Wouldn't she have effective and sufficient medication to deal with most attacks, leaving only major events requiring medical intervention? The big question is: if they didn't go into town, where did they spend those few days when absent from the farm?"

"It amazes me how you can turn a 'fact' into so many questions. The unfortunate thing for you is, I don't have answers to any of them. I know she wasn't here. Beyond that, I just accepted the story. I can't think of where else she might have been if she wasn't in Millhaven."

"Okay, here is a different question. Where was Lyle Rogan during the time the valley was isolated by floodwaters? Was he marooned up there in his shack ... Or did he escape to town as well?"

"Rogan…? I don't know. I assume he was at his shack. His shack became cut-off by floodwater as did Tanwood. So, I suppose he was flood-bound the same as we were here. The road down the range to Tanwood cleared quicker than the road into Millhaven. After the police arrived, and the road re-opened, Rogan came into Tanwood for fresh supplies. I don't think he came near Kirk Michael Farm. From local gossip, the police caught up with him at the store and spoke to him there. Word has it he was quite shaken up by the news."

"I imagine the police would speak to him again after the initial meeting at the store."

"Several times… If you believe everything you hear, the police were keen on him as the culprit for a while. I don't know what changed their mind, but they seemed to discount him late in their investigation. Maybe someone came forward to vouch for Rogan's having been at his shack at the time of the crime. If I'm honest, I think that outcome disappointed the community."

"Imagine being disliked so much by your community, they would rather see you charged with murder than cleared as a suspect." Ned gave a noncommittal shrug in reply. "If I may backtrack for a moment, Ned, you said you didn't think Rogan came out to the farm when he came into Tanwood after the floodwater receded and the road cleared." Ned nodded. "Was that unusual? Earlier, you mentioned Rogan always hung around this farm."

"I never saw him lift a finger to help Thomas, but he always seemed to be here; spent more time here than at his shack."

"That's the problem I have. He was always here yet, when he came into Tanwood after the road cleared, he didn't come out here to check everyone was okay. That strikes me as out of character, and strange."

"Are you suggesting he didn't come to check on those on Blaine's farm because he knew no one was here? He might have known Rita and the child weren't here. In which case, he probably knew Thomas was here on his own. If he were Thomas' mate as he claimed, he would come to the farm to see if Thomas needed a hand with anything."

"Without suggesting anything but, if we are into speculating, the scenario you described is a plausible one. Another possibility is, Rogan knew about the real situation here and deliberately distanced himself from it."

"Sonny, I don't know much about Lyle Rogan other than he seemed always to be here. I heard the first time the police spoke to him was at the store. Nothing like these suggestions we're dreaming up now ever entered my mind before. One comment about your possible scenario though, for Rogan to know what the situation was here before the police spoke to him, he would have to be the murderer. Am I right?"

"It's possible – except the police were able to satisfy themselves he was not involved. Here's another remarkable thing about all this: we spent so much time this morning discussing this issue, only to end up where we were when we started." It gave us both something to chuckle about.

"It looks like your saucepan is boiling. Are you going to make coffee?"

For a few moments I was undecided whether to fetch the coffee making stuff, including a Thermos flask, from the box I brought with me, or to carry the pan of boiling water across to the house to make the coffee there. The latter option seemed the least involved. I added another piece of wood to the fire and raked up the coals before rushing to the house with the hot water. Ned strode along behind me. It was obvious something bothered him. He asked the question as I made the coffee and filled the Thermos.

"Why did you bother building up the fire again? Do you think you'll be making more coffee as the day goes by?"

"That's a possibility, but I brought a quiche with me. It's a bit cool today, so I think our lunch might be nicer warm, rather than cold. Just before lunch, I'll put the quiche in the over to warm up. In my cooler are milk and sugar. Make yourself a coffee while I fetch Lucy to join us."

Again, I felt panic when I realised I couldn't hear a sound coming from the office. I pushed the door open a little wider without a sound, and peeked inside. Lucy had the third drawer of the filing cabinet partially open, and sat sobbing as she looked at its contents. After a few quiet steps back from the door, I took heavy steps back to the door, calling to her as I did. "Lucy, we are waiting for you for morning tea. Could you leave what you are doing for a few minutes, please?"

Making as much noise as might be considered normal, I pushed open the door and strode into the office. She made a futile bid to hide her tears. I rushed over and wrapped an arm around her shoulders. "What is it, Lucy? What have you found?"

Unable to speak, she waved her hand over the contents of the open drawer. As I moved around to see what she indicated, I saw her swallow hard twice before managing to croak, "Look … Look in there."

"Do you recognise any of these things?"

"Any of it…? I recognise all of it. It's all mine; everything of mine he saved from when I lived here, even all the letters and postcards I sent him after I left."

No wonder she was a mess. Without touching anything, I took another look at the contents of the drawer. There were items belonging to a toddler and a young child, among bits and pieces from a teenager. Baby's bootees mingled with a couple of dolls of different sizes, a stack of cheap bright coloured plastic bangles and a fancy little beaded purse. Everything was neatly and carefully packed and labelled. The label on the bangles read 'Lucy aged about 12 years'.

A lump formed in my throat. I swallowed hard. Having me blubbering as well would not help Lucy. I gave her shoulder a squeeze. "Come on, morning tea is ready. You need to take a break. This will all still be here when you come back after smoko." I gently closed the drawer, and caught her under the arm to lift her.

"Do you need a hand? Is there anything I can do?" Ned stood in the doorway, a concerned look plastered across his features. I shook my head at him.

"No thanks, Ned. We are okay here. We'll be out in a moment. Come on, Lucy. On your feet; let's go. I'm sure coffee and a lemon meringue tart, or cupcake or two, are just what you need right now."

After wiping her face and blowing her nose, she followed me out to the kitchen. Where to have morning tea was the next issue to deal with. Should we go outside somewhere, or perhaps go over to the cottage? Would having it here in the kitchen add to the trauma of Lucy's morning? Lucy settled the issue for me by drawing out a chair from the dining table and flopping onto it. I noticed Ned had wiped the table while I was in the office.

It only took a few moments to unpack the morning tea, spread it out, and pour coffee into the three disposable cups I brought from home. No conversation intruded during the couple of minutes it took me to hand out disposable plates and everyone faffed about stirring coffee and selecting their preferred sweet treat. Once everyone was engaged with munching and sipping, I judged it safe to initiate conversation … with a question.

"Lucy, how much of the filing cabinet have you looked at so far?"

"I had a quick look in all of the drawers and then came back to the one I was looking at when you came in."

"What was in the other three drawers?"

"The top two drawers held documents. They look important and I intend studying them later. So, I left those two drawers and moved down to the last two. You saw what was in the third drawer. The bottom drawer is full of stuff which belonged to my mother, and a few things I saw that were sentimental to both my parents. He saved everything. It blew me away when I saw all the things of mine."

She couldn't go on. The tears welled up again and her voice choked. I searched for something – anything – to say to help. While I still floundered, Ned stepped in

"He loved you very much, Lucy, and your mother too. Losing your mother was difficult for him, but having you around kept him going. He thought he was doing the 'right thing' by marrying again so you would have a woman around to help you through your teenage years. He hated sending you to boarding school, but knew you had to get away from the unpleasant situation here. He knew it was possible you would never come back. It almost broke his heart. The letters you wrote kept him going. He told me he hated what happened, but accepted it was the best thing he could do for you." Thank God Ned finally finished. Jesus, he almost had me in tears

It was no surprise tears were running down Lucy's face. "I hope he knew how much I loved him, and missed him," she sobbed. "Then, when I learned he died, I wasn't sure I could go on. The only thing to pull me through was the thought he would expect me to make the most of the opportunity he gave me by sending me away." That did it, I was sniffling too.

After a couple of deep breaths, I felt sufficiently under control to speak again. "Good God, what a party this is. That's enough tears for today. Lucy, what do you want to do now? Do you want to go back into the office, or would you prefer to explore other parts of the house?"

"I want to do both, but right now, I want to go back to that filing cabinet for a better look at what's in it. I'm feeling guilty about abandoning the pair of you. Are you okay if I spend more time doing that?"

Neither Ned nor I had any complaint, so Lucy went back to the office and Ned and I cleared away after morning tea. It had grown dark and threatened rain. I thought about Ned and his stock. "Ned, it looks like bad weather settling in. If you have things to do on your farm before it rains, please feel free to go and take care of it. Lucy and I are okay here on our own. Once you've finished, please come back to have lunch with us."

He confirmed he wanted to check on his animals in case it did start raining, but assured me he wouldn't be long, and he would return as soon as he finished what he had to do. I was becoming used to his being around and felt a little sad to see him go. Don't sit there moping, I told myself, go upstairs and have a poke around in the bedrooms. You never know what you might find … And then think about how whatever you find might affect Lucy.

Chapter 18

The mezzanine floor contained three rooms, a master bedroom and two others. Of the latter two, the first was large, while the second one was quite small. There were also a bathroom and toilet tucked away in one corner. I started my search in the master bedroom.

Size-wise there was nothing surprising about the master bedroom. It was average and sparsely furnished. A queen size bed occupied most of the space. Other furniture in the room included a pair of bedside tables, a dressing table, and a bank of built-in cupboards running the length of one wall. With nothing more than a pair of rumpled and grubby sheets to see, nothing about the bed grabbed my attention.

The built-in cupboards were the most promising place to start my search. They consisted of three separate sections. Moving from left to right, I flung open the doors at the left-hand end of the installation. It was obvious this had been Rita's wardrobe.

Several pieces of well-worn clothing remained. They presented a forlorn picture of perhaps once favourite items now abandoned. Nothing looked clean but, after two years, it wouldn't be. I checked each item of clothing, including a scuffed and well-worn pair of shoes, but found nothing interesting. A little disappointed, I closed the doors and moved to the next section.

This one held a few items of men's clothing. Again, there was nothing interesting amongst it, but I checked every pocket. With nothing to entice me to waste more time there, I moved on to the third and last section. After flinging open the doors, it took me a moment to recover from my surprise.

More men's clothing, but this time it looked like someone left their full complement of clothes behind. After inspecting a few pieces on hangers, I returned to the middle cupboard for another look at the few items left in there. While both cupboards contained men's clothing, those in each one were for different sized men … and men with different tastes.

Those garments in the previous cupboard I looked at were of modern styling and would fit a 'medium sized' man, whereas the ones in the last section told a different story. They were for a much larger man, and one who preferred more conservative styles. I felt safe assuming the middle cupboard of the three was Lyle Rogan's wardrobe, while the third one held Thomas Blaine's clothes. How could Rita and Rogan live with such a situation? I perched gingerly on the end of the bed to think about it.

So few clothes in the cottage meant almost all Thomas' entire wardrobe remained in the cupboard in the main house. If he and Rita became estranged some years before his death as Ned suggested, Thomas was obliged to continue visiting this room to access his clothes. At least Lyle Rogan's belongings weren't in the other cupboard until after Thomas' death. Thomas didn't have to suffer the indignity of a usurper taking over the master bedroom.

Did it happen that way, or am I making up stories, I asked myself? I'm an investigator. Investigators don't jump to conclusions. They look for evidence. There was nothing to suggest when another man's clothes made themselves at home in the master bedroom. I suppose I could ask Ned about the timing of when it happened, but I doubt he would know.

I heaved myself upright again and moved to examine the bedside tables... and wished I hadn't. These too contained remnant traces of the last residents: an almost empty box of condoms, a box of tissues, sheet of analgesic tablets with only two tablets remaining, and a tube of lip balm which I couldn't bring myself to touch.

The dressing table was next, and I felt it would tell the same story as every other repository in the room. I wasn't surprised. It held more discarded bits and pieces of Rita's belongings. The half-used containers of make-up were old brands, suggesting they were replaced by new products which Rita took with her when she left.

With nothing more to achieved in the master bedroom, it was time to move on to the other two rooms. My first impression of the room adjacent to the master bedroom was 'girlie'. The furniture was white and decorated with pink flowers and butterflies. Most other objects in the room tended to be pink – except for the mobile.

Hanging from the ceiling near the window was a once bright plastic mobile comprised of animal shapes suspended on plastic ribbons. There for so long, the plastic had lost much of its bright colour. This room told much the same story as the previous one. Items not wanted on the journey remained strewn about; a couple of story books, a colouring-in book, an assortment of small toys, and a few Barbie doll's clothes.

A look in the cupboard confirmed my developing suspicion. This room started out as a nursery for a baby girl and developed into her bedroom as she grew. The cupboard contained a significant amount of discarded clothing. Garments ranged from those to suit a toddler to increasingly larger pieces echoing the growth of the toddler into a young girl. While not 'frilly', almost everything in the cupboard was pastel coloured and 'pretty'.

There was nothing more to be gained from the room, so I moved onto the third and last bedroom on the upper floor. Compared to the size of the previous room, this one was miniscule. It provided just enough room to walk between the bed, a small desk and a small wardrobe. Everything in the room looked as though it was acquired from a second-hand shop. The single bed was a narrow steel-framed model topped with a thin lumpy, uninviting-looking mattress.

Distressed from the abuse of what I suspected was a long line of previous owners, the desk was small with three shallow drawers on one side. A mirror in a wooden frame sat above the drawers. About 250 millimetres square, it had lost part of its silvering due to old age. Nothing remained on the desk, and the drawers contained only the accumulated crud of ages.

The small wardrobe, with its shiny veneer chipped off in places, screamed 'old'. Its interior just as sad as its external appearance. There was nothing in it but dust, and a few tiny scraps of paper on its floor. No clothes or other personal items remained.

Based on nothing more than instinct, I assessed this to be Lucy's room. Not for one moment did I think it started out as such. This is where Lucy was relegated to after the arrival of the new baby. The thought of what it must have been like for her – and for Thomas – brought a lump to my throat. I swallowed hard, and asked myself an important question: why did Thomas allow this to happen to his adored daughter, Lucy?

While it would be a difficult conversation to initiate with Lucy, I knew it was one I had to have at some time … not just for the sake of curiosity, but to help me understand what her life was like before she escaped. Dark thoughts about Thomas and his apparent indifference to what was happening to his daughter accompanied me from the room.

I forced myself to take a quick look at the bathroom area. It was every bit as depressing as the rest of the floor. Although unused for almost two years, it told me Rita was not into scrubbing shower recesses or cleaning toilets. Even the hand basin sported a generous coating of mould and grime under its more recent coating of dust. The mirrored cabinet above the hand basin told much the same story as the master bedroom. A half-used tube of toothpaste and containers of various creams remained, along with a man's razor, and a toothbrush which looked as though it was used to scrub the floor rather than clean teeth.

Repulsed by the area, I beat a hasty retreat to spend a few moments in thought at the top of the stairs. There was something about what I found up here on the mezzanine floor. It was trying to give me a clue about some aspect of the case, but the communication channels weren't receptive. Regardless of what it's trying to tell me, everything I've seen up here is disturbing.

After checking the time, I bounded down the stairs and into the kitchen. It was time to put the quiche in the oven to reheat for lunch. While I was upstairs, misty rain set in, making the day even more miserable. I dashed from house to cottage without getting too wet. Ned followed me in. As I put the quiche in the oven, he explained, "I finished everything I needed to do on my farm, so I decided to come back to see how things were going here."

"Drag your chair over and sit closer to the stove to help you dry off and warm you up a bit."

"Yeah, I might do that. I thought it was only a light mist but, by the time I'd walked here, I was soaked. So, what's happened while I was away? Is Lucy still beavering away in the office?"

"She is still in there, but I've no idea what she's doing. Whatever it is will be personal and I don't want to intrude."

"What about you, what have you done to fill in time?"

"I investigated the rooms on the mezzanine floor. You probably know, but there are three bedrooms and a bathroom up there. No point boring you with the details, but I found it disturbing. While everything about those rooms was depressing, there was something else about it. Something I can't yet identify, but I know it's important. I'm sure it has something to do with the way the mob left.

God, I must stop calling her 'the child.' She has a name. Her name is Sarah. It's time I paid her more respect. As a child, she can't be held responsible for whatever went on here, even though she might have been the root cause of it all."

"I think you're right. I've always believed her arrival was the catalyst for everything that happened afterwards. I've been giving it some thought. Perhaps her birth brought things to a head, but she wasn't the cause of it. Rogan was the cause. Regardless of his involvement, his continued presence here was enough to create a serious problem."

"You share my thoughts, Ned, but I wonder if we're not misjudging the situation. I admit to being a sceptic from way back, but I can't help wondering if Rita's efforts to insert herself into family life here weren't part of some grand plan. Don't ask me to explain those thoughts. They would sound more ridiculous put into words."

"Perhaps so but, sometimes putting thoughts into words, helps clarify your thinking. You might want to give it a go."

I wasn't going to try explaining my thoughts to Ned. They weren't clear enough in my head for me to understand, let alone try to verbalise them for someone else. Besides, while Ned was speaking, a vague thought drifted in from left field. I allowed it silence in which to develop. Within moments, it did.

"Ned, you're right about talking things through. I know what was disturbing about everything I found on the mezzanine floor. It was the way Rita and her mob departed. Theirs wasn't a midnight flit, but it was not a well-planned exodus either. They left in a hurry. Something happened to precipitate it. What do you know about the time immediately before they left? Was there anything significant, either here or in the community, which might have caused them to flee?"

"The problem is, I'm not sure when they left. I have a rough idea. For a couple of days or so, the vehicle hadn't gone out, not even to take Sarah to school. As we weren't on close terms, I couldn't go over to check if everything was okay. So, a few days went by before I realised the place might be deserted. Jessie at the store said she thought they were gone because of a couple of things Rita did. But, I can't say

I'm aware of anything happening anywhere to cause them to pack up and leave."

"It seems strange for them to leave. I wondered if there was something behind it. Why would they leave a cushy set-up which provided them with a roof over their heads and income from the farm?"

"They had a roof over their heads, but there was no income from the farm. They never worked the farm; not a day's work was done on the place after Thomas died. As for Rogan, he was too tired to get out of his own way."

"Did Rogan have off-farm employment?"

"Nah, early on, he supposedly worked at one of the mines somewhere out in the central area, and worked one of those funny rosters involving one week on and one week off. He never seemed to be employed after moving in with Rita. Maybe he never was employed. I don't know much about him. It seems nobody in the valley got to know him well."

"Well, how did they survive? If he wasn't employed, and there wasn't any farm income, where did their money come from? Rita only inherited about five thousand dollars from Thomas. It wouldn't last long without other income to supplement it. So, the question remains, how did they survive?"

"That's an interesting question I hadn't thought about before. They must've had 'invisible means of support'. There wasn't even a vegetable garden to help keep them going. And, they were never home. I don't know where they went, but most days they went out."

"Sarah had to be taken to school every day."

"Yes, they left at the same time every morning to take Sarah to school, but they often didn't return until after collecting her after school. And, they went out at night a fair bit too. Another mystery about them is how they always seemed better dressed than everyone else up here."

"What do you mean by 'better dressed'? Did Rogan get round in suit and tie?"

"That's not what I meant. His clothes always looked good quality, newish, and the latest style. She always wore make-up and had her hair done on a regular basis."

"Maybe they had a secret income stream … from a different form of cultivation perhaps. If that were the case, things might have gone bad. They might've fallen afoul of someone and needed to flee. What do you know about the shack Rogan had somewhere further up the valley?"

"It's an interesting line of thinking you've got going there. I don't know much about that shack; never been there. It's somewhere on Bob Joyce's property."

"Do you happen to know this Bob Joyce bloke?"

"Yeah, pretty well... We served on a couple of committees together. He's one of the world's decent blokes; a gentleman and as straight as they come."

"I would like to look at that shack sometime. Do you think Mr Joyce might be amenable to us having a poke about?"

"I don't think he'd have a problem with it."

"Would you be able to arrange for us to visit the shack, without sharing with him any of the stuff we've been discussing?"

"Shouldn't be a problem, I don't think. Let me know when you want to go and I'll call him to see if I can set it up."

"Time is getting away, and the quiche will be hot enough. Let's go back to the house to entice Lucy out of the office long enough for lunch." With the quiche back in its container, I opened the door. "Argh hell, Ned, look. It's decided to rain properly now. It looks like we're both going to get soaked going back to the house."

"Give it a few more minutes while we boil a saucepan of water to make coffee." I pulled the saucepan full of warm water forward onto the heat and, within a minute or so, it was boiling. Then, I carried the quiche and Ned carried the saucepan as we made a mad dash for the house.

Lucy still beavered away in the office. We set everything up for lunch before calling her to join us. I could see she had been crying. Her eyes were a bit red and puffy. Discretion suggested I shouldn't mention it, so I didn't.

We might have been eating lunch in a morgue. For the first several minutes, no one spoke. Lucy looked preoccupied. I guessed her mind remained focused on whatever she'd been dealing with all morning. When Ned broke the silence by commenting on the quality of the quiche, it opened a floodgate. Lucy began telling us about her discoveries.

Chapter 19

Lucy's excitement was almost palpable. She was still dealing with the filing cabinet which created so much emotional stress for her. "I've spent the whole morning going through the top two drawers of the cabinet. They are full of documents. I'm convinced Dad set up those files with me in mind. Perhaps he hoped one day I would return and they would help me understand much of what went on here. I won't elaborate. So much of it is personal. It will take me a while to come to terms with it, before being able to discuss it with others. I hope you understand and don't feel too offended."

We both reassured her. Our only concern was for its impact on her. Despite spending all morning on it, she still had one full drawer and part of the top drawer's contents to read. It was good she recognised the importance of the information in the documents, and realised her need to read every scrap of paper and absorb its information.

"It seems those two drawers of the filing cabinet are going to keep you occupied for some time. Do you intend focusing your efforts in there for the foreseeable future, rather than investigating other aspects of the house?" I asked.

"The answer probably is yes and no. There are things I need to put in place regarding the house but, once that's done, I should be able to give the office my undivided attention. Ned, sometime soon, I need to sit down with you to discuss the farm." Ned nodded and said he would be available whenever she was ready. "One thing from this morning thas left a bitter taste. A computer and printer are missing from the office."

"It's a while since you were in the office. Are you sure there was a computer and printer there in recent times?" I asked.

"Yes, quite sure… I remember Dad had a computer before I went away. I'm sure it was upgraded over the years. There is a mark on the desk which indicates where the computer sat, and I think the little cupboard beside the desk held the printer. A couple of reams of paper are still in the cupboard. While there are some handwritten documents in the filing cabinet, most were printed on what I think was a laser printer. Anyway, the bottom line is, there is no computer or printer there now."

"Much as I hate to say this," Ned said hesitantly. "A computer and printer might be desirable objects to take with you when you leave. Is it a possibility in this case?"

"Of course, I thought about that. I suppose Sarah is now required to use a computer for some of her schoolwork. While it is possible they took those things, somehow I don't think that's the case. The office was locked when we arrived, and Dad went to great lengths to make sure it stayed locked. If they knew there was a computer and printer in there and wanted to take them, they had to force the door. That's the conundrum: if they took the equipment, how did they do it?"

While the loss of the computer was upsetting – and galling – for her, I wondered how important it was in the overall situation. "Maybe the key concern here is what your father kept on that computer. Perhaps it was nothing of any consequence, or perhaps it was used to maintain financial records and farm production information."

Ned suggested another scenario. "It's possible the other mob didn't abscond with the computer and printer. No, I'm not saying they didn't… I'm just suggesting the machine might still be here." Both Lucy and I had our eyebrows crawling up our foreheads. Lucy's voice dripped disbelief when she replied.

"It's nice you to think the best of people, Ned, but this time, I think your trust is misplaced."

"As I said, while I can't be sure, there is a possibility the missing items are still here."

"For goodness sake, Ned, why keep saying that? They are not in the office, and we found no computer when we searched the cottage yesterday. How can they still be here?" Lucy snapped.

Ooh dear, it seems Lucy is not as together as she would like to appear. I rushed in to save the situation. "Do you know something which suggests somewhere else we might search, Ned?"

"Well, I know it's bucketing down outside, but I was going to suggest searching the shed."

"The shed…?" Lucy and I chorused in unison. I recovered first and jumped in before Lucy snapped at him again. "While I'm sure there's a sound reason for suggesting the shed, I can't imagine why Thomas might consider the shed a safe place to hide anything."

"I saw him using it over there … and it was a perfectly safe place to hide it. Rogan never ventured in there. He never went in the shed while Thomas was alive, and he had no reason to go in there later ... because, as I've said, he never did a tap of work on the farm."

Ned had Lucy's undivided attention. "Okay, but where in the shed could you hide a computer and printer … and have them okay after being hidden there for so long?"

"You spent quite a bit of time messing about in that shed when your father was working in it. Take a minute to think back on it. I can think of the best place ever to hide something. We will get wet going there now, but how about we take a look?"

He was right. We were soaked galloping from house to shed. It was cold, but I seemed the only who noticed. I could almost feel the excitement wafting from Lucy as Ned led her to the far end of the building. An area was fenced off and its gate padlocked closed. "Bugger…!" Lucy exclaimed. "We have to find another key. Before we go key-hunting again, Ned, are you sure this is where Dad might hide the equipment. It doesn't look the best place for it."

"Yes, I know it looks like any other farm tool room, but this is where I saw your father using the computer on a few occasions. And, this is not just another ordinary farm tool lock-up. This one has a secret. Do you remembered what it is, Lucy?"

Her brow furrowed and her eyes squinted as she delved deep into her memory banks. "No-o, I only remember a lot of tools and stuff in there, and Dad always kept it locked. I don't remember anything else about it." When she started speaking, Lucy had her hands resting on the mesh fence of the tool room. As she spoke, she drew herself in closer until her face was resting against the wires of the barrier. "It doesn't matter what I remember. We don't have a key. So, if the computer and printer are in there, we either will have to accept defeat, or attack the lock on the gate."

"Or, we could use the key to unlock it." Ned smirked as he walked to a narrow timber bench running a short distance along the side wall of the shed. After scrabbling around under the bench with his hand, I saw a look of triumph spread across his face. A beaming smile replaced his earlier smirk as he walked back to Lucy standing beside the locked gate. He held out a key to her. "Would you care to do the honours?"

Within moments, we three stood in the tool room. "Please stand clear while I organise a few things," Ned said. Lucy and I moved to the entrance while Ned fiddled about with the chain from a chain block affixed to a steel beam under the roof. He brought the chain to hang above the centre of the tool room, before shifting a piece of equipment which reminded me of a milk separator. Then, he slipped the hook on the end of the chain through a metal loop in a recess in the floor previously concealed by the separator. After wiping his hands down the sides of his trousers, he gave us a wry grin. "I'm not as young as I used to be. If this becomes too much of a challenge for an old bloke, I might need assistance."

I rushed forward to stand beside him. "Let's avoid the possibility of damaging your ego – and any other parts of your anatomy. I'll give you a hand. Show me what you want me to do." With one raised eyebrow, he looked me up and down.

"Aw, come on. I'm probably fitter than you are. I'm a regular at the gym – well, maybe not too regular, but I do work out and I am fit. So, let's get on with it shall we?" I thought I detected a chuckle.

"Okay. Grab hold of this chain and, when I tell you to, haul down hard on it. I suspect the crud of ages will make it more difficult than it used to be."

Our first haul down on the chain made no impression on a recalcitrant object and nothing happened. Maybe Ned was right in organising himself assistance. The next solid pull on the chain met with success. A large concrete slab in the floor started to rise up from its resting place. Then, a bit of hand-over-hand work hauling on the chain had the slab standing upright. "Right; now, Sonny, I need you to do something while I keep hold of this chain. Attached to the wall behind us is a short chain with a big hook on the end of it. Hold that hook. When I pull this concrete slab over far enough, slip that hook through the same steel ring in the slab as the chain block is attached to."

It sounded as though I was about to perform some strange precarious operation. In reality, it was nothing of the kind. In hindsight, I realised the whole operation is quite easily managed by one person. With the concrete slab then secured back against the wall, I had a chance to inspect the result of our labours.

A hole a bit over a metre square in the floor appeared to lead down into a form of subterranean pit. "What the hell is this?" I asked as I peered into the blackness below.

Lucy, now standing beside me, exclaimed, "Oh yes, I remember this from when I was quite young. I think it went out of use or something. I don't remember seeing it open when I was older. It is a tank of some sort. What was it for?"

"Go to the top of the class. Your memory serves you well. As you know, we use molasses as supplemental stock food. In the 'good old days', as we call them, on-farm storage of molasses was difficult in summer. It ferments in the heat. By storing it underground, it was kept cool and at a relatively constant temperature all year round. If your underground tank was in the floor of your shed, it was shaded all year round, and that helped maintain its cool temperature. There's one in the floor of my shed too, but mine is round. At some point, people decided round ones were easier to clean. You can still get a whiff of the molasses stored this one, even after all this time."

"Does this still contain molasses?" I asked. While I assumed it didn't, I thought it worth checking. Ned would hardly think a computer and printer might be hidden in this tank if molasses remained in it. Then again, he wouldn't know whether there was or not, until we lifted the lid. He was quick to reassure me.

"It was emptied and cleaned out long ago. Like so many other things in life, these tanks went out of use. Better materials and different ways of doing things meant these tanks became obsolete. And they were a pain to use. It was difficult to get the molasses out of the tank without making a mess everywhere. On some farms, when they became obsolete, they were filled in. In other instances, they were used to store stuff that you didn't need to use too often. Even that went out of practice after a while, they just sat there as empty spaces."

If nothing else, this investigation was improving my knowledge of farming practices. If we were going to investigate what might be hiding in that black hole in the ground, we were going to need a torch. "As I'm confident none of us has a torch in their pocket, I'll duck back to my car to fetch one."

No one argued. I ran back in the rain to the house, and then through it and out to my car. A couple of minutes later, and much wetter, I was back in the shed with two torches. Ned grabbed one and started to move away. Lucy followed, leaving me in possession of the second torch. Lined up along the edge of the tank, we shone the torches into the blackness before us.

A steel ladder affixed to one wall of the tank lead down to the bottom. I felt my pulse start racing as I swept my torch around the lower reaches of the tank. No molasses ... but there were lots of other things stored down there. Lumpy items of various shapes and sizes were covered with old blankets and bits of tarpaulin. One box appeared stored with particular care. The tank's contents presented a tantalising scenario. What had Thomas considered so precious he went to the trouble to store down there? "Shall I lead the way down?" I asked.

With no opposition forthcoming, I swung myself over onto the ladder and began picking my way to the bottom. I heard Ned tell Lucy, "You should go next." Almost immediately, I heard the ring of Lucy's shoes on the rungs of the ladder.

While I found items stored there fascinating, for Lucy, it was an absolute treasure trove – and another emotional wrench for her. She blundered about throwing back the covers to reveal those objects Thomas considered important enough to preserve for her. Not for one minute did I consider he hadn't saved them for her. But, as I stood there casting my eyes over the assemblage before me, a stray thought tried making its way through to the forefront of my thinking. A squeal from Lucy interrupted its progress.

"They are here. The laptop and printer are here. Thank you, Ned, for being so clever. I wouldn't have found any of this stuff Dad hid down here. ...Because, he did hide it here, didn't he? He hid this stuff here to keep it safe for me."

Some careful manoeuvring had the laptop and printer up out of the tank. We were still damp from our dash from the house to the shed and, in my case, soggy from my extra romp in the rain to fetch the torches. I was beginning to shiver, and

I was sure the other two were just as cold. I checked the time. Good… "It's coffee time. I move we adjourn to the cottage to sit by the stove and have coffee while we dry off. Ned, if you stoke up the fire, I'll bring the coffee-making gear from the kitchen."

Soon, with our mugs of coffee, we were perched anywhere comfortable as we munched our way through the remaining sweet treats I brought with us. A heavy silence hung over us for some time. It was obvious Lucy was dealing with her thoughts and emotions. In order to help accommodate the process, Ned and I allowed the silence to prevail until Lucy broke it.

"I want to take the laptop and printer when we leave, but I'm concerned about getting them wet on the way to the car."

"That's not a problem. You can use the Esky that held the food. I'll shove whatever is in it into the other plastic box so you can use the Esky. I think both the laptop and the printer should fit in it. As soon as I finish my coffee I'll fetch it for you."

"I don't have a printer, so it will be good to use that one, and I do want to see what is on the laptop. I just hope it is not password protected." I did not give voice to the thought which ran through my mind. If Thomas was so careful about protecting everything else, it is unlikely he wouldn't password protect his laptop. We'll deal with that when we come to it.

Another trip from cottage to house and back again, undid much of the drying sitting by the stove accomplished. Packing the two pieces of equipment into the Esky presented no problems. As Lucy tested it for weight, she announced, "There are a couple of things in the office I want to take with me as well. I'll take this to the office and add them to it."

"The car is unlocked if you want to load the box into it when it's ready to go." She nodded and strode out into the rain.

Ned and I did a quick clean up and made sure the fire in the stove was extinguished before following Lucy. While we were about it, I took the opportunity to ask Ned about the local schoolteacher. "I want to have a chat with her if she is willing. It's just another avenue to explore in the search for clues about what happened here. What can you tell me about her?"

"…Came here as a single woman and married a local. She's been here about eight or nine years now. I hear, she's a good teacher, and everyone in the community seems to like her. Her name is Sally Matthews. You drove past her house on your way here. It is that two-storey white place amongst the trees. She comes home from school between four and five o'clock every day."

"Thanks. If she has been the teacher here for so long, she might remember Lucy as a student at the school." I didn't tell Ned why I wanted to talk to Sally Matthews. I'll wait until I see how the event pans out before I mention it. Right now, I need to convince all the players to go along with the plan I'm trying to put together in my mind.

Chapter 20

All three of us appeared to have come down with a severe dose of lethargy after this afternoon's coffee. Lucy wasn't inclined to do any more today, and I was happy to leave early. After loading everything into the car, we climbed aboard and set off for Ned's house.

As we sloshed and bumped our way along the track, Lucy spoke over her shoulder to Ned in the back. "I'll be back up here again tomorrow, Ned. I don't know what time I'll arrive but it won't be early. I've a couple of things to do in town first. Don't bother coming over tomorrow unless you want to. I'm only letting you know so you aren't concerned when you see a strange vehicle arrive at the house."

"Am I required tomorrow?" I asked.

"Thanks, Sonny, but I'm sure you need to spend time looking after your business. I intend working in the office first. Once that is done, I'll start going through the rest of the house."

I sent the gods a silent thank-you. It meant I could pursue other avenues of investigation tomorrow without Lucy tagging along. While Ned climbed out of the car, I rescued the remainder of the quiche. "Here you are, Ned. It's a bit second-hand by now, but you might like to warm it up for dinner tonight, or save it for tomorrow's lunch." He was happy to accept the quiche. As I handed it over, I said quietly, "If convenient, could you try calling Bob Joyce tonight to see if I might visit Rogan's old shack tomorrow?"

"If *we* might visit the shack…," he corrected me. I assume he still doesn't need to know why?"

"It might be better if he wonders about the reason than knowing why."

"Good … because I'm not sure why we are going there anyway." I gave him a wink and tapped the side of my nose before climbing back into the vehicle.

Once out on the road, I kept an eye out for the white house set back among the trees. Some distance before we reached it, I saw a car turn in and drive up to the house. I hoped it was Sally Matthews arriving home from school. At the entrance to the property, I swung off the road and headed up the driveway.

"Where are we going?" Lucy demanded. "I thought we were going home."

"…Soon, but I have one small thing to do here first. It shouldn't take long. If you prefer, wait in the car while I talk to the woman who lives here."

"Okay. I don't remember the house or who lives there, so I might wait in the car. Who is it you are going to see?"

"Mrs Matthews…"

"I remember a Matthews family lived around here somewhere. Should I know this woman you are going to see?"

"She is the Tanwood schoolteacher, and has been for eight or nine years – or so I've been told."

"Hmm … no, I don't think that's right. Eight or nine years ago, I was a student at Tanwood School. The teacher then was Miss Dingle."

"That's possible. As I understand, the once Miss Something who was teaching here stuck around, married Mr Matthews, and now lives in the house ahead of us."

Sally Matthews was unloading groceries from her car when we pulled up beside her. I introduced myself and asked if she could spare me a few minutes. She was happy to do so after she finished taking her groceries inside. We loaded ourselves up with bags and were about to go inside when she stopped. "I see someone is waiting in your car. Invite them in too. We can have coffee while we chat." I persuaded Lucy to follow us into the house.

As I dumped the bags of groceries on the kitchen bench, I said, "Mrs Matthews, do you remember my friend, Lucy

Blaine. I think you taught here when she attended Tanwood School." She spun around to face Lucy.

"Goodness, it is Lucy. I didn't recognise you in the car. It's been so long, it's great to see you again. Are you visiting someone in town?"

This conversation was not going where I wanted so, to nudge it off in the required direction, I jumped in before Lucy could answer. "After being away for quite a while, Lucy has only been back in the area for a few days. I'm helping her sort out a few things at her old home, Kirk Michael Farm. While cleaning out stuff, we came across a few things belonging to Sarah Blaine. They look like a little girl's treasures overlooked when they packed to leave. We wanted to see if she wanted them before we threw them out, but nobody seems to know where they went. If I remember correctly, when parents pull a child out of one school and transfer them to another, they have to lodge some sort of transfer form. I hoped it was still the practice, and Sarah's form might give some indication of where her new school would be."

"Ye-es, the form is still in use and parents are required to complete it. I remember Sarah's case. I think they left the district on a weekend. If my memory serves me right, when Sarah was absent from school for two or three days the next week, I tried contacting her mother to find out if there was a problem. I heard the child had health problems but, if she did, they never prevented her attending school."

"Are you saying no form was submitted, and only Sarah's absence from school alerted you something might have happened?"

"That sums it up. There was no transfer form, and Sarah never came back to school. I asked around here, but the consensus was the family had moved away."

"Oh well, we thought we should try locating them, but it looks like there will be few more things to throw out."

"I'm sorry to disappoint you. If you do manage to locate Sarah, please let me know. You're not the only ones with things they'd like to return to her. Three or four books belonging to her, and her report card, are still held at the school. Legally, I can't destroy them, so they'll just sit there for a few more years – or until we locate Sarah and I can send them to her."

"Perhaps you shouldn't hold your breath. Coming to talk to you was a last resort in our quest to find her."

"They did seem to just disappear into thin air. I suppose an emergency of some kind caused their hasty departure. Now, Lucy, what are your plans? Are you just visiting, or are you planning to move back onto the farm?"

Lucy wrinkled her nose and shrugged. "The safest answer, Miss Dingle, is the jury is still out on that one. But, I will be spending a bit of time in Tanwood for a while."

Sally Matthews giggled. "I haven't been Miss Dingle for quite a few years. It's Sally Matthews now, and I think you're old enough to call me Sally."

With nothing more to gain from taking up more of Sally's time, we said goodbye and headed for Millhaven. As we left Tanwood, Lucy questioned my reason for visiting her former teacher. I kept my reply vague and hoped it satisfied her curiosity. "I thought it might be a way of finding out where they went. That's all there was to it. I wasn't looking to forward anything onto them, wherever they might be."

My answer must have done its job. She didn't pursue the matter further, and she sat deep in thought for quite a few kilometres before speaking again. "I think I'm starting to get my head around what I have to do on the farm – in the house anyway. So, don't worry about me. I'll be all right on my own tomorrow. If I do encounter trouble of any sort, I'll just yell for Ned to rescue me. Once I finish sorting out the house, I'll need some long talks with Ned about the rest of the place."

I assured her I wouldn't worry about her, and wasn't offended by being told I wasn't required tomorrow as I had a few things of my own needing attention. Conversation was sparse for the rest of the journey to my house for Lucy to collect her car. It allowed me to devote some thought to how Lucy might manage her time at the farm. As she helped me carry my bits and pieces into the house, I shared some of those thoughts with her.

"Life is a bit primitive on Kirk Michael Farm at the moment, and I don't think you should fuss about lighting the wood stove in the cottage. I have a stack of camping gear in my shed. If you take the camp stove and gas bottle, and that Esky when you empty it, you should survive your day in relative comfort. To sustain you, you need to do a bit of grocery shopping for whatever takes your fancy."

To my surprise, she accepted my offer without hesitation. I had expected at least a token argument. "Thanks, Sonny. I'm sure my client contract doesn't include your looking after me like this, but I do appreciate it. I've taken up all of your time over the last couple of days. Thank you. My only hope is it might have helped you in some way with the case."

"Time at the farm has given me a few ideas and several possibilities to pursue." By the time she drove off, I was more than ready for a shower and a hot meal.

As I stepped out of the shower, Ned called to report on his conversation with Bob Joyce. "He's happy for us to look at the shack, although he couldn't understand why we wanted to. It is years since he went anywhere near it, and suspects it is in poor condition by now. If we want to go tomorrow, could we make it early, as he has an appointment in Millhaven at eleven o'clock?"

"What do valley residents call 'early'?"

"I think we need to be at his place by nine o'clock at the latest."

"Okay, I'll pick you up at eight o'clock. Will that give us enough time to be at Bob's place by nine?" He assured me it gave us 'heaps' of time. "While I think of it, Ned, do you know the registration number of Thomas's vehicle?" Of course he did. I scribbled it down as he rattled it off.

"Is it important? I know they scarpered in it, but I'm not sure they still have it."

"At this stage, Ned, I think everything is worth investigating. You never know what might prove important." Ned's call meant an early start tomorrow.

While on my way to the kitchen to start preparing dinner, Ben called. In spite of being busy all day, he would be at my place soon after seven o'clock – but he hadn't given any thought to what to bring for dinner. I assured him dinner would be ready when he arrived as I was making lasagne.

As I checked on it in the oven, I heard Ben's car pull up out front. He came in with a bottle of wine in each hand – one red and one white. "I forgot what sort of pasta you were making, so I tried covering all possibilities," he said, brandishing the two bottles of wine at me. Because the pasta was ready, and we both admitted to being hungry, we didn't waste time on conversation and a pre-dinner drink before sitting down to eat. It wasn't until later, when settled in the lounge with coffees, that conversation about the days' efforts began.

Ben asked about progress on my Blaine investigation. "I spent a bleak, miserable sort of day on Blaine's farm. There's little of significance to show for it, but it was disturbing in a number of ways. I guess I need to sit and stare into space a while for my thoughts to crystallise and make sense."

"…Might help to talk it through. I'm not in a hurry to leave tonight. Do you want to go through what you've found so far? Don't worry about making sense of it, or putting it into any proper order. Just tell me about anything that sticks out in your mind."

"I know how the game works. I'm not stalling … just trying to unscramble a headful of thoughts to find things worth discussing." Ben and I have done this many times in the past. It usually amounts to a rambling dialogue devoid of structure. It's like comparing a passing parade of thoughts which often have nothing in common but seem linked in some way.

The strategy wouldn't work tonight. My gut told me I wasn't ready for it yet. The 'information soup' gathered from Blaine's farm over the last couple of days remained too murky. My thoughts needed to clarify further before I could isolate specific points from amongst them. Nevertheless, there was one thing I wanted to discuss with Ben.

"I don't know if this is important to the investigation, but I wondered if you could track down Thomas Blaine's car. When the other mob scarpered, they left in that car. I thought finding the vehicle through its registration payments might tell us where they went, or even where they are now." I gave Ben the registration number. He gave it no more than a cursory glance before shoving it in his pocket.

"I'll have a look, but I don't hold much hope of finding anything useful. They probably disposed of the vehicle. And, depending on why they left, it might have been prudent to change the number plates. Nevertheless, I will see what I can dig up. So, what did you do at the farm today?"

"Let's see… I was soaked through several times thanks to the rain, boiled water in a saucepan on a wood stove to make coffee, poked about in cupboards in bedrooms, and explored inside a tank. And I stopped by the local schoolteacher's house on the way home to ask if the child's transfer form gave their intended new location. There was no form, so no help there.

Tomorrow I'll go up the valley, but without Lucy this time. It has the potential to be a waste of time, but I'm always hopeful. So, if I'm lucky, I might have something to share with you tomorrow night."

"It doesn't matter how your day goes tomorrow, you won't be sharing anything with me tomorrow night. I'm driving to Ralston tomorrow afternoon, and I'm not sure whether I'll be away one or two days. I spoke to the daughter of the senior investigating officer on the Blaine case, and set up a meeting with her father while I'm there. Don't get your hopes up. She wasn't keen on the idea and, from what she said, my chances of getting much from him don't sound promising. So, at this stage, I can tell you I won't see you tomorrow night or the following night. I'm not sure about after that."

He didn't stay long as he had a stack of work to do before leaving for Ralston. As I walked out to his car, I asked him to let me know if he located the whereabouts of Thomas Blaine's vehicle. He agreed to either call or text me, but again warned a search might not produce anything useful."

*****

This morning I was dashing about with the speed of the gazelle as I prepared to head up the valley. After encountering a delay at roadworks, I arrived at Ned's place about five minutes later than intended. Ned was waiting and jumped in the car the moment I arrived. With no idea how long the trip to Bob Joyce's property would take, as soon as Ned was belted in, I headed back out onto the road.

We seemed to be about the only car heading further up the valley. The lack of traffic to delay us had me shaking Bob Joyce's hand a few minutes before nine o'clock. "Good of you to make the effort to arrive so early. I apologise for the situation, but I have an appointment in town at eleven o'clock. Still, this won't take long. I'll show you how to find the shack and then leave you to your own devices. As I told Ned on the phone, I've no idea what you'll find there. I haven't been near the place in years, even while Lyle Rogan was living there. I didn't bother checking there after I heard he left town."

"Didn't he tell you he was leaving?"

"No. Like I said, one day at the Tanwood store, I heard people talking about his leaving the area.

"What about his rent, did he leave with that in arrears?"

"Rent…? Wait till you see the place, then you'll know how silly that question was. Of course I wasn't charging him rent to live there. Anyway, he was only there part-time, thanks to those funny rosters the mining people work."

191

"How did he come to live there in the first place?"

"I needed a bit of labour to help clearing scrub from a big paddock. I think he heard about it in the pub and came to see if I'd give him a job. He was having a couple of weeks' holiday at the time, so he worked full-time for those two weeks. After going back to work, he came here again on his next lot of days off to see if I needed help with anything else. We cleared as much of the paddock as I wanted by then, so he gave the boys a hand mending fences. I think that's when he came across the shack and asked if he might stay there when he wasn't out at the mine. I'd forgotten it even existed and was surprised it was still standing. He didn't seem a bad sort of bloke; one of those always willing to pitch in if you needed a hand with anything. I told him he could stay there rent-free for as long as he liked – or until the place fell down."

"Did you see him come and go, or know when he was at the shack if you needed him to give you a hand with something?"

"No, I can't say I saw him at all, except for the few times he worked for me."

"So, he didn't work for you on any regular basis. Over what period did he help out here?"

"I suppose it was over a few months, but it was only for the odd days here and there when he had days off, and only if we had a labour-intensive job happening – like clearing that paddock."

"Did he pay his own power bill, or was the arrangement to work it off in kind?"

"Power bill…? There is no electricity connected to the shack, and the cost to run a supply to it would be prohibitive. No, the shack is a no-frills place. Hell, it doesn't even have the basics. There is no running water. An old rainwater tank was there from years ago. He knew about the spring in the rocky ridge behind the shack. It had never run dry, even in my father's time. I remember him telling me he set up a system to plumb the water from the spring into the old rainwater tank, so he only had to go outside to fetch water instead of having to climb the ridge to the spring for it."

"So, he used the shack as his home base for quite some time, but only worked on-and-off for you over a period of a few months. Was there a reason he stopped working for you?"

"I suppose there were a couple of reasons. Work on opening up the new paddocks was complete, so no further need for extra labour. And, my son came home to help me run the place – and mend his broken heart. Between us, running the place became easy, and we only needed a hand sometimes with mustering."

"Did you use Lyle Rogan to help with mustering?"

"No, Lyle was a labourer. He wasn't a horseman. I don't think he liked horses. Sometimes, Tom Blaine helped with a muster, if he wasn't busy on his own place. If he was busy, we used one of the lads off a neighbouring property. After that initial period of casual work, I had nothing to do with Lyle, and maybe only saw him once or twice in passing. We should go if you want to look at the shack, or I'll be late leaving for town."

Bob led us onto a well-made track through the property. After about half a kilometre, the track opened up into a wide clearing beside a pumping station. Bob stopped in the clearing and I pulled up beside him.

"If you don't mind, I'll leave you here. You won't have trouble finding the shack; just follow the track leading off from this clearing. It will take you to the front door. Will you be able to find your way back; back to the road I mean?" Ned, displaying more confidence than I felt, assured Bob 'we'll be right, mate'.

I drove across the clearing and onto the new track. It was obvious this part of the world had not suffered a close encounter with a vehicle in a long time.

Chapter 21

Long grass growing up through the compacted dirt all but obliterated wheel tracks. Scrub closed in along the edges and we bashed our way through overhanging branches. If there were such a thing, the only good point was there were no wheel ruts to make the track any rougher. We bumped and fought our way along for what felt like twenty kilometres, but was probably no more than a few hundred metres. Then, up ahead and almost hidden in scrub, I saw what I thought might be the shack.

Our luck ran out at about twenty metres away from our destination. A dead tree had come down across the track. Our two options were to walk the rest of the way, or to try removing the tree. The thick scrub came right up to the edge of the track, eliminating the option of driving around the tree. "Looks like we're on foot for the rest of the way," I said as I opened my door and unbuckled my seatbelt.

"Maybe you should think it through a bit before we start walking. We need to move that tree." I looked at him in surprise. Ned's comment was almost a rebuke.

"If you think we're going to move that tree, I hope you had your porridge this morning. We're going to need all the strength we can muster."

"If we don't clear the tree off the track, you should think about how you're going to get out of here. Do you intend reversing all the way back to the pump station clearing before you can turn around? Even a multi- point turn isn't possible on this narrow track without damaging your vehicle."

Christ, what was I thinking? Of course I couldn't reverse all the way back along the narrow track. "Okay, you win. Let's attack that tree." My initial assessment of the problem was highly inflated. The main part of the termite eaten out trunk lay off the left-hand edge of the track. Only scraggy branches from the upper part of the tree littered the actual track. After about fifteen minutes spent removing them, we drove onto the cleared area surrounding the shack.

In truth, it was a cleared area once but, as with the track, the scrub was reclaiming its own territory. For a few moments I stood out front gazing at the structure before me. It was dilapidated, filthy, and had all the hallmarks of being uninhabited for some time. The dilapidation looked to be of long standing rather than a recent development. As if offering an invitation, the front door stood wide open.

It felt eerie. I cringed as I stepped inside. If possible, the interior was even more depressing than the exterior. Dead leaves and dirt blown in through the open door had piled up in drifts in various places. Spiders had been busy. Their webs adorned every corner. My eyes took a second or two to adjust to the darkness before I could see what furniture remained. Once I could see, I realised there wasn't much to see.

A distressed looking wooden table about the size of a card table was pushed up against one wall. Two dodgy looking chairs and a three-legged stool kept it company. Four wooden packing crates stacked in two columns appeared to provide cupboard space, and the large plastic bowl on top might have been used for washing dishes.

The grubby remnants of a fabric curtain designed to partition off a narrow section at the end of the hut hung from a wire stretched across the building. Not feeling particularly brave about venturing into that area, I peered around the curtain. An ancient looking double bed, complete with sheets in no better condition than the curtain, occupied the space.

Spending as little time as possible in the building seemed prudent if one wished to avoid catching some terminal disease. The back door had come off its top hinge and hung at a crazy angle and with it bottom corner buried in the dirt. Opening the door would require digging it out of the dirt. We opted to sidle out through the narrow gap of the partially open door.

Makeshift bathroom facilities were located a short distance from the rear of the hut. I knew instantly I didn't need to look in there, and was content just to survey the surrounding area. What I found sent me back to inspect the back wall of the shack where a small concrete sump covered in thick grease and grime was installed. The sump was of little interest to me, but the poly pipe leading away from it was. A pipe from both the shack and the bathroom led away into the scrub.

Ned came over to see what grabbed my attention. I gestured towards the pipes. "The wastewater management system is a little out of keeping with the rest of the place. While it looks like it's been installed for a while, it wasn't part of the original construction. Now, why would anyone go to so much trouble and expense?"

"You had to ensure you took the waste water away from the immediate area. Otherwise, in no time, you would have a vast area of boggy, stinking ground at your back door."

As he explained, I started following the pipes into the scrub. He made sense, but my gut told me that wasn't the story in this case. After pushing a few metres into the scrub, I noticed an area not too far ahead looked different. It was an area thick with different looking plants. I didn't need to reach the patch of ground to realise why it was different. Only a stranger to this planet wouldn't recognise those plants. I pushed on through the scrub for a better look.

Ned, following close behind, barrelled into me when I came to a sudden halt. "What…? What's happened? What did you find?"

"We don't need to go any further, Ned. I've seen enough." He stood beside me as we surveyed the area in front of us.

"This area looks to have been cultivated at some time. Maybe Rogan had a vegetable garden. It explains those pipes we followed. He was using his waste water to irrigate his garden."

"Yeah, you have just about nailed it. Right, let's get out of here before the mosquitoes carry us off, or we end up needing blood transfusions." We fought our way back through the scrub and into the shack. I cast one last quick look around inside. "Unless you have something else you want to do here, I suggest we head back to Tanwood." He assured me he had seen enough.

I executed a tight turn on what was once part of Rogan's front yard. Then, we bounced our way along the rough track to the clearing at the pump station before picking up the better track to leave the property. Part way along the track, I checked the time. "We won't have to call at the house to say goodbye to Bob Joyce. About now he should be in town and in the throes of dealing with his important appointment."

"Good, Ned murmured. "Let's hit the road. It's nearly lunchtime. I'm hungry so much as missing my morning cuppa."

"We could call in at the Tanwood coffee shop on the way. Apart from their great food and coffee, I could have a chat to Jessie if she is not busy."

For a few kilometres, Ned was quiet. It appeared deep in thought, and soon confirmed it. "Well, it was a different kind of morning. I know inspecting the shack was about crossing another item off your list of things to investigate, but was it worthwhile? Did we gain anything from it? I mean, did you learn anything useful this morning?"

"I wouldn't say it was a complete waste of time. In terms of my investigation, the best comment I can make is that it was an interesting morning. That's how investigations go I'm afraid. It's not like you see on TV where they just go, poke around a bit and, hey presto, we know who did it. Reality involves a lot of hard graft and dead ends. I don't mean to be negative. If I'm honest, I do have a better picture of what went on both before and after Thomas' murder.

While I can't say how useful any of it will be, it is suggesting a few possibilities." Ned nodded but looked completely confused. I tried a different tack. "What about you, Ned, did you gain anything from our time at the shack? Did anything catch your attention or stand out in some way?"

"Nah, the only thing to strike me was how someone could live in those conditions. The place was worse than primitive. I suppose it would explain why he spent so much time at Thomas' place. I'd be looking to spend my time somewhere else too if I lived there. Did I miss seeing something of interest? I sense you're suggesting there was something."

"There were a couple of things I'm not sure about. One thing I did find interesting was the single bed in the main living area of the shack."

"You would have to pay me to sleep on that thing. It was old and a bit narrower than a normal single bed, and the rolled-up mattress on it was one of those old coir jobs. Was there something important about that bed?"

"Maybe not… Did you not wonder why Lyle Rogan would want a skinny, tatty single bed in his shack?"

"Yeah; he'd hardly invite a guest to stay over. I see your point: why did he need a single bed? Or perhaps the question should be: who was it for?"

"That is the question, isn't it? No, don't look at me like that. I don't have the answer, but I'd damn well like to know."

We were the only vehicle in the coffee shop's parking lot. It meant Jessie wasn't busy and might be encouraged to sit and chat. The problem is, I would prefer to speak to her alone rather than have Ned included in the conversation. I needed to keep today's discussions basic rather than ask the questions I wanted to ask. Who knows, once we get her talking, she might tell me things I want to know anyway. But, it's looking like I'll be making another trip to Tanwood for coffee, and a deep and meaningful conversation between just me and Jessie to go with it.

Jessie was pleased we broke the monotony of her day and rushed to take our orders. Before anything else, we needed coffee to drink while she prepared our lunch. When she brought lunch to the table, I invited her to join us for a chat. She remembered my asking about the Blaines last time I was in the shop and asked how my investigation was going. Rather than give her a long progress report, I simply shrugged and said, "I'm not sure it is. It's feels like I'm spinning my wheels and going nowhere."

"Damn, I'm disappointed to hear that. Is there anything I can help you with? Mind you, I don't know much about what happened on the farm, or about some of the people involved. But, if you have questions, try me. You never know, if nothing else, I'll give you the local gossip."

"The most intriguing thing about their disappearance is, they made like the proverbial Arabs … they rolled up their tent and disappeared into the night. So far, I haven't found anyone who knew they planned to leave and, it was only by a process of osmosis, people discovered they'd gone. I don't suppose they gave you a forwarding address before they left."

She guffawed loudly. "Oh, they would hardly tell me they were leaving. They left owing this business more than the odd dollar or two. No, there was no forwarding address. I'm confident they told no one they were leaving, or where they were going. We only found out through the mail run."

"How did the mail run enlighten you?"

"I told you we deliver fuel and oils to farmers in the area. My son-in-law does a mail run three days a week at the same time he delivers fuel and oils. On the Monday, he placed mail in the farm's roadside mailbox. Then, on his next run on Wednesday, he had more mail for the farm. The mail he left there on Monday was still in the box. It rained on Tuesday and wet some of Monday's envelopes. As it was still showery on the Wednesday, he didn't feel inclined to leave more, and was concerned about the mail he delivered on Monday. So, he brought the whole lot, both Monday's and Wednesday's deliveries, back here."

"You didn't think they might be in town for a few days or something … or that the little girl was ill and they were in town while she received medical attention?"

"Such thoughts did occur to me. I decided to wait a few days to see what happened. More mail arrived for them on Thursday. So, on Friday, when my son-in-law made the next run, he took all the accumulated mail for the week and placed it in the mailbox. The weather was fine, so we thought the mail would be all right there over the weekend."

"I suppose it was a dead giveaway something was amiss when it was still there on Monday."

"It would have been if we knew about it. There was a problem with the truck and no deliveries were out on Monday. Nobody was desperate, so we left everything until the normal Wednesday delivery run. After the truck returned with all the mail from the farm Wednesday, we stopped trying to deliver mail there. And, by then, word was spreading about that mob having left."

"In such situations, what happens to the mail?"

"I held the mail for another week before returning to sender all of the envelopes with a return address. There were plenty without a return address, so they sat here until we completed the Postal Department's annual returns at the end of the year. As part of the year-end processes, any unclaimed mail hanging around for a while is bundled up and sent back to the main Brisbane postal depot."

"Was much mail for the farm sent away?"

"Yes, quite a bit… We're only a small post office in a small community. Most years, we don't have any unclaimed mail at all. That year, a reasonable bundle – all for the farm – was sent to Brisbane. I think they all were unpaid bills."

In quick succession, after we asked for another coffee, three lots of customers arrived. We were early for lunch, so they were the first of the lunchtime rush. With no further opportunity to talk to Jessie, as soon as we finished our coffees, we were on our way out to the car.

I had a dilemma. Instead of driving off as soon as our seat belts were fastened, I sat there with the engine idling. "Ned, there's a bit of a problem. When Lucy said she didn't need me to come with her today, I was relieved. I wanted to look at the shack without her tagging along. So, I didn't mention I might be coming up here today.

It wasn't a problem this morning because I knew she was in town dealing with other matters before coming to the farm. Our plan to be on the road early would have us gone before she arrived. I was confident she wouldn't know I was up here, or that I collected you this morning. This afternoon is another matter. I'm sure she will be at the farm when I drop you at your house. That's why we're using my other car today. Lucy won't know this is my car."

"A strange car coming up my driveway so early in the morning did have me wondering for a moment or two. I didn't want to appear rude and ask you about it. What if this devious plan of yours doesn't work and she does know you were here today?"

"In that case, my story would be that I made a spur of the moment decision to come to Tanwood and organised to have you show me around the area. It might not be the truth, but I need it to be that way for the moment."

He raised his eyebrows in surprise. "So, if I'm asked, I had a lovely time driving around the countryside with you, showing you the sites of Tanwood and its surrounds. That shouldn't cause her any indigestion I don't think." He dropped me a knowing wink, and again I knew we were of the same mind.

Without lingering more than a few moments at the house after dropping Ned at his front door, I was on the road and heading back to my office in the city – and two days' worth of unread emails and unanswered messages to deal with.

Chapter 22

By about seven o'clock, most of the basic admin tasks were under control and I was ready to go home at the end of a long day. With no Ben or Emily coming tonight, I could luxuriate in the laziness of reheated leftovers for dinner before indulging in a long period of reflective practice.

My hot chocolate accompanied me through to the lounge where I sat reviewing everything from this week. Some way through my reflecting, I realised I still hadn't asked Ned the hard questions about Thomas Blaine's death, including about the crime scene when Ned found him. The police file should have photos, but I haven't seen any and Ben hasn't mentioned them. The trouble with Ben at the moment is, his 'real' job is keeping him so busy, he doesn't have headspace left to devote to his Blaine cold case.

While a bit unusual, I found myself wishing Ben wasn't in Ralston tonight. I needed to tell him about the interesting horticultural endeavour at Rogan's old shack – and about that intriguing single bed. I remembered Ben's meeting in Ralston with the former Blaine case senior investigating officer. It was while pondering the possible outcomes from that meeting, my phone chirped. Ben must be psychic to call just when I was thinking about him. I know we are close, but such a coincidence is ridiculous. It was just after nine o'clock.

"Sorry it's so late, but I guessed you wouldn't be in bed yet. I wanted to ask what your plans were for tomorrow. I'll be back in Millhaven by lunchtime, and was hoping to meet with you afterwards. Any time in the afternoon is fine. I plan to take the afternoon off."

"In the morning, I'll be in my city office, but I was thinking I might spend the afternoon working from home."

"That works for me. I would prefer our meeting to be at your house. When I know how my timing is going, I'll call to check where you are."

If Ben wants a meeting tomorrow, I should spend time tonight making sure my case notes are up to date. The meeting could only be about the Thomas Blaine case. Perhaps he learned something critical about the police investigation from the former SIO. I didn't think I had much to do … until I started tidying my case notes. It was midnight before I crawled into bed.

*****

I was in my city office before nine o'clock this morning to do a few things before my potential new client arrived for her interview at ten o'clock.

We discussed her problem at length when she rang for an appointment, so there wasn't much left to discuss at the interview. Nevertheless, it took about half an hour to complete the usual processes, and finalise details and timing of the investigation. It was another of those run-of-the-mill cases which aren't exciting, but are the mainstay of my business. The only concern was the timing. I wouldn't be able to begin my investigation until towards the end of next week. That created some degree of emergency about finalising the Blaine case.

After she left, I wrote up my notes and created a case file for the client. Then, I took a long, hard look at my Blaine investigation and its apparent lack of progress. With, the Blaine case file, my priority list for the next couple of days, and a few other things stuffed into my oversized tote bag, I was ready to go home, via the supermarket. I felt certain Ben would expect lunch when he arrived and, depending on how our meeting went, he might still be there for dinner tonight.

My early getaway from the office was ambushed when Lucy arrived. A bit taken aback by her unexpected appearance, I checked my memory banks for any appointment to see her today – that I'd forgotten about. No… no recollection was forthcoming.

"Apologies for dropping in like this, but could you see me for a few minutes. If you are expecting someone else, I can come back later. I was dithering about knocking on your door, when I saw the other woman leave. I hoped to catch you between appointments."

"You're fine; take a seat. I was about to be out of the office for the rest of the day, but when I leave is not critical. What brings you here today? …And, how did your day at the farm go yesterday?"

"Yesterday was okay I think. I sorted out electricity and gas supplies before I went to the farm. The gas mob told me the man from the Tanwood store is their agent in the valley, and he will install it and set up everything for me. That was a bit of a relief. Then I went to the Tanwood store to tell Gary I organised for gas to be reconnected, but he would have to delay the work until my new stove was delivered. I left the farm early and bought a new stove as soon as I was back in Millhaven. Delivery will be next Tuesday or Wednesday. They will let me know so I can be there when it arrives."

"What about reconnecting the power?"

"Because it's been disconnected for so long, somebody has to come to do something to reconnect it, and that will be sometime next week too. As for the rest of it, I've been busy, but you can't see what I've done. Anyway, that's not why I came to see you."

"I'm getting the distinct impression you're thinking of spending some time on the farm. Otherwise, why would you go to all the trouble of having the power gas reconnected?"

"Yes, I have decided – well, sort of decided – to live there. The problem is, I feel like I'm trespassing while the stuff Rita bought is still there, and everything about Rita and the child are still around me. Is it now legal for me to assume the property is technically abandoned and I'm free to do things … like throwing stuff out, for instance?"

"That's probably a legal question rather than one I should answer. Although, I think it is okay for you to go ahead with that ... but I do recommend checking with a solicitor before you do anything too rash. A solicitor would probably run something in newspapers to confirm that, now it has been abandoned for some time, you are taking possession of the farm in accordance with the terms of your father's will. It's unlikely you require any more than that, but it might just help tidy things up if there is any comeback."

"My problem is, I don't really have a lot of confidence in solicitors I don't know."

"You mean you don't have confidence in the local solicitors because you haven't had previous dealings with them?"

"Nothing against the local blokes, but I would prefer to use the Brisbane firm which did the work on my trust account for me. They were good, and I feel as though I know them now. You're right. I should put something in place before I do much more on the farm. I'll phone for an appointment with the Brisbane solicitors on Monday, and book a flight for some time over the weekend. If I can see someone on Monday, I'll return either Monday night or first thing Tuesday morning."

With her concerns dealt with, Lucy thanked me and left. I allowed her to be down the stairs and out of the building before grabbing my bag and following her. After a quick trip to the supermarket to accommodate provisioning requirements for the rest of the weekend, I was home by a little after midday. Ben arrived around one o'clock.

After a quick lunch, it was down to business. The first item on the agenda was a report on Ben's meeting with the Blaine case's former SIO. His time with the man was disappointing due to the former officer's having only sporadic lucid moments these days. "His daughter warned me I was wasting my time. She believes he became aware of the onset of his dementia a short time before he retired from the service. In fact, it probably was his recognition of the problem for what it was which led to his retirement and moving from Millhaven."

"It must've been hard for you to find him like that. Is he living with the daughter or in a care facility?"

"At first, he lived with his daughter. Her marriage had broken up, so there was plenty of room in the house and she thought he would be company for her. The arrangement lasted a bit more than two years. When his dementia worsened to the point she felt she couldn't cope with him, he went into a care facility. She says they discussed it whenever he was lucid, and it was what he wanted. It helped ease her conscience a bit."

"Nevertheless, such a situation can't be easy to deal with. Did you find him lucid enough to discuss the case at all?"

"When I first arrived, he seemed alert and I thought his daughter was exaggerating. After only a few minutes into our discussion, the truth became apparent, and I had to abandon the meeting."

"Did you get anything from him – anything useful I mean?"

"He remembered the case quite well. I think leaving an unsolved case behind galled him at the time, and continued to do so afterwards. It was hard listening to him telling me he believed he was already suffering the onset of dementia when working the Blaine case. He blamed it for conducting such a poor investigation, and it was the reason he took early retirement. Thomas Blaine's death was his only unsolved case. It continues to bother him today.

I tried for his opinion on whether Blaine's death was suicide or murder. There wasn't a straight answer but, from what he said, I formed the opinion he was not convinced it was suicide. Just when I thought I was getting somewhere, his mind wandered off. I waited and kept talking to him, but trying to continue the interview was pointless."

While I was disappointed, discovering the truth about the police investigation must've been gut-wrenching for Ben. If, as the former officer intimated, it was more likely murder than suicide, a more diligent investigation might have seen someone charged and behind bars … and saved Lucy several years of anguish. I was still mulling over how a possible murder investigation could go so wrong when Ben's voice brought me back to reality.

"On a different note, and with no better outcome I might add, I had a look for the missing vehicle. No sign of it anywhere so far, but there are other avenues to explore. All I did was a quick check on the state records. It's been a while now, so anything could have happened to it during that time; sold, gone interstate, had the plates changed, or any combination of those things. I think their hasty departure from Tanwood suggests they were on the run. If that were the case, I'm sure they tried everything to hide their future whereabouts. Anyway, there are still other avenues to investigate."

"Ah yes, as to their hasty departure, I think I might have…" That's as far as I got before Ben's phone interrupted.

He checked caller ID before walking to the kitchen to take the call. All I heard from the lounge room were snatches of a one-sided conversation; meaningless and frustrating from my point of view. The call ended, he ambled back to his chair. It was obvious he was preoccupied, so I didn't interrupt. Then, having barely planted his backside down, he bounced up again. "…Have to make a couple of calls," he murmured absentmindedly as he went past on his way out onto the deck.

The calls looked like taking some time, so I made fresh coffees and brought them back to the lounge room. They were a few degrees cooler by the time Ben reappeared. Again, he was lost in his own thoughts, so I sat in silence and sipped my coffee until he remembered I was there. About a minute later, he looked up and said, "Sorry; where were we? Oh yes, the car … Yeah, those other avenues will be investigated in the coming week. I still don't hold much hope of finding anything. Look, I might as well admit, now I know about the mishandling of Blaine's death, I am considering opening a new investigation into the case, but there are a couple of things I still need to organise."

Somehow, the news of a possible investigation into the police's handling of the case did not thrill me. It was likely to make my job more difficult rather than help me. An odd thought occurred to me. "Ben, do you think the other young officer who worked on the investigation became aware of the senior officer's problem, and it influenced his decision to leave the service soon afterwards?"

"I hadn't thought about it. In case I do decide to go ahead with an investigation into the handling of the case, it would be best if I kept an open mind until the findings were in. But now you've mentioned it, maybe he was so embarrassed – or disillusioned – by the outcome of his first big case, he decided to chuck it in. Perhaps it will remain one of those things we will never know for sure. Uhmm … I think you were about to say something before my phone call interrupted you. I don't remember what we were talking about at the time."

"We were talking about Rita and her mob, and their hasty departure from Tanwood. I might have a theory about their rush to leave. Yesterday, I visited the old shack where Rogan was supposed to be living before he moved in with Rita after Thomas' death."

"Right; …find anything useful?"

"…Not a lot in the shack itself. It has no power or running water, and calling it 'primitive' is an exaggeration. What I did find interesting was the remnant of a previous horticultural project, complete with plumbed irrigation supply."

"Are we talking drug cultivation?" I nodded but he didn't wait for my answer and rushed on. "Ye-es, if a deal went bad, or something similar happened, it would account for their need to leave in a hurry. Was there anything else interesting about the shack I might want to know about?"

Before I could answer, his phone demanded his attention. Again, he opted to take the call out on the deck … and out of my hearing. I told myself I shouldn't get off-side about it. He has an important, demanding job, and helping me with my investigation is generous of him. I should be grateful. Regardless, the constant interruptions were bringing my dark side to life. My hope is, after this, there are no further interruptions until we finish our discussion. When he came back to the lounge, he looked pleased with himself, and I wondered whether he would share his good news.

Then, he looked up and blinked a couple of times as if seeing me there for the first time. "Right… I think we were discussing Rogan's horticultural pursuits when we left off. Did your visit generate any other ideas about what was going on up there?"

"Yes and no… From what I'm told, subsequent to Thomas' death, all work on the farm ceased. While it's not surprising Rita didn't continue running the farm, it's interesting Rogan didn't do anything on the farm once he moved in. The sum of money Thomas left Rita in his will was not a significant amount. I imagine the amount didn't impress her. With the animals gone and no crops planted, no income was being derived from the farm. Yet, by Tanwood standards, the couple lived the 'high life'. Word has it they were always going out, wore the latest fashions, and were the best-dressed people in the valley. I believe their 'invisible means of support' came from Rogan's horticultural pursuits."

"It seems a likely scenario. I wonder where they banked; might be something else to investigate."

"Would they use a bank? I mean, if it's tainted money, would they be brave enough to put it through a bank account?

I had visions of them keeping it in a bottom drawer or stuffed under the mattress – anywhere not as obvious as a bank."

"Under other circumstances, that might apply. In this instance, there was a farm involved. It might look odd if they appeared solvent, but no money was going into a bank somewhere. At least, if money was going in and out of bank accounts, any interested onlooker would be forgiven for assuming it was income from the farm. That is, until they looked at the farm and realised it wasn't being worked and, therefore, couldn't be producing income."

"Okay, I see your point. Perhaps checking on bank accounts might be a sound move, but it would be for you to do. No bank is going to provide me with information about its customers' financial situations."

"True… And I'll keep that in mind. So, was there anything else to report about your visit to Rogan's shack?"

"One thing intrigues me. Apart from a double bed, there was also a single bed … perhaps more a narrow cot than a single bed. It suggests Rita and the child spent time in the shack. The problem I have with it is, by the time the child was born, Rita was well established on the farm as Thomas' wife. The farm became her principal and only residence for the duration of her stay in the area after her marriage to Thomas. So, the questions are: why was there a single bed in the shack? Who slept in that bed, and when were they there?"

"I just know you will have a theory about it, so perhaps you should share it with me."

"Oh, I think I'd rather let you dwell on it for a while." The look Ben gave me indicated I should review my suggestion. "Okay, but it's only a vague idea and not a theory. If it was the child who slept there, was it at the time Thomas was killed? Were Rita and the child staying at the shack, when they claim to have been in town?"

"Jesus, you do manage to come up with the most interesting questions. Finding out where they stayed during those days they were supposed to be in town just moved closer to the top of the things-to-do list."

Ben's phone was working overtime. Another call came in and he took it out on the deck. I saw him make himself comfortable out there and realised the call might be lengthy. I bought lamb shanks for dinner. They needed to cook long and slow, so I went to get them started. I had no sooner dealt with dinner than my phone wanted my attention.

For the next while, discussing Thomas Blaine's death was on hold while we both dealt with other matters in our working lives.

Chapter 23

The remainder of Friday afternoon was devoted to phone calls. Ben dealt with several while still occupying his perch on the deck. I dealt with two case enquiries in quick succession. My life looked set to become busy. Closing the Blaine case as soon as possible was critical. As Ben still had his phone welded to his ear, I called Ned Edwards and left a message, and made a mental note to try him again later if he didn't return my call.

I was wondering about doing some work in my office to fill in time, when Ben honoured me with his presence again. When he wandered back in, he looked so pleased with himself, I knew something had gone right. But, there was something more about his demeanour than that. There was a hint of smugness about him. I decided not to rise to the bait and ask him what was going on. My resolve didn't last two minutes.

"Whatever your calls were about, they seem the have brightened your day. Anything you care to share with me?"

"Yes, I do have something to share. From Monday, an investigation into the handling of the Thomas Blaine case will commence. I told you I was inclined to do this, but certain issues needed sorting out. Most important was how to go about it. While I was in Ralston, I discussed the Blaine case with my Ralston counterpart, Pete Messell. It clarified a few points in my own mind. Pete confirmed my thinking when he outlined how he would do it. We were both of the opinion it needed to be undertaken by someone from outside my precinct. After that, sorting out the rest of the details became academic."

"Okay, so there will be an investigation into your Thomas Blaine cold case, and you will bring in an outsider to conduct it. Am I allowed to know who the outsider might be?"

"The big issue was finding someone I respected and trusted, and who is a competent investigator." That did not satisfy my curiosity at all, but he continued. "So, our old friend, Sam Keller, will arrive in Millhaven over the weekend to take on her new role – her new temporary role – from next Monday. Pete Messell was a tad reluctant to lend me his top detective, but he was persuaded. Sam can work the case for up to three months. It won't take that long to complete but, agreeing a long period up front avoids having to renegotiate the terms of the arrangement every week or two."

"Where is she staying while in town? Do you want her to stay here with me again?"

"Not this time; I've no idea how long the investigation will take. She will stay in one of the holiday apartments in the city. As it might take some weeks, hotel accommodation wasn't an option. Although, she might end up spending as much time at your place as Emily and I do, I don't think you want somebody underfoot for however long this investigation takes. And, she needs the flexibility to come and go and work independently as she sees fit. You're not offended by the arrangement, are you?"

"No and, as I've two small cases due to commence in the next few days, I'll be working quite a few nights anyway."

"Good… Now, where were we with what your investigation has uncovered so far?"

"I don't think there's much more to tell, but I do have a question – or two. They both relate to the murder weapon. What can you tell me about the bullet and the weapon involved in the crime?" Nonplussed, Ben stared at me for a moment. I thought the question must've been confusing, so I tried again with more direct wording. "I'm asking whether the bullet which killed Blaine came from the weapon found at the crime scene."

"Yes, I understood what you asked, but I can't answer the question because I haven't checked the evidence. I didn't notice anything about that in the police file. Perhaps we should comb through the file now for any mention of the bullet or the weapon." His suggestion didn't raise any argument from me.

"Before we do that, are the crime scene photos in your file?"

"Yes, there are photos in a sleeve at the back of it. We could look at them first if you wish." I did 'wish', so he unclipped the sleeve from the folder and upended it onto the coffee table. "The others must be stuck. I'll shake it."

In spite of a vigorous shaking and a visual inspection of the sleeve, the photos in the file totalled two. After a quick glance at them, I wasn't sure what to say; what it might be safe to say. The obvious question was: *is that all there are?* Discretion advised against asking that question. While I struggled with what not to ask, Ben carried out a frantic flip through the folder. No further photos emerged. Stunned and accepting defeat, Ben pushed the folder aside and spread the two photos out on the table.

One appeared to be taken from just inside the front door. It showed much of the living area, excluding the actual area of the crime scene. "What use to anyone is that?" Ben demanded. I hoped it was a hypothetical question and not one he expected me to answer. I picked up the second photo for a closer look.

It showed the crime scene, but was taken after some work on the scene, and not when the police first found the body. "Is that one any more useful?" Ben asked. The disgust in his voice did not go unnoticed.

"Maybe … It does show the crime scene, but it looks as though it was taken after the police had scratched around a bit. See how the body is positioned. To me, it looks as though it has been rolled onto its side; so they could check the back for an exit wound. I was told a rifle was near the body when it was found. It led to the suspicion of suicide. Although it shows quite an area of floor around the body, there's no rifle in the photograph. Isn't it standard procedure to take close-up shots of the body and immediate surrounding area before anything is disturbed?"

"Yeah, that's how it is supposed to happen. …And the next question you are about to ask, and which I can't answer, is: where are those photos? If you have any bright ideas about where they might be, share them with me – please!"

The flood of vitriolic comments about the handling of the case I was expecting was avoided when Ben's phone intruded at just the right moment. His initial reaction suggested he would ignore the call but, after noting the ID, he rushed out onto the deck to take it.

Bugger! More time this afternoon was spent dealing with interruptions than on progressing the Blaine investigation. To work off my frustration and fill in time yet again, I went to check on dinner. While I prodded the lamb shanks in the oven, my phone also demanded attention. It was Ned Edwards returning my earlier call. His timing was perfect. With Ben occupied with his call, I could chat to Ned without being overheard. I went to my office and flopped onto a chair at my desk.

"Thanks for calling back, I know it is Friday afternoon, but there is something I need to discuss with you as soon as possible. While I hate to intrude on your weekend, I wondered whether you might have some time if I came to see you."

"Sonny, I'm a farmer. Weekends don't mean much to us. They're the same as any other day as far as we're concerned. But, you don't have to drive up here to talk to me. I'm coming into town tomorrow. It's the local turf club's race meeting tomorrow afternoon. I usually make a day of it in town and come into Millhaven sometime during the morning. I don't have anything else to do in town tomorrow, so I can come in as early as you like and spend all morning with you if needed."

We agreed to meet at my city office at about ten o'clock. I made a quick note of the most urgent questions I wanted to ask Ned, before I wandered back to the lounge room. As I sat down again, Ben strolled in from the deck. I couldn't read anything in his face, so decided to test the situation. "… Everything all right?"

"Yeah … I'm hoping it's better than all right. That last call was from the daughter of the former officer I spoke to yesterday." My stomach tightened. I half expected Ben to tell me the man had passed away or some other tragic event had befallen him. "She told me she has quite a few boxes of her father's stuff stored in her garage. After I told her why I wanted to interview her father, she remembered he kept banging on about a case from just before he retired. He often pulled out one of the boxes and went through its contents."

"Did he keep a file on the Thomas Blaine case? I suppose he kept copies of various bits and pieces from the police file at home while he worked the case, and couldn't bring himself to get rid of them when it was over."

"It might have started out that way, but I think the case continued to haunt him after he retired. His daughter said he was obsessed with whatever was in that box. His obsession became a problem as his dementia worsened. In the end, while he still lived with her, she hid the box under all the other boxes he had stored in the garage so it was harder for him to find it. When he went into the care facility, the box remained in the garage. She couldn't remember where she hid it. Her call was to tell me she found the box, and a brief look at its contents suggested they related to the case I mentioned to her."

"It's a pity she didn't remember it before you left Ralston. I don't doubt you want it, but how are you going to collect it now you're back in Millhaven?"

"There isn't a problem. I arranged for Sam Keller to collect the box and bring it with her when she comes on the weekend. The woman couldn't tell me much about what the box contained. She only needed to read the labels on the first couple of folders to know the material related to the case I mentioned to her. So, when Sam arrives, we could be in for a pleasant surprise – or another disappointment."

With the phone calls dealt with, I returned the conversation to what was in the police evidence locker. "If Sam is arriving over the weekend with a box full of material relating to the case, I wondered if, before she arrived, it might be worth knowing what evidence the police hold here."

"The weekend would be a good time to ferret around in the evidence locker while there aren't too many officers on duty. I don't want to advertise the fact the case is under scrutiny, and won't tell them about Sam and her investigation until it becomes necessary. That might be after a few days, or a few weeks, if progress is slow."

As strange as it seemed, there was little more about the case to discuss as the afternoon faded into twilight. It made sense to end our discussions and adjourn to the deck for a pre-dinner drink and a bit of a 'wind down'. It was cool outside and the dew drifted in early. So, we didn't linger long out there before returning inside for dinner.

Ben received another phone call as I was clearing away after dinner. This time it was about something local and urgent. He didn't elaborate, but simply told me he'd been alerted about a serious crime in one of the town's poorer neighbourhoods. Moments after receiving the call, he was on his way to the scene of the crime, and I had the rest of the evening to myself.

*****

After a late-ish night updating my Blaine case file and fine-tuning the list of questions I wanted to ask Ned, this morning saw a brisk start to my day. With Sam Keller about to arrive in Millhaven, it was possible both she and Ben would spend time at my place over the weekend. I needed to free up whatever time that might involve. So, a few minor but pressing domestic chores were dealt with before I left for my city office and my meeting with Ned.

Sam Keller occupied my mind all the way into the city. After an interesting beginning, our friendship goes back a few years now. I managed to upset a few of the wrong kind of people while working a particularly unpleasant case in Ralston. It resulted in my being placed under police protection for a while and then having two police officers accompany me on my return to Millhaven.

The officers were supposed to be accommodated in a nearby motel while they took turns at patrolling my property. Sam refused to stay at the motel and was asleep on the couch in the lounge room when an armed intruder broke in to attack me. A vicious skirmish occurred in the lounge room. The would-be assassin went to meet his maker, and Sam was seriously wounded. She required major surgery and extended rehabilitation. While she was in hospital in Millhaven, she made Detective, and was nominated for a bravery award. Later, she lived with me while serving under Ben as a detective at this precinct. After returning to Ralston, she became top detective at that precinct, and has remained there ever since. I have called on our friendship to assist with my investigations on a couple of occasions since then.

My late arrival in the city allowed me just enough time to scurry up to my office with a chocolate cake and set the coffee machine up before Ned knocked on my door. We settled in my ancient lounge chairs with our coffees and huge wedges of chocolate cake. Then, it was down to business without adhering to the niceties of dealing with coffee and cake first.

"Ned, in all the time I've spent with you over this week, I haven't asked you to describe the crime scene you encountered at Thomas Blaine's house that morning about three and a half years ago. I understand it will be difficult to discuss but, the reality is, the information is vital to my investigation. Do you feel up to telling me about it?"

"Yes... and it's about time too, if you don't mind my saying so. I suspected you stayed away from the topic to avoid upsetting me. I'm here to tell you such an approach wastes time. Let's get down to it. You ask your questions and I'll answer them. It was a traumatic event, but I adjusted to it … and, since then, I've lost my wife, Norma, as well. All things take on appropriate perspectives with the passage of time. Everything develops its own relevance."

Philosophy so early on a Saturday morning was not what I expected, but I complied with his instruction to 'get down to it'. "I suppose the best place to start is when you went to Thomas' house that morning. Tell me what the house was like when you arrived."

Chapter 24

The long and tortuous session to establish all there was to know about the Blaine crime scene began. "About what time was it when you arrived at the Blaine house?"

"Early by city standards I suppose, but not for farmers; probably just before eight o'clock."

"Earlier you told me about Thomas putting a cow down and, because of the rain and the state of the paddock, he had to leave the carcass there. The next morning, you went to see Thomas. What prompted you to go to see him?"

"The carcass was still in the paddock when I went to check my stock. It made sense for Thomas to leave it there until the rain eased off. Next morning, there was only a drizzle, before becoming heavy again later in the day. But, there was no sign of Thomas anywhere in his paddocks. I felt uneasy and thought something might be amiss, so I went across to see if he was all right."

"When you arrived, was there anything unusual about the house?"

"No. Well, not at first … I noticed lights were on inside, but that wasn't odd. It was a dark, miserable morning, so you would expect lights to be on."

"So, what did you do when you found everything looked okay?"

"I called out a couple of times but nobody answered. At that stage, I didn't know Rita and the child had gone into town. I suppose I half expected her to come to the door. When nobody responded, I went around to the cottage. It was closed and there was no light from inside. I went back and pounded on the front door. Still no response, so I tried the door. It wasn't locked and swung open a little way."

"Did you go inside as soon as you discovered the door wasn't locked?"

"It didn't feel right to do that, so I stood at the door and called out to anyone inside. No response; so I tried calling Thomas a couple of times. When there still wasn't any response, I knew something was wrong. I tiptoed up, stuck my head around the door and called out again. While waiting for a response, I glanced around the living area. That's when I saw Thomas on the floor."

"I'm sorry, Ned, this next bit will be difficult for you, but I have to ask the questions."

"Of course you do. I'm not some delicate petal, so get on with it."

"Right, can you describe the scene for me? Tell me about the state of that area of the room; where everything was. Include details which might help me develop an image of what you found."

"Yeah, I'll try." I watched him trying to organise his recollections. Then, he sat bolt upright as though an idea had struck him. "Can you get me a pencil and paper, please? Maybe if I do you a bit of a sketch, it will help as I try explaining how it was."

If I was going to get him some drawing materials, I might as well take our plates with me and reload them with another wedge of cake while I was up. I brought him a few sheets of copy paper and a selection of pencils and pens and left him to begin work on his sketch while I fetched our cake. His sketch was well developed when I settled back into my chair. Soon after, he was ready to explain his sketch.

"So, as you glanced around the room, Thomas lying on the floor caught your eye, and this was how the scene looked?"

"No, that's not quite how it happened. When I looked over to that side of the room, I didn't see Thomas at first. He was hidden by the table. He wasn't under the table. The table blocked my view of him. See on the sketch where the table and Thomas were. I looked around the door from where I was over here." He traced a line with his finger from the door across to the table and onto Thomas beyond it.

"Ah, I see my problem with understanding it. The table isn't there now. It's on the other side of the room, adjacent to the kitchen."

"I can't blame them for moving it across the room. I wouldn't want to eat my meals in the place where someone was killed." He had a point, but I wanted him to move on with explaining the sketch.

"So, you saw the table first. Tell me about the table. What made you go over to it?"

"I saw the table was set-up for something. When closer, I could see he had been cleaning his rifle. A brightly coloured beach towel covered the table, and a large rag – possibly a piece of an old sheet – was on top of it. The rag was folded into a long narrow pad and was close to the front edge of the table. Beyond the rag, all the cleaning gear was set out; the oil, the pull-through, and all that stuff."

"Was it a surprise to find Thomas had been cleaning his rifle?"

"No. He used it to put the cow down, and it was normal to clean it afterwards."

"Okay, you went to inspect the table … and then what…? You found Thomas?"

"Yes … It's not a great sketch, but that's more or less how he was lying. His rifle was there on the floor, a short distance from the arm he had flung out in its direction. And, over here on the other side of Thomas, one of the chairs was lying on its side on the floor. The whole area was wet. The window almost right above Thomas was open and the rain had come in. It was the only window open in the whole house."

"Wouldn't it have been unusual for the window to be open when it was raining so much?"

"No … that sudden storm came against the other side of the house. It is likely there weren't many windows open in the place anyway. When it's continually raining like that, you keep the place closed up as much as possible to keep the damp out. I think, when the storm hit, Thomas raced around closing any open windows, but left at least one open. He had a fire going in the fireplace sometime during the day. While the fireplace had adequate draught, it's good to have a bit of fresh air coming in. And, he would keep the window open near where he was working to help get rid of the smell of the oil he was using."

"Where was he shot?"

"Eh…? I know the sketch isn't great and I probably haven't explained things well, but that's where he was shot." Ned tapped his finger impatiently on his sketch.

"I'm sorry, that's not what I meant. What I should have asked was: where was the wound; head? Chest…?"

"Oh, I see; … Head … almost in the centre of his forehead."

"So, if the door was unlocked, someone might come in and, when Thomas looked over at him, he shot Thomas. Did you notice any footprints across the floor when you arrived?"

"Footprints…? No, there were none. There was nothing to indicate someone came in through the front door – or even the backdoor."

"What about when you came inside? Your footprints would have caught the police's attention."

"Nah, I didn't leave any. When I decided to go inside to find out what was happening, I took my boots off at the door and only wore my socks. I didn't leave footprints. The ground was so muddy, the boots of anyone coming in through that door would have traipsed in quite a deal of mud. There was none."

"So, unless they came in, shot Thomas, cleaned the floor after them, and shut the door behind them on their way out, it's unlikely anyone came in through the front door." At least that brought a wry smile to Ned's face. "Is there anything else you can tell me about the immediate area around Thomas' body?"

"Not that I can think of … There was blood … And then with the rain coming in … You would have to see it to…"

"I've had the unfortunate experience of seeing such scenes in the past. Don't trouble yourself trying to describe it to me. The chair lying on its side on the floor, had it come from the table?" Ned again tapped the sketch to indicate where the chair had been. "Because the table is no longer in the same position, I can't picture the scene properly. I presume Thomas had occupied the chair. When it was at the table, how far from the window would you reckon it was?"

"It was close to the window ... No more than four feet away – or whatever that is in the new measurements. I could convert it for you."

"No need; I'm fluent in both feet and inches and metric." We both fell silent for a while. Ned appeared to be dealing with his memories, while my mind ran at warp speed in an endeavour to process his details of the crime scene. I picked up his sketch and studied it for a few moments before breaking the silence.

"Ned, there are a couple of things about this which don't sit comfortably with me."

"I'm happy to try explaining them. Like I said, I probably haven't done such a great job so far, and the sketch isn't exactly a work of art, but…"

"It's not that. You've done brilliant job. While I didn't know Thomas, I had developed a picture of the man. I think he was house proud; proud of the home he created in that old church. More than that, I think he paid attention to detail. So, as I said, there are a couple of things about the crime scene which don't fit with my picture of him."

"You just about summed him up. Thomas was all those things, and more. He was hard-working and meticulous in everything he did. So, what things are causing you indigestion?"

"If we are to believe he committed suicide, why did he do it there? His home was his pride and joy, and shooting yourself in the head makes an awful mess. If he was hell-bent on doing away with himself, why didn't he take himself off somewhere else – somewhere out in the bush, in the shed, or the cottage?"

"I agree it was out of keeping with the man. But, do people plan to do away with themselves, or is it more a spur of the moment thing? I have to admit I don't know much about it, let alone why they do it."

"I'm no psychologist either, but I think there is a lead up to the event and a definite intent, rather than a spur of the moment action."

"You said there were a couple of things. What else is bothering you?"

"Maybe it's not bothering me. Perhaps I find it an anomaly. Why did Thomas clean his rifle before shooting himself? Was he afraid a dirty bullet might infect him? I'm sure that's not the case. So, why did he clean the rifle and then use it again… immediately … and on himself?"

Ned didn't reply. Instead, he stared unseeing at some indeterminate spot on my bilious green carpet. I was happy to let him be, until I saw his eyes light up. It was obvious he had a lightbulb moment. I sat forward in my chair in anticipation, and somehow managed to hold my tongue for the few moments before he turned to face me.

"He didn't clean the rifle. Thomas … had not yet … cleaned the rifle. He was all set up to do it, but he hadn't started. The rag he folded into a pad was there to lay the rifle on while it was cleaned. He didn't want the oil he used messing up the towel, so he put the rag down. But, the rag was *clean.* There was no oil on the rag. He hadn't started cleaning his rifle yet when he was shot. You are right. He wouldn't just decide 'to hell with cleaning the rifle, I think I'll shoot myself instead'. Does this mean it wasn't suicide?"

"It doesn't provide definitive evidence against it. But, while it is not proof, it is strong enough evidence to consider the alternatives."

"The only alternative I can think of is murder."

"Y-e-s, I agree that's about the only other alternative. Then, that raises the question of who, and how? The WHO might be difficult to determine. Who was around the time? Who would be roaming around out in the storm? But, if we put that to one side for the moment and think about motive, does it help narrow down the candidates?"

I saw Ned's brow furrow and his eyebrows draw together until they almost touched across the bridge of his nose. I rushed on to explain what I meant. "If we are looking for motive, we need to ask ourselves who might benefit from Thomas' death."

"Well, that's not hard to answer: Rita. She was his wife, so I imagine she did all right out of his death."

"That's a reasonable assumption – but it holds true only if she knew what she might gain in the event of his death. We now know from Thomas' will, her cash benefit was hardly worth the effort. True, it was cash she didn't have while he was alive. And, she and the child retained a roof over their heads for as long as they needed. So, yes, I agree there was some benefit to Rita from Thomas' death."

"Okay, we narrowed the field a bit. Who else benefited from his death? You're not thinking about Lucy?"

"What…? Lucy…? Of course not. She wasn't even in the country at the time. Even if she was, why would she suddenly turn on her father like that? They were close, and had maintained contact right up until his death. No, there is no question about Lucy's involvement. But, there was somebody else who benefited. Who found himself living in what amounted to absolute luxury compared to a cold, primitive shack further up the valley?"

"Rogan…! Are you saying Rogan did it?"

"No, I'm not saying that. All I'm suggesting is he also benefited, albeit indirectly, from Thomas' death. Before you get too excited, we haven't found any evidence pointing to his being there, or anywhere near the farm, on the night in question."

"Yeah, okay, so how do we go about finding some? It won't be easy. It all happened too long ago now for us to find something the police didn't find when they were poking around up here all those years ago."

"What we are going to do is keep an open mind. So far, all we have established is others besides Rita benefited from Thomas' death and, therefore, might be considered as having motive. We have nothing to point the finger at either Rita or Rogan, so we can't jump to conclusions."

"Well, I don't like where the WHO bit took us. Am I likely to be any more impressed with the HOW when we examine it? If Thomas didn't shoot himself, do we have any ideas about how it did happen?"

"After talking to you this morning, I think I do, but there is something else I need you to think back on: did you notice any footprints around the outside of the house? You said the ground was boggy from all the rain. Someone wandering around outside the house in those conditions would leave deep footprints in the mud."

"The ground was boggy enough for that to be the case. While walking across from my place, the mud squelched up over my boots. But conditions at the house were a bit different. The driveway and the path across the yard to the front door are compacted decomposed granite. It was hard like concrete. Sure, walking on that stuff, the soles of your boots would pick up sloppy water and a bit of mud, but you wouldn't leave footprints in it."

"What about if you left the path and walked around the side of the house? Would you leave footprints then?"

"No. Once you reached the bottom of the front steps, you were on that wide concrete path running around the house. There might be footprints on the concrete as he walked along the path, but they wouldn't be there long. It was still raining. By morning, the concrete would be washed clean. No sign of footprints or anything else would remain on the concrete. How is this important?"

"I think Thomas was shot through the open window – probably while sitting at the table preparing to clean his rifle." Ned sat forward in his chair, his excitement almost palpable. "Don't get to excited, Ned. We have nothing to prove any of it. But, if you allow me a couple more days of digging about, I just might come up with something."

"You've already found more than the coppers did. Just keep digging – please … for me and for Lucy. She lost her father, but I lost my best mate, who was like a son to me. I have difficulty living with the thought I didn't do anything to prevent it. I wasn't there for him when he needed help … like he was for me when Norma died. Maybe knowing he was murdered, and didn't commit suicide, will help me come to terms with it."

It was almost lunchtime. Aware Ned was supposed to be going to the races in the afternoon, I suggested we go for an early lunch. I took him to my favourite bistro again. We both worked hard at lightening the mood after the morning's heavy discussions. Our conversation while we waited for lunch was light and of no particular consequence until Ned mentioned Lucy.

"I expected to see Lucy at the farm this morning, but she hadn't arrived by the time I left for town."

"I think she is spending the weekend, or part of it, in Brisbane. By the way, maybe you soon will have a full-time nextdoor neighbour. She has arranged for the power and gas to be reconnected. It should happen sometime during the coming week."

"So, by next weekend, she could be back in the house."

"Maybe not; I think she wants to remove a lot of stuff from the house before moving in – stuff having anything to do with Rita. It's likely she will return to Millhaven sometime on Monday, so you probably will see her there again come Tuesday."

"I look forward to her moving in. It will be great to have her home again."

We didn't linger long over lunch. Ned wanted to catch the first race, and I needed to spend at least a few minutes in my office. Back in my office, I decided to check my emails before tackling anything else. One of the enquirers I sent information to had responded with a request for an appointment on Monday if possible. I replied confirming an appointment for ten o'clock.

This was the second potential new client this week. Closing the Blaine case had become urgent if I was to look professional about managing my new clients.

After washing up our morning tea things and attending to a few minor admin tasks, I loaded the remains of the chocolate cake into its box, stuffed my Blaine case file in my tote bag, and headed for home. Whether Ben was coming for dinner tonight or not remained a mystery. I hadn't heard from him all day. It wouldn't be a bad thing if he didn't. An evening alone to digest everything Ned told me this morning would be nice.

Chapter 25

Ben called just after six o'clock to say he was bringing Chinese for dinner. While I was looking forward to a night home alone, I wasn't feeling inclined to cook. Chinese would go down well and, with any luck, he might leave early. I spent time before he arrived updating and tidying my Blaine case file. I had no doubt we would be discussing Thomas Blaine again tonight.

At seven o'clock, Ben arrived with an enormous selection of take-away containers from the local Chinese restaurant. "My tastebuds were not communicating well. I couldn't work out what I wanted to eat, so I tried covering all bases and picked a bit of a wide variety of dishes."

Ben's bout of indecision was a clear indication he was strung out … not surprising given his heavy work schedule. The thought of Sam Keller's arrival lifted my spirits. Apart from delving into the police investigation into Thomas Blaine's death, I knew she also would find time to assist Ben with other matters.

To ensure the food didn't have time to get cold, we indulged in the serious business of eating as soon as he arrived. Confronted with such an array of dishes, I ended up eating a bit of far too many of the offerings. Then, it was off to sprawl in the lounge chairs until we felt sufficiently comfortable to sit up straight again. That's when I stirred myself to make coffee. Little conversation occurred while we went into virtual hibernation after dinner, but the coffee restored life.

I felt obliged to break the silence. How else was I going to find out what he discovered in the evidence locker if we weren't conversing? "How was your day? You seem preoccupied, or worn out tonight."

"I only went into work this morning to sneak down for a poke about in the evidence locker. It was late this afternoon before I did that. Before you ask, yes, I found the rifle collected from the scene of the Blaine crime. No, don't get excited. It doesn't help much."

"Why not…? Was it the weapon used to kill Thomas Blaine or not?"

"Short answer: dunno. Yes, the rifle is the same calibre as the bullet removed by the coroner. The bullet in question is not amongst the evidence collected. So, I don't know whether this is the rifle which fired it, or not. All I know is the calibre of the rifle matches the calibre of the bullet as recorded in the coroner's report."

"So, without the bullet, there can't be a ballistics comparison to see if it was fired from that rifle?"

"That is correct. While I was there, I scratched around for any other photos which might be mixed up with the other evidence. There was none. I'm beginning to think Sam has a hell of a job, and I am beginning to regret deciding to look into this investigation."

"Was the rifle in its case?"

"What case…? I don't know anything about a case. A lot of farmers don't even bother to keep their weapons in a locked gun cabinet, although the law requires it. I'm sure they don't bother putting a rifle away in its case."

"This one did. When the body was discovered, the case for that rifle was open on the table and was a component of the crime scene."

"See… I told you I was beginning to regret opening this investigation. Nowhere in the file is there any mention of a case for the rifle. The two lousy photos we have don't show enough detail to know whether there was a case on the table or not. I'm sure, if there were a case there when they found the body, they would have logged it."

"The police didn't discover the body. Blaine's neighbour found the body and called the police … who arrived twenty-four hours later. And, before you ask, yes, the case was still on the table when the neighbour led the officers to the body."

"Why did it take twenty-four hours for the police to arrive? Was something else happening at the time?"

"The road was flooded. They waited until the floodwaters receded before driving through to Tanwood."

"So, how did you hear about the rifle case being on the table? Is it a local rumour?"

"No…," I took a deep breath to control my irritation before saying more. "Thank you for selling me short. I don't ever put much faith in local gossip. For your information, I spent most of the morning with the neighbour who found the body. That's how I know about the rifle case – along with a few other details about the crime scene. And, that's why there is chocolate cake for dessert, if you are interested."

"You haven't been baking?"

"Why would I, when there is a fantastic cake shop next to where I work?" He decided a slice of cake and a fresh coffee would be nice. He followed me to the kitchen.

"What other details from the crime scene did chocolate cake manage to elicit from him."

"Well, it didn't score me a photo, but I do have a sketch of the crime scene as it was when he found the body. We referred to it as he explained the various aspects of the scene. I also heard about the events which led to his discovery of Thomas' body."

"You must enlighten me … or, better still, give me a copy of your notes and the sketch."

Before I did that, I had an important question to ask. It bothered me since discussing the rifle in the evidence locker. "How long is the rifle they took from the crime scene?"

"What do you mean by 'how long'? It's a rifle. Rifles have long barrels, as a rule. That's why they are called 'long arms' … as opposed to 'short arms' which often are called 'handguns'."

"If you want to see the stuff I collected this morning, don't be so patronising. I want to know the approximate length of the weapon from the stock to the end of the barrel."

"I don't know. I didn't measure it because I didn't know you were going to ask for its measurement."

"Oh, for God's sake, hold your arm out straight. Right; how long was it compared to the length of your arm?"

"It would be at least that long. Why? How is the length of the weapon important?"

"Having never met Thomas, I have no accurate idea of the size of the man, but I have seen his clothes. While he was of solid build, he wasn't a tall man. 'Stocky' might be a reasonable descriptor. If my assessment is correct, his arms would not be as long as yours are."

"And that is important because…?"

"Oh, I don't know that it is. I was trying to put my picture of the man together with a rifle I haven't seen. It was just a few moments of mental gymnastics, nothing more." At that point, I thought it wise to fetch my case file before Ben asked further questions which might lead him in the same direction as my thinking was heading.

Ben devoured every detail of my notes from this morning's session with Ned, and studied Ned's sketch for some time before commenting. "This is more than exists in the police file. I do want copies of your notes and the sketch map please." I obliged. As I handed him the photocopies, he asked, "You don't happen to have a spare folder do you? I'll need to keep anything not in the official police file separate from everything else." I fetched a new two-ring binder from my stationery cupboard for him.

Again, he scrutinised each piece of paper as he place it in his new folder. The task completed, he snapped the binder closed and sat staring at it for a few moments before turning his attention to me. "Did you draw any conclusions, develop any theories, from all this?" he asked as he waved his hand over the folder.

"Perhaps… At this stage, all I have is a few thoughts to pursue. Maybe they will develop into theories in time."

"…And that's not the truth. With only one read of all this, I developed a theory – well, maybe more of a suspicion. I don't believe for one minute you don't have some ideas after your session with that bloke this morning. So, come on … share."

"You might be right. I do have a half-baked suspicion, and this morning added weight to it." Ben made a 'give me' gesture, and I decided it might be worth sharing it with him. "I don't think Thomas Blaine committed suicide. While I don't have any evidence to support it, I am leaning towards murder."

"That's the good thing about our working together. As a rule, we are on the same wavelength. You should have joined the police. You would have made a fantastic detective … still would if you joined up now."

Okay, so Ben also now thinks it was murder. Maybe that doesn't change anything, or advance my investigation, but it is nice to have your hunches supported. For lack of evidence of one way or the other, my belief it was murder can't be more than a hunch.

With little more to discuss tonight, Ben prepared to leave. On his way to the front door, he paused. "I forgot to mention it earlier, but Sam will arrive in Millhaven by lunchtime tomorrow. I thought we all might have dinner here tomorrow night. We could kick around a few ideas about the Blaine case to help familiarise Sam with the investigation."

"Sounds good; I'll do a baked dinner, and aim for us to eat by about 7:30."

*****

Having promised a baked dinner tonight, as soon as the supermarket opened, my critical task this morning was to shop for a joint to cook. Before heading into town, I spent time planning the coming week. So many avenues still to explore and, by the end of the coming week, I would have two other cases begging for attention.

Mid-afternoon, a call from Emily told me we would be four for dinner. Something light for dessert after the baked dinner might be appreciated. I settled on a lemon meringue pie on the basis that, if we didn't have it for dessert, it might be nice with coffee later in the evening. By the time the dessert was made and the dinner was progressing nicely in the oven, most of the afternoon had disappeared and I barely had time for a quick shower before people started arriving.

Thanks to all the catching-up with Sam, we sat down to eat a little later than anticipated, and everything else over the evening was pushed back accordingly. The Blaine case was not mentioned until we were settled in the lounge room after dinner. Sam had a few questions about how I became involved. Emily remained silent during the early stages of our discussions. I knew she was absorbing everything being said as she came up to speed on my investigation. At last, an opening occurred for me to ask the question nagging me all night. As I was about to do so, Ben scuttled my attempt.

"Sonny, remember I told you Sam was going to collect a box of stuff from the woman in Ralston. We only managed a quick look through its contents this afternoon, but there are some interesting items. Foremost amongst those was a bullet. As I said, it was a quick look at the contents, but I didn't see anything about a ballistics test on the bullet. I can't swear there isn't one, but I have a strong suspicion there isn't."

"You know I can help with that if it's required," Emily said. "I don't just mean the bullet, but anything else you need tested as well. Some tests won't be much use after all this time, but still worth a try."

While Emily spoke, it gave me time to marshal my thoughts. "I don't remember details of the autopsy. Was there an exit wound?"

"Yeah, I think so. Give me a moment while I check." Ben flicked through his file for a few moments before continuing. "Here it is and… Yes, an exit wound at the back of the skull. Why did you ask, Sonny?"

"I was wondering about the condition of the bullet. If it exited the skull, where did it end up? If it hit something hard like the floor or a wall, it might be too damaged to compare the striations with a shot fired from the rifle."

"No, it wasn't damaged. It buried itself in one of a lounge chair. Its soft landing resulted in no apparent damage," Sam said.

"Jesus, the bullet travelled some distance after hitting its target. Those lounge chairs were across on the other side of the front section of the house." I had difficulty picturing the bullet travelling such a distance to conveniently bury itself in something soft.

Sam had a string of questions about the house. She saw Ned's sketch of the crime scene, but she needed something to place it in the context of the house and its surrounding environs. Your client… "What's her name…Lucy? … If I went to the house tomorrow, would she be there and would she let me in so I can turn it into a crime scene again, or will I need to organise a warrant first?"

Emily sat upright in her chair. I could tell by the set of her jaw she took offense at Sam's comment. Before I could intercede, Emily let Sam know how she felt.

"Lucy is the daughter of the man who was killed. And, as you well know, as a police officer, your request to enter the house and look around can't be refused – not without creating a whole lot of problems for herself anyway. So, what's the game here, Ben? Is this a legal investigation or some covert operation … or is it another case of police employing bully-boy tactics … and to what end? It's beginning to look like the latter. And, it's beginning to look like you've brought in someone from out of town so the locals don't know what's going on. I suspect this case was handled in a dodgy way from the outset, and bringing in Sam to do whatever she is going to do is just another exercise along the same lines. I don't want to risk being any part of this. Thanks for dinner, Sonny. I'll catch up with you again some other time – when you are free."

"What the hell are you on about? Sit down and explain yourself?" Ben demanded.

"Stop it! All of you, shut up and listen. You are guests in my house, and I won't tolerate such behaviour. Sam, your comment was insensitive at best, and has me wondering whether you are the right person for this investigation which Ben decided is necessary due to the anomalies we uncovered. And Ben, if you want to carry on like a copper, go back to your office and throw your weight around there amongst your own – not in my house. Does anybody not understand any of that? No? … Well then, you can all start behaving yourselves, or leave now."

The red mist had come down and my dark side was on brilliant display. I had bounced up out of my chair to deliver my ultimatum, and then stood glaring down at them. A few moments of uncomfortable silence followed, during which feet shuffled and heads were bowed.

"What was all that crap about? All I asked was a sensible question, so I would appreciate someone from those mortally offended present explaining what got up their noses." Sam gave a haughty toss of her head as she finished speaking.

My red mist deepened. "This case is about real people … People who might have suffered serious injustice as a result of the original police investigation … and about a young woman grieving for more than three years for the loss of her father, and still not knowing why or how it happened. It seems you have forgotten police cases are about real people, and have become just another arrogant copper."

"Sonny…" Ben tried to intercede.

"Don't bother, Ben. While I acknowledge lively debate is sometimes useful in solving problems, tonight's efforts have not helped. And, as much as I don't make a habit of taking sides in any such debates, tonight I am with Emily on this one. I am disgusted with yours and Sam's behaviour, and embarrassed a guest in my house had to suffer it."

Having vented my spleen, I rushed around gathering up coffee mugs and heading for the kitchen. Emily followed me around collecting port glasses and side plates, some still contained uneaten portions of lemon meringue pie. I had finished stacking everything in the dishwasher when Ben knocked on the breakfast bar. When I turned around, I was confronted by a contrite and awkward looking Ben with an embarrassed Sam peering out from behind him.

"May we offer our apologies and seek forgiveness. Both of us were way out of line. Please give us a chance to make amends … and, please, may we have more coffee and another slice of that pie?"

Emily giggled, and my red mist receded. While things remained a bit stilted for a while afterwards, peace was reinstated. Conversation was about nothing in particular while we drank coffee and ate pie. After mugs were drained and plates cleaned, conversation returned to the Blaine case.

In the few moments it took to again be settled in the lounge room, I realised it would be in my best interest to work with Sam and Ben, rather than alienating them. If I was to begin working my two new cases at the end of the coming week, I needed either to have closed my Blaine investigation for Lucy, or be able to assure her the police investigation was about to achieve her desired outcome.

Sam's agenda for the coming week entered the conversation. She admitted to no clear plans yet, but her top priority was to meet with me as early as possible tomorrow. We agreed soon after teno'clock would be good. The only other progress worthy of mention involved Emily. Ben promised to look for ammunition to suit the rifle in the evidence locker to enable a test firing so Emily could check the ballistics on the bullet.

Tomorrow was a working day for all of us, so nobody lingered too late. Still troubled by events earlier in the night, I fell into bed soon after eleven o'clock knowing an unsettled night was ahead of me.

Chapter 26

Not at my sparkling best this morning, I hadn't given any thought to Sam's visit, but I didn't have long to worry about it. She arrived at my office at about 10:30 with salad rolls for lunch. It was a little early but we went ahead with it anyway – and the rolls served well as a peace offering after last night. Her excuse for not arriving on time was having spent a couple of hours going through the police case file and some of the material in the box she brought from Ralston. While I wasn't sure how this morning was to proceed, Sam had definite ideas.

Sam started our discussion by asking what I had looked at so far. For some unknown reason, I decided to be economical in how much I shared with her. So, I told her about the house that once was the local parish church, and its general interior layout. I made passing reference to the cottage, but didn't mention anything I found there, or in the shed.

In spite of my best efforts, I could see she didn't grasp most of my time had been spent researching the people involved and those in the wider local community and their relationships. As an example, I mentioned my visit to Rogan's shack on the property further up the valley. It caught her attention. "Who is this Rogan you mentioned. Maybe, before we go any further, it might be best if you outlined Blaine's family situation for me."

She received a somewhat potted version: first marriage, one daughter, Lucy, then widowed … second marriage, one daughter, then Blaine dead … second wife's lover, Rogan, moved in. There were a couple of perfunctory questions regarding Lucy's story before her focus swung back to Rogan and his shack. It seemed an appropriate moment to mention Rogan's 'horticultural' plot in the scrub behind the shack.

Mention of the plot convinced Sam the shack was the best place for her to begin. Always happy to cooperate, I called Bob Joyce to ask if we might visit the shack again. He was okay with it, but said he might be busy with a few things today. I assured him we wouldn't bother him, but would call by the house in case he wanted to speak to us before we went to the shack. With our visit approved, we piled into my vehicle and headed up the valley to Bob's property.

As we drove onto the property, I told Sam about doing the right thing by calling at the house first. There was no sign of Bob, but a young chap strolled out and was waiting when we pulled up adjacent to the front lawn. Expecting trouble, I scrambled out and introduced myself.

"Dad said to keep an eye out for you. He's on the phone at the moment. He and another couple of suppliers are arguing on a phone hook-up with an agent about the next live shipment of cattle. He said you wanted to visit the old shack. Do you need me to show you the way? Oh, by the way, I'm Connor Joyce, Bob's only son and heir."

After I told him this was a return visit and I would be okay to find the shack without a guide, he shook his head as he scuffed up the gravel with the toe of his boot. "I can't imagine why anyone would want to go there in the first place, let alone a repeat visit. The place gave me the creeps, but it suited that creep Rogan. I didn't think he would ever leave."

Now there's something I just had to explore. "I take it you weren't a fan of Lyle Rogan. Was there anything specific about the bloke?"

"No, nothing specific, just everything about him. I always thought he was up to no good. Argh, I don't have anything to base it on. There was just something about the bloke made me feel he was no good. All I can say is, I didn't like him, and I didn't like his mates either."

"Were there many mates? And, was there anything about them that caused you concern?"

"I suppose I only ever saw two blokes – apart from that woman. Mind you, I didn't think much of her either. What sort of woman would live in that place with him? All right, I know it sounds like a lot of biased rubbish, but there was something about him, and his mates that made me wary of them. I wanted Dad to tell Rogan to go, but Dad couldn't see any wrong in him. Dad thought Rogan was a good worker – handy when you needed him – and he wasn't doing any harm down in that old shack."

"Were his services required much after you came back to the property?"

"Nah, I only used him once I think. It was handy he was here when Dad was clearing and fencing that back paddock, but he wasn't a horseman. Once the work in the back paddock finished, the only thing we needed a hand with was mustering, and he was useless at that. Anyway, we put in place a good arrangement with a couple of the neighbouring properties. When we needed a hand with mustering, we borrowed a couple of their blokes and, when they needed hand, I went over to help, and sometimes Dad came with me. So, after I came home, we didn't need Rogan's help."

"I don't suppose you could count on him being around when you needed him anyway. I imagine he was away from the place quite a bit when he was at work."

"When I first came home, I asked a lot of questions about him. Dad said he worked at one of the mines out west somewhere and only spent time in the shack on his days off. I can't say I ever saw any evidence of his working away from the place – of working at all. If I'm honest, I didn't trust the bloke, and I made a point of keeping a bit of an eye on him. He used to come and go a lot; erratic, not as regular as work hours."

"Those mates you mentioned, what can you tell me about them?"

"One came more often than the other. In fact, the second bloke only came a couple of times as far as I know. Of course, he could have been here more often, but I wasn't aware of it. Neither of them ever came to the house, and there was something sneaky – 'covert' is probably the right word – about their visits. I think the one I saw only a couple of times was a bikie belonging to one of those motorcycle gangs. The first time I saw him, he was in a vehicle but, the next time, he was on a motorbike. It was one of those big black things with a throaty growl, and the bloke wore leathers with fancy coloured things stuck all over his jacket."

"Was Rogan here for long after you returned to live here?"

"Ah, that was a bit strange. He was here for a while, coming and going as he did. Then, all of a sudden, I only saw him come onto the place every so often. There were still a few bits and pieces of his stuff in the old shack, but I had the feeling he wasn't living there anymore. If he'd found somewhere else to live, I can't understand why he kept coming back. Anyway, if he were living somewhere else, I think it was somewhere close; convenient for his visits to the shack. That situation lasted for the best part of two years I think. Then, he stopped coming, and I never saw him again."

"Maybe he told your father what he was doing, but didn't tell you. After all, the arrangement for him to live in the old shack was with your father."

"I doubt it. Dad knew I was unhappy about Rogan being here and wanted him off the property. If Rogan told Dad he was leaving, I'm sure Dad would tell me."

"So, you think your father was unaware Rogan abandoned the shack?"

"Yeah, and I think he probably still is unaware."

Sam remained silent while Connor Joyce and I conducted our question-and-answer session. I began feeling uneasy about her. She might not be interested in any of what Connor had to say, but I was – and I still had questions to ask. Sam was not shy, and I felt sure she would let me know if she wanted to move on. I decided to test my luck and pressed on with questioning Connor about the shack, and Rogan and his mates. "At least, after Rogan moved out, you wouldn't have to worry about his mates visiting the property anymore."

"No such luck; one of his mates, the one who visited a fair bit, came a couple of times afterwards until I caught up with him in the clearing at the pump station one day when I went to check on the pump. I warned him off, told him to stay off the property."

"How was that received? I don't imagine he was too receptive. Did he have a reason to be there when Rogan no longer lived on the place?"

"He was a bit put out about it and became aggressive. I always carry a rifle in case I have to put a beast down, so I showed him I carried it and meant business. I never saw him again. I was sick of people treating the place like the Queen Street Mall and coming and going at strange hours."

The big question I wanted to asked might challenge his memory. After all, the event was more than three years ago, and I wasn't sure Connor had returned to live on the property then. I mentioned the date of the storm and the flooding it caused. "Had you returned to live here by then, or were you still living down south at the time?"

"No, I was back here. The storm was a beauty. I think they called it a super cell, or something like that. We had a few trees come down and a bit of fencing damaged."

"Now, here's a question to challenge your memory: was Rogan at home in the shack on the night of the storm?"

"That's not hard. Yeah, he was here; him, the woman and the kid. The storm must have made for an interesting night in that shack."

"You're sure it was the night of the storm?"

"Positive… I was up most of the night keeping an eye on the storm. When I saw Rogan drive out, I wondered where the hell he was going at that hour of the morning and in a raging storm. At some time between three and four o'clock, the storm passed and the rain eased off a bit. I knew trees were down and it was a no-brainer fences would be down too. I went to check on the stock down by the creek. I ran into Rogan on the track. He said he was driving around checking fencing and the stock. It was a lie. He had just returned to the property from wherever he went."

"Did you challenge him about his story, or where he had been?"

"Nah, I had better things to do than waste time talking to Rogan. Wherever he went, it couldn't have been far. He wouldn't have been gone more than half an hour."

"…And you are sure he wasn't checking the property as he said?"

"Yeah… I saw him drive out the gate and disappear down the road."

"You said the woman and child were in the shack with him that night. How sure of that are you?"

"On that first time when I ran into Rogan, I told him to go back to the shack. I would look after the stock. He was useless at rounding them up. I managed to move most of the animals into a secure paddock, but I knew there were still a few roaming in the scrub. At first light, such as it was that morning, I rode out to round up the escapees. When I found the five of them, they were almost at the shack. Instead of taking them back through the scrub, I drove them out onto the track – the one that leads to the shack – and walked them along the track to the first secure paddock I came to. As I went past the shack, I saw the woman, and heard the child inside talking to someone. I assume she was talking to Rogan. His truck was where he always parked it."

"When he left the property that night, he probably wasn't gone long because the road was cut and he couldn't go anywhere."

"No, that's not right. The creek did flood the road to Tanwood, but it wasn't until about the middle of the next day. The road was still open when he left. Then, it only remained flooded for the rest of that day, unlike the road from Tanwood to Millhaven, which remained closed for a few days I think."

"Do you remember how long after the storm Rogan vacated the shack?"

"Well, I know he was still around for a couple of months after the storm, but I don't think he spent much time at the shack. He came and went a fair bit, but it looked like he still lived there. Then, in April, a cyclone late in the wet season drifted down the coast before turning into a rain depression and moving inland. By the time it passed over here, it was only a bit less of a storm than the one we had in January. It dumped about 250mm of rain on the place in a few hours. Again, trees and fences came down. That time, the cattle that escaped from their paddock made it all the way to the shack.

There were a few more than I could handle on my own and they were spooked. I was desperate enough to ask Rogan to give me a hand to move them along the track to the next paddock. He wasn't home. Nobody was in the shack, but he was living there still, part-time anyway. I remembered seeing his mate come onto the property just before the heavy rain started. At the time, I assumed he was going to the shack, but nobody was there when I went to ask Rogan for help. It struck me as odd because I saw the mate come, but I never saw him leave again. A week or so later, I happened to be at the pump station along the track and decided to check on the shack. It was obvious no one lived there any longer, but Rogan continued to come and go for quite a while afterwards. For another year or more, I sometimes saw him on the property."

"Did something happen to put an end to his 'visits'?"

"Not that I know of, but he never took up residence there again, although he continued to treat it as his place. And then, it occurred to me I hadn't seen him for some time. I checked the shack again. I could see nobody had been near the place for a while. Then, a bit later again, I heard at the store that he had moved in with the Blaine widow."

"Was the Blaine widow the woman you saw at the shack the night of the storm?"

"I don't know the Blaine woman, so I can't tell you whether she was the one at the shack or not

"What did your father make of Rogan's behaviour? Did you discuss it with him?"

"No, I never mentioned it. It would have been a waste of time. He considered Rogan a decent chap. We differed on that point, and any mention of Rogan always ended in an argument. So, I was happy to assume him gone for good, and left it at that."

Time had slipped away and we still hadn't been to the shack. After apologising to Connor for taking up so much of his time, Sam and I headed for the shack. I hoped our time there would be short. My stomach was starting to rumble and I was having obsessive thoughts about a Tanwood coffee and maybe a home-made pie.

We weren't long at the shack. "This place makes my skin crawl. Was there something in particular you wanted to show me?" Sam asked.

"It is no palace, but it probably has deteriorated a bit after being abandoned for so long. I agree though, you would have to be desperate to live here … Or have a very good reason to stay in the place. If you follow me out the back, I'll show you what I think Rogan's 'good reason' was."

On our way to the patch of scrub out the back, I pointed out the irrigation system installed to support his horticultural endeavours. Sam took a lot of photographs of the overgrown plot and, once we were back in the car, sent a couple off to Ben along with the GPS coordinates for the plot. "He can claim an anonymous tip made him aware of what went on up here, and he can send a team out to deal with it. That way, my presence in Millhaven and my role remain oblivious to the rest of the precinct."

As we bumped our way along the track, I intended calling at the house again to tell people we were leaving. It was unnecessary. We encountered Connor at the pump station clearing. I made a decision about something I'd been mulling over since before we arrived on the property. I told him about Sam and her investigation – and suggested it might be wise not to mention it to his father yet.

"I should warn you too. Police will be coming to investigate the spot of drug cultivation that went on in the scrub behind the shack. Probably best not to mention that to your father yet either." He smirked and tapped the side of his nose. I think I made his day.

Sam spent most of the drive to Tanwood staring out of her window at the passing scenery. There was no conversation and I wondered whether she was unhappy (sulking perhaps) about the way the morning panned out. I wasn't going to apologise for spending so much time talking to Connor. Apart from his being a good-looking personable bloke, he was a wealth of information. Sam's silence allowed my mind to analyse all I learned from Connor.

Chapter 27

Tanwood coffee shop was deserted. The aroma of pies straight from the oven was overwhelming. I led Sam in and selected a table. Jessie was up for a chat. I wanted her to join us, but I needed one of her pies and a coffee first. As she placed the famine relief on the table in front of me, I introduced her to Sam – without mentioning her occupation or rank. Conversation was delayed further while Sam selected from the menu.

At last Sam and I were eating, and Jessie and her coffee joined us at our table. I commented on the pies. "I'm pleased you baked these, but isn't it a bit late in the day? The lunchtime trade is over by now."

"Yes, but a lot of customers call in on their way back from town or after picking the kids up from school. They take pies home for an easy dinner or to reheat for tomorrow's lunch, especially in this cooler weather. I ran out today, so I thought I'd better make another batch. Were you working at the Blaine farm again today?"

My phone interrupted the conversation. A delay in information gathering occurred when the caller ID showed me it was Lucy and I took it outside. She wanted to let me know she wouldn't return to Millhaven until tomorrow sometime, and also that she had found another key to the house. If I needed to go into the house while she was away, she explained where she hid the second key. While we didn't need to go into the house, it was good to know we could if we wanted to.

Back at our table, Jessie was explaining something. It only took me a moment to work out Sam had asked about the area's strange name: Tanwood.

"The area's earliest settler, fresh from England, took up the first land grant in the valley. In those days, the land grants were in excess of 1200 acres. A few months later, his son joined him here and secured the adjoining land grant. It gave them a combined area of more than two and a half thousand acres. Over the years, they added other small areas to their holdings to end up with more than 3000 acres between them. They amalgamated all holdings and called it Tanwood Estate."

"The family must be worth a fortune. Do they still own all that land?" Sam asked.

"Nah, fortunes ebb and flow. Over the years, some of it was sold off to prevent bankruptcy, and the government reclaimed some of the land for subdivision. Bob Joyce's place is the original home area. It's still a big property for these times, but it's nothing like it was last century. The rest of the original Tanwood Estate was subdivided into smaller holdings and sold off. Bob Joyce's place is still called Tanwood Estate. This area known as Tanwood covers part of the original estate."

While the history of the area was interesting, I was trying to work out how to redirect the conversation to Rita and her mob, and their subsequent disappearance, when Jessie solved the problem. "So, Sonny, how is your digging around in Blaine farm matters going? Are you any closer to finding out where they went or why?"

"Perhaps the best answer is: the jury is still out on that one. I do have a couple of questions for you though, if you have time."

"Unless someone comes in, I have all the time in the world, but I don't know I can help you much."

"What can you tell me about Lyle Rogan? I know it's a difficult question, but I wondered whether he had much to do with the store."

"Yes, we did see him on occasion, but Rita came in most of the time. Rogan was a strange bloke. He seemed a bit 'shifty' to me. You know the sort of bloke. One who makes you want to do a stock-take and check the till the moment he leaves. Don't get me wrong, I don't think he ever pilfered anything, or did anything else illegal. It was just how he was. I suppose it was his manner; sort of sly somehow. And, he wasn't friendly. Never made any attempt to fit in around here."

"What about his mates, what were they like?"

"Did he have any? If he did, it wasn't obvious. I never saw him with anyone, or talking to anyone."

"I don't suppose you get many strangers up this way. If there were, they would stand out like the proverbial in a place where everyone knows everyone."

"That's true. As an example of that, from time to time, a scruffy bloke came into the store. I think he belonged to one of those motorcycle gangs. He always wore some black leather outfit. A nasty looking piece he was. The other one, I would describe as a hippie. Do they still call them hippies these days?"

It was a serious question, so I nodded and replied, "Yes. I know what you mean by hippie, but could you describe him for me?"

"Oh, now you're asking … Scruffy, lots of tattoos, beard, earrings, chains and things hanging around his neck, often in bare feet, and hadn't seen a dentist in a long while. I don't suppose that tells you much, but he was the sort of bloke who, in the good old days, you would want to take out and give a good dunking in carbolic before letting him come too close. I'm not suggesting he ever did anything wrong, but he did look as though he had a mean streak. In short, I didn't trust him, and the rest of the staff kept a close eye on him whenever he was in the place."

"Have either of those blokes been around in recent times?"

"Since you ask, I think it's been quite a while since I've seen either of them. I mean, at least a year – maybe more."

It was Sam's turn to take over the questioning. "Did the people from Blaine's farm run an account here?"

"Yeah, as do most of the locals. If they run out of something or maybe need a couple of items, rather than running to the store, they call and we send it out on the truck with the mail and fuel run. We keep the accounts separate; those for the store, and those for fuels and lubricants. Blaine's farm ran both accounts. When we became fuel agents, Thomas installed a tank on the farm and we kept it topped up. They never used much fuel in his day, but they churned through it after he died."

"Did they settle their accounts before they disappeared?"

"No such luck; they left owing us quite a bit. We weren't the only ones stung, not by a long shot. She had a fair bit on the store account, and then came in … I think it might've been the Friday before they disappeared over the weekend ... Anyway, it was just before they disappeared. Rita came in and picked up a fair load of groceries and put them on the bill. A couple of days before that, the fuel truck filled the tank on the farm. It was filled the week before but already was about three parts empty. So, all up, they left owing us quite a few dollars."

"I don't suppose you could do much about being paid when nobody knew where they went," I suggested.

"We just had to kiss it goodbye. It leaves a bad taste when it happens in a community like this. A small business like ours takes a while to recover. We did manage to minimise the damage a bit. When we realised they'd gone, we waited a week or so, and then the truck went back to the farm and drained the fuel tank. We reduced the amount owing on the account by the cost of the amount of fuel reclaimed. I don't know whether it was legal or not, but it helped us. Now, there is something you might be interested in. I think the fuel tank was filled on the Wednesday and they left on the weekend. When the boys went to drain the tank, it was only half full. They had two cars, Rogan's old truck, and Thomas' SUV which she drove. I don't know what she did with the old wreck she used to drive before that. Anyway, the boys said the amount of fuel taken out of the tank was more than would fill both vehicles. Maybe they filled a few containers to take with them."

Sam returned to something said earlier. "Jessie, you said you weren't the only ones left with unpaid accounts; others were ripped off as well. How do you know that?"

"I'm also the local postmistress. I returned anything with a return address, but I still ended up with a pile of unclaimed mail for the farm. I'm sure some of them are bills, and most of the ones I sent back were accounts."

"What sort of accounts?"

"Oh, the usual household stuff: electricity, gas, a local mechanic, vehicle registration; those sorts."

My mind went into a spin. What about house insurance and local government rates? If those renewals remained unpaid, the place could be in a precarious position. The farm could end up being auctioned off by the Council to recoup unpaid rates and, if household insurance was unpaid, the house was unprotected – and had been since Rita and her mob absconded. While I was preoccupied with my nervous twitch on Lucy's behalf, Sam had identified herself to Jessie and asked to see any remaining unclaimed mail for the farm.

Jessie dumped a few envelopes on the table. "I'll need something from you to say you've taken them. In my capacity as postmistress, I can't just hand over mail – even to the police." Sam promised to drop back with the requisite document in the next day or two.

A couple of customers came into the coffee shop. With nothing more to be gained from lingering there any longer, we climbed into my car. "Well, Sam, what would you like to do now?"

"I'm not sure. I was wondering whether you should introduce me to the bloke you've been talking to, the bloke on the neighbouring farm. Is it a possibility while we are here in Tanwood?"

"I can take you to Ned's place. I don't know what he'll be doing or where he will be but, if he is around, I'll introduce you. In case we do find him, how do you want to be introduced?"

"Uhmm … Maybe in this case, I should be introduced as a copper. It might make him feel a bit easier about answering questions." I doubted her reasoning but didn't say so.

I was right. Introducing Sam as a copper was the wrong move. Ned became wary of Sam, and was stiff and standoffish even with me. It took a while, and was hard work, but I managed to talk him around enough to invite us in for a cuppa. The coffee and general conversation seemed to work. Ned relaxed enough to cope with Sam and her questions.

Her first question was predictable. "Ned, during the time Lyle Rogan lived nextdoor, did they have many visitors?"

"Visitors were rare. But, now I think on it, there were a couple of blokes turned up at different times. One of them came a few times soon after Rogan moved in. He seemed to come and go a bit for a couple of weeks or so and then never came again. …Might have had something to do with the almighty row I heard one day between him and Rogan. It probably was the last time I saw him visit the place."

"You said there were two blokes who visited. What can you tell me about the other bloke?"

"Him? …Fancied himself a big-time biker. He used to arrive on one of those big noisy motorbikes. I only saw him there a couple of times. Always dressed from head to foot in that black special sort of biker's gear. His last visit was only a day or so before the mob nextdoor disappeared. That was another interesting occasion; more shouting. I saw the bloke come out and straddle his bike but, instead of roaring off, he started yelling back at Rogan standing on the doorstep. The only bit I understood of what he yelled was: *time is running out, (expletive), and that's no idle threat.*

I wasn't happy about him coming out this way. Before we knew it, he might bring his mates with him. That one was a bad-looking lot … both Rogan's visitors were. It was good they never came again after Rogan and his lot scarpered. I kept an eye out in case either of them returned and planned on getting up to no good over there."

While Ned's information spoke volumes to me, Sam didn't consider it merited more than a couple of words in her notebook. Today was proving frustrating. I couldn't wait to get home to add all the bits I'd learned today to my Blaine case timeline, especially the information Ned shared about the visitors. My thoughts were interrupted by Ned's question. "Sonny, what's going on with Lucy? I know you said she was going to Brisbane over the weekend, but she hasn't been here today. Is everything all right with her?"

"She's fine, Ned. She called to tell me about a change of plans. It now looks like she won't return to Millhaven until tomorrow. I don't know what happened, she didn't say. She did tell me she had found another front door key in the office and she has hidden it in the shed. Her information about the key was in case I wanted to enter the house before she returned."

Sam sat upright and looked excited. "If she is happy for you to enter the house while she's away, is it possible for us to go over there now? I'd like to look at the crime scene."

Should I take Sam over to have a look at the crime scene, or not? I considered the question for a few moments. While Lucy had, in effect, given me permission to enter her house, she didn't know about Sam. I felt reluctant to take a stranger into the place while Lucy was away. Before I could put together a response, Ned realised my predicament. "Sonny, I'm sure Lucy wouldn't mind if it's going to help with the inquiry. After all, she gave you permission to let yourself in while she is away, so she won't have a problem with it."

Ned was right. Lucy wouldn't have a problem with it, but I wasn't any easier about it as I drove the three of us along the rough track to Kirk Michael Farm. Having Ned along made me feel a bit happier. Once we were inside, adopting something of a 'tour guide' performance, Ned took over.

He began by explaining the changed layout since the time of the murder. Then, he went on to point out where the body was lying, the location of the table, chair and the rifle. I spent the time perched on a stool at the kitchen counter. As I examined every inch of the room from my perch, I was half tuned in to Ned's running commentary. It was apparent Ned had not quite accepted Sam. The tour of the site he gave Sam was an abbreviated version of his knowledge of the gruesome sight he encountered the morning he discovered Thomas' body. Somehow, that pleased me.

As he finished speaking, I climbed off the stool and ambled towards the other two, but Sam had started asking questions and taking photos. I detoured to walk past the office – and tried the door on my way past. It was locked. It seems Lucy still is not confident the others will not be back. While Sam clicked off shots of the now lounge room, Ned roamed around and ended up next to me.

It provided an ideal opportunity. I signalled Ned to follow me over to the stove. While we stood in front of it, I announced in a voice loud enough for Sam to hear, "I can see why Lucy is replacing this one. It doesn't look like it has ever been cleaned." At about that point, Sam announced she was going outside to take a few shots of the front and side of the house. I took advantage of her absence to wise-up Ned on my intention not to take Sam out to the cottage or the shed.

"Okay; but why not take her out there, Sonny? Is there something I'm not aware of?"

"Dunno; it just doesn't feel like the right thing to do. Ned, earlier you told us about a blazing row between Rogan and one of his visitors. Can you give me a rough idea of when that happened?"

"Do you think it's important?" I shrugged but didn't reply. It was too hard to explain my gut was telling me it was. "Well, I think it was the last time he came here. Now when was that?"

He took a few moments to think about it. "…Might have been in April. Yeah, I think it was April; not long after Rogan moved in with Rita. Something makes me think it was around the time of the other big downpour we had that year. It caused a bit of flash flooding too. If the exact date is important, I can look it up. I don't know if I recorded anything about the row, but I know I noted the downpour. My journal for that year would give the date, even if I didn't make a note of the row. Would you like me to look it up for you?"

"Yes please, Ned, but there's no hurry. Whenever you have some spare time will be good."

By the time Sam finished taking her photos and came inside again, it was late. I was anxious to leave. I wanted time alone to write up my notes and consider all I learned today. So, I was pleased when Sam announced she was finished and was ready to leave whenever I was ready. Ned almost was knocked over in my rush to shove everyone outside, lock the door and hide the key in the shed again. Then, it was a quick trip to drop Ned off at home before we were on the road to Millhaven.

After dropping Sam off, I called in at my city office to check messages and emails. As I was about to pack up and head home, Ben called. He and Sam were coming for dinner. He would bring something.

Damn! I wanted a night at home alone. Still, if Ben and Sam discuss their case while they are at my place, it might give me an insight into Sam's assessment of the case so far. I hadn't heard from Emily, so assumed she wouldn't be joining us for dinner. That might be a good thing. If she wasn't there, Sam might feel more relaxed about discussing the case.

Chapter 28

Ned's call came soon after I arrived home and was about to write up my notes from today's sessions with him and Connor Joyce. He found the date of the April downpour he mentioned this afternoon. "…And I did make a note about the row between Rogan and that scruffy bloke. It occurred in the afternoon before the downpour happened. My note says I couldn't hear what was being said except for the word 'money' being mentioned a couple of times."

"That's brilliant, Ned. Thanks for looking it up for me, but I hope you didn't go to any trouble to find it."

"It was no trouble and, while I was on the go, I decided to check my journal for any mention of the run-in Rogan had with the bikie bloke. It was on the Friday before Rogan and the others disappeared sometime over that weekend."

There wasn't more to say, except for me to offer my profuse thanks for his invaluable information. Then I made a note for myself to ring Jessie at the Tanwood coffee shop as soon as a respectable hour rolled around in the morning. Ned's information left me with one burning question, and I thought Jessie might have the answer to it.

I felt a story was emerging, but it was as though shrouded in fog and I couldn't quite grab hold of it. For the first time during this investigation, I felt on the brink of discovering what happened at Blaine's farm on the night Thomas was killed.

Ben said he would be running a bit late with dinner tonight, but he arrived only a few minutes after seven o'clock. Sam arrived about five minutes later. She looked a bit drawn and tired. I refrained from commenting. We sat down to eat almost as soon as Sam arrived. Conversation during the meal was scant and of no consequence. It wasn't until we adjourned to the lounge room afterwards that conversation flowed.

It was as though Sam just noticed Emily's absence. "Emily is not here tonight. Were you expecting her?"

"No, she doesn't always come for dinner. I didn't hear from her today, so I wasn't expecting her tonight. She is able to join us less often these days. Her workload is heavy and, if there's been a crime spree in the area, socialising and sleep become dispensable."

"That's a relief. I was concerned I might have offended her last night. It's a bit disappointing she is not here though. I was prepared to make abject apologies for my behaviour, but I suppose there will be other opportunities."

To say we discussed the Blaine investigation after dinner would be misleading. What happened was Sam updated Ben on her case so far. I felt it might be enlightening – even beneficial – to sit and listen rather than to contribute. Towards the end of her report, Sam's comment to Ben riled me: *So, it was a big day of talking to people but, so far, I haven't heard anything to discount the suicide theory.*

Her subsequent assessment of research into Lyle Rogan and his relationship with others at the farm as 'nothing more than a waste of time' stirred my dark side. The red mist began descending again. Sam's comment seemed to accuse me of diverting interest away from Thomas to focus on Rogan. While I bit my tongue to control my rising anger, Sam rubbished everything which suggested Thomas's death was anything other than suicide. I lost the internal struggle.

"Sam, in case you hadn't noticed, I'm still here – and you are a guest in my home. You might at least have the good manners while sitting in my lounge room not to rubbish me and discount my research. For the record, I don't share your assessment regarding Thomas' death. Still, I don't expect that's of any consequence to you. From here on in, you're welcome to conduct your own investigation, just as I will conduct mine in my way." Perhaps not unpredictably, Sam took offence, said she thought I was being overly sensitive, and left in a huff. Ben looked uncomfortable about the way things had developed but had the good grace not to comment – not until after Sam left. Then, Ben admitted to being stunned by what happened between Sam and I tonight.

"Sonny, what is going on with you two? You and Sam are good mates and have worked well together a number of times. What is wrong this time?"

"Okay, firstly, I am not happy about being used by Sam. I'll come back to that. Perhaps the most negative aspect of trying to work alongside her is the way she is throwing her weight around when talking to the locals – or not talking to them at all. It's bound to produce a negative reaction which will be counterproductive to both our investigations."

"What do you mean about how she is interacting with the locals?"

"She either ignores them – doesn't as much as say a single word of make a comment – or she speaks to them as though they are yokels and not too bright. Ned reacted badly to her the moment I introduced them. It took a bit of talking to persuade him Sam was okay and he should talk to her. In the end, he did, but in a guarded way. This is totally out of keeping with her character. What has happened to the 'real' Sam? The person you engaged is a look-alike, but is not our Sam."

At that point, Ben's phone played its tune, interrupting discussions for a few minutes. I heard him answer the call as he walked out to the kitchen. He greeted the caller as a friend, and not as somebody from the precinct. Good; it probably means it will be a short call and he won't go dashing off to some crime scene before we finish thrashing out whatever the problem is with Sam. While I couldn't hear what was being said, a few moments into the call, I heard Ben bellow 'what report'. Oh dear, maybe this isn't such a friendly call after all.

In spite of my best efforts to look as though I wasn't trying to eavesdrop, Ben's next explosive comment caused me to spin around to face him ... only to find him looking at me. He shrugged at me and, while the call appeared to continue, Ben walked to the drinks cabinet and took out a bottle of single malt scotch and waved it at me. I nodded enthusiastically and mouthed, "Yes, please."

A few moments later, the call ended. He shoved the phone back in his pocket with a tad more force than required, and poured our drinks. As he made his way back to the lounge room, the firm set of his jaw told me the call had not gone well. While I didn't really need or want a drink, the glass put down in front of me held a good two fingers of scotch. Unsure about how to proceed, I contented myself with sipping my drink while I waited to see if I was to learn anything about his call, or if we were to resume our earlier discussion. Seconds ticked by as he continued to stare at his boots stretched out in front of him.

Then, after a deep breath, sat upright in his chair and demanded, "Where were we? Oh yes, Sam... I admit I noticed a change in her tonight, and last night too. Last night, I thought she might be tired and a little awkward about not having studied the case yet. I had to support her then, but I am not impressed with her behaviour tonight. Before I took that call, I put her behaviour down to her seeing this as a big break for her career ... trying too hard to be a 'hardened investigator" to impress her superiors. Now, I suspect it's something else. Nevertheless, I will try to 'ease her down a bit'.

"Whatever you choose to do with your investigator is your business, and has nothing to do with me. There is something you need to know though. I won't spend any further time working with Sam on this investigation. To be blunt, I don't want to work with her anymore. I have my own case to deal with, and I intend continuing with it alone."

"Sonny, I hear what you're saying, and I understand where it's coming from. But, if that is how you wish to proceed, it is likely to make life quite difficult for me. I know I can't ask you to work with Sam, but will you at least think about keeping me informed on your progress?"

Of course I would keep him informed. That's how it always happens. That's why our relationship has been mutually beneficial over so many years. Why would I change my practice of discussing my cases with him after dinner most nights? I assured him I did not intend making his life difficult – not at this time anyway.

"Thank you. I hoped whatever was going on with Sam would not impact on our relationship. Perhaps I should tell you about that call I received earlier. It was from Pete Messell. He wanted to confirm Sam would be back at her job in Ralston by the end of the week."

I suspect my jaw hung slack as my eyebrows shot towards my hairline in surprise. "I thought your arrangement with Pete was for a possible long-term investigation, and not only a matter of a few days. Why would he expect Sam to return by the end of the week?"

"Ah well, that's another mystery in the 'what's wrong with Sam' saga. It appears Sam has been reporting to Pete, and has given him to understand she will wrap this up within the next couple of days. He says she is mystified as to why I brought her in to sort it out, when it was evident it was a straightforward case of suicide."

Pete's revelation left me dumbfounded for a few moments. In the end, neither of us could work out what was going on, and we agreed there appeared to be some hidden agenda involved. With nothing to be resolved on that matter, we drifted back to discussing the Blaine case.

"I get the distinct impression you don't share Sam's opinion that Thomas Blaine's death was suicide. Would you like to tell me about it?"

"You're right. I don't believe it was suicide. I'm not talking about a hunch. Yes, if you asked me yesterday, I would have cited gut feeling or instinct, or some other nebulous reason. After today, I *know* it wasn't suicide. I'm sure he was murdered. There is a story emerging, but I can't quite put it together yet. Give me another day or so, and I think I'll have it."

"Okay, keep working on it, but is there anything that gut of yours is telling you – anything you would like to share with me, that is?"

"Well, I think Thomas knew something was going to happen to him. While I haven't spent much time at the house, much of what I've seen suggests he was preparing for it. It looks as though he was 'putting things in order' for when he would no longer be around. It's clear it was done with Lucy in mind, and in the hope she would return to Tanwood in the future."

"If you look at it a different way, putting things in order might indicate Thomas planned to suicide. Perhaps he was tying up all the loose ends before he went. I don't see how any of that suggests he was murdered."

"Yeah, I agree it might sound that way to someone who didn't know what he did, and who didn't know about the strength and depth of Thomas and Lucy's enduring relationship. After the work I did today, I'm convinced it was murder, and that Thomas knew it might happen."

Our discussion ended with our agreeing to disagree. Ben remained unconvinced it was murder. The temptation was to keep pressing my argument, but I knew Ben well enough to realise it wouldn't work and might prove counter-productive in the long run. So, I moved on to something else from today's interviews.

"I know you won't be able to answer this off the top of your head, but I wondered if any bodies were discovered during April of the year Thomas died. Perhaps there was one somewhere in the valley, or near the valley… It would have been around the time of another downpour and when another bit of road flooding occurred."

"No, I can't think of any off the top of the head, but I will check. Is there anything else I should know about this possible body?"

"There's not much I can tell you. If it's who I think it was, when he was alive, he was scruffy, bearded, tattooed, and wore an earring and other jewellery. But, even if you did have one who doesn't match that, I still might be interested."

Ben left soon after. Then, I spent time just going over everything I learned so far about the case. It was well after midnight when I went to bed. Sleep was elusive thanks to thoughts about the case plaguing me into the wee hours of the morning.

*****

Tuesday morning already and I still don't have anything definitive to tell Lucy … and, I'm in a quandary about what to do today to progress things. I know I'm close to solving the case, but I'm missing one or two vital pieces of information. It's like almost finishing the jigsaw except for a couple of pieces which seem to be lost. Oh well, maybe inspiration will come as the day wears on … and I do have to call Jessie at the Tanwood coffee shop later this morning. Maybe that will trigger something for me to follow up.

To fill in time until a sufficiently civilised hour to call Jessie, I created case files for the new investigations I would work during the coming week. The task reminded me I had to put the Blaine case to bed in a hurry. Emily arrived while I was absorbed with such thoughts. She bounded in looking pleased with herself.

"…Thought you might be interested in a copy of this before I give it to Ben." She waved an envelope at me as she came towards my desk.

"Quite possibly… what is it, and will it help me solve the Blaine case for Lucy?"

"To quote you, *quite possibly*... It's the result of the test firing of the rifle from the Blaine case evidence."

"Ah hah… and did the striations on the bullet removed from the body match those on the test-fired bullet?"

"Not even close; that rifle wasn't the one used to shoot Thomas Blaine."

"Oh, I do like it when my day starts this well. Anyway, why are you here and not slaving away over your test tubes or whatever it is you do all day?"

"Day off… I've chalked up too many hours again this month. Are you going to copy this report?" I snatched it and headed for the photocopier. "While you are doing that, bring me up to date on your Blaine investigation." After handing her the case file to peruse, I delivered a verbal report. Although succinct, recounting it verbally seemed to help clarify a few things for me.

By the time I finished copying her report, Emily had skimmed through my file. "What do you make of this hippie bloke who seemed to drop out of the picture after his row with Rogan?'

"Interesting isn't he? I've asked Ben to check if there was a body found around the time of that downpour in April of the year Thomas was killed. The downpour was only a couple of weeks after Rogan moved in with Rita. I might be way off beam with this one, but my gut keeps insisting the hippie is significant in the overall story."

"I could check our files. It was before my time, but all the existing files came across when we set up the new arrangement. After five o'clock this afternoon, come over to my office. If we look at the files together we could see something I might miss on my own. By the way, what's going on with Sam? The person at dinner the other night looked like Sam – but it sure wasn't the Sam I knew."

"We all noticed. Even Ben admitted he was stunned by her behaviour. In order to keep something resembling an open mind, we put it down to her trying too hard to impress." Emily's only response was a loud snort of derision.

She stole a glance at the clock. I took the hint and handed the original of her report back to her to slip back into its envelope. "I had better be off. I'm sure you have things to do and I expect Ben will be waiting for this. I told him I was bringing it over. After I've delivered it, I am available if you would like a hand with anything."

"Your assistance would be most welcome … and collect something for morning tea on your way back please."

Chapter 29

With Emily on her way to Ben's office, I toyed with the idea of calling Ned, but abandoned it. Instead, I thought about what else Ned might be able to contribute. Sometimes people don't think they know anything until a stray question unlocks a hidden memory.

Emily returned with a selection of muffins for morning tea. "I didn't expect to see you back so soon. I felt sure Ben would cross examine you about your findings." I made the comment as we settled into my ancient lounge chairs.

"I half expected that myself. He wasn't as surprised by the results as I thought he would be. It was as if he already doubted the rifle being tested was the weapon that killed Thomas. Maybe he already suspected murder and not suicide."

…A step in the right direction, I told myself. Perhaps time spent explaining to Ben what I'd found so far was worthwhile. For me, there is no doubt it was murder. All I have to do now is find sufficient evidence to prove it. I feel I'm so close, it's frustrating not to be able to reach out and grasp it. "Emily, do you fancy a drive up the valley? I intended to ring Jessie at the Tanwood coffee shop this morning, but my gut is telling me I should take a drive and talk to her face-to-face. I don't know if it will produce anything useful. In this instance, I think I'm running on instinct instead of common sense."

By the time we reached the coffee shop, I had a topic to focus on: Rogan's mates. My questions would focus on both the hippie and the bikie. As soon Jessie was able to join us at our table, I asked my first question. "Can you tell me anything about the scruffy looking hippie bloke who supposedly was a mate of Rogan's?"

"Don't know if I can tell you much at all. You're right, he was scruffy looking; unkempt and in need of a good scrub. He had a number of cheap rubbish-looking things hanging around his neck, and unmatched earrings. Apart from that, the only other distinctive feature about him was his tattoos. His arms were covered in them – and up his neck. I don't mean it was a continuous pattern. It was just a series of bits and pieces all jammed in everywhere, and a big spider's web on one side of his neck. Maybe something in those tats will be helpful to your investigation. They are a bit hard to describe. If I draw them, it will give you a better idea of what they were like."

She grabbed a couple of napkins from the holder and a pencil before coming back to our table to begin her artwork. Her efforts began with an outline of a neck, upper chest and two arms. On the outline, she then set about sketching in the tattoos as they appeared on the bloke's upper body, starting with the spider's web on the side of his neck. "Argh, it's no good. I can't get these couple to look right," she said, and threw down her pencil in disgust.

"What's going on here? Mum, have you decided to take up art to fill in your spare time?" A tall slender young woman stood beside Jessie. So engrossed in Jessie's artistic endeavours, I didn't notice the woman come in.

"What spare time? I was trying to give Sonny an understanding of the tattoos on that scruffy hippie bloke who used to hang around here a while back. Do you remember him at all?"

"Oh yes, I remember who you're talking about. This drawing isn't quite right. Here, give me the pencil and I'll show you what it should be like." Her revised sketch took a couple of seconds to complete. Then, she stood up straight and studied the napkin. "Yeah, that's not too bad. But, you've left out the most important one."

"There weren't any others. What other one are you talking about?" Jessie asked.

"The big pornographic one on his chest… It was huge and looked like a page from the Kama Sutra."

Jessie's mouth gaped slightly and her eyebrows mingled with her hairline. "What are you on about? I never saw anything like that."

"No, you wouldn't. Those shirts he wore always had the sleeves cut out to show off the artwork on his arms, but he always kept the shirts buttoned up to the neck so you couldn't see that tat."

"Oh, I see. And just how did you get to see it, may I ask?"

"Relax, Mother Dear. The top button on one of his shirts was broken. There was only about half a button hanging there, but it kept his shirt done up – until he stretched across to reach something. The button popped open and pulled the one below it open as well. That's when I saw the tat … well, some of it anyway. He didn't know his shirt was open until he saw me looking at his chest. Once he realised, he did up the buttons again, and then continued to hold the shirt closed with one hand until he left the store."

"I don't think we need you to sketch that one for us, thank you very much."

"That's a relief. I don't think I could draw it anyway."

"By the way, Sonny, this is my daughter, Tina. She runs the general store section of this empire." After the usual introductions, Jessie continued. "Tina, did you have a reason to come in here this morning, or was it just to shock me?"

"Mrs Taylor asked me to put this pack of envelopes in her mailbox for it to go out with her next mail delivery. She also wants a book of stamps please, Mum."

Perhaps it was time to divert attention from the artwork and test Tina's memory about other matters. "Tina, you seem to remember the bloke well enough, what can you tell me about him? Do you recall him as a mate of Lyle Rogan's?"

"Yeah, I always thought he was until one day when I saw him giving Rita a hard time out there in the car park. He was giving a mouthful and poking her in the shoulder as he laid down the law about something. It's funny. I expected Rita to burr up and put him in his place. She could be quite vicious. Instead, she seemed to just take it, and then she seemed to plead with him … or placate him somehow. I couldn't hear what it was all about but, as he went to walk off, he turned to her and said, *a deal is a deal. Remind him of that if he wants me to keep quiet.*"

"Nice work, Tina." I exclaimed. "I don't suppose you have any idea when this happened?"

"Well, I'm pretty sure it was the last time he came into the store. Do you want something more specific than that? I could look up the accounts."

Jessie cut in before I could open my mouth. "Why would you check the accounts? The bloke wasn't running an account was he?"

"No, not until that last day. He bought a few things and then was five dollars short when it came to paying for them. I gave him the option of putting something back on the shelf, or putting it on the slate. I explained if he didn't pay the money within a week, the debt would increase by a dollar a day until it was paid. He never came back. The debt is still there."

"I can't believe you let him get away without paying. You should have made him put some of the stuff back so he could cover the cost of what he took away." Jessie's tone said she was most unhappy about what happened.

"Yes, but I thought it might be worthwhile letting him take the stuff. It was stuff I really wanted him to use, like soap, toothpaste and toothbrush, comb, and a couple of other things I can't remember, plus some potatoes and carrots. Don't worry about your five bucks, Mum. I had a thumb on the scales when I weighed his potatoes and carrots, so I probably charged him two or three dollars more than I should have. I saw how much he had his wallet and knew he couldn't pay for everything. We probably lost about two dollars on the deal. Now, Sonny, did you want me to have a look at that account card?"

What a silly question to ask, of course I did. She ducked back into the store and returned about a minute later carrying a small card. She explained, "We run a proper computerised accounting system for all our regular customers but, for those casual, once-off type accounts, we keep a card system."

Tina gave me the date the account card was created. I felt a surge of excitement. It was only a couple of days before the date of that big downpour in April. Too much about this bloke is focusing on that date in April and the fact he hasn't been seen since. At last I felt game enough to ask the big question. The question I knew Tina would have an answer for. "You don't happen to have a name for this bloke who owes you five dollars, do you?"

She chuckled. "How else could I keep an account for him? He told me his name was Cass, so I asked what it was short for. He gave me an unpleasant look and told me it was 'Casper'. I said, 'Okay, as in Casper the friendly ghost? He lent across the counter in an aggressive way and said, 'yeah if you like'. So, I wrote *Casper Ghost* as the name on the card."

"That's bound to be useful," Jessie said without hiding her disgust.

"Not as useful as the name on his credit card I suppose." Tina dropped her mother a look. "While I scanned the items he bought, I saw him slide his credit card half out of his wallet. He looked at it for a few moments, as though trying to decide whether to use it or not, before shoving it back in the wallet. Maybe he didn't have enough cash left in his account, because that's when he checked the notes in his wallet and raided his pockets for loose change. I knew he was a doubtful character." She showed me the two words in tiny writing at the bottom right-hand corner of the card: Trevor Griffiths. "That's the name I saw on the credit card. It might prove useful. You never know, it might even be *his* credit card and *his* real name."

The place was quiet for a few moments until Jessie spoke. "Tina, it looks like you have customers. I'll put a book of stamps in with Mrs Taylor's mail." By the time Jessie finished speaking, Tina was already on her way out of the coffee shop.

Emily and I exchanged looks. I felt stunned. This was more than I hoped to achieve today. Through the chaos in my mind, I heard my name being called. "Sonny, Sonny… Are you all right?" Jessie asked.

"Better than all right… At the risk of pressing my luck too far, you don't happen to know anything about a bloke who dresses in black leathers and rides a big motorbike do you?"

"Don't know anything about him, but I do know who you mean. He's a bad piece of work that one is. He's never come in here and I don't know that he's ever been into the store. He did buy fuel for his bike one day and started an argument with Gary when he went to pay for it. Said he was being ripped off. The bowser was rigged. It showed more than he took. Insisted his bike couldn't hold as much as the bowser said; was aggressive and refused to pay. An off-duty copper was there at the time. He took the bloke outside and changed his mind."

"Was he a regular around here, a local maybe?"

"Nah, he wasn't local. He might've called in at the store one other time, but that was it. On occasions, I saw him tearing up the road on his bike, but he wasn't a regular. Thinking back, I haven't seen him go past in quite a while now. He was supposed to be another mate of Rogan's, but I never saw them together. The hippie, the biker and Rogan; they were all a bit strange."

Sometimes gold is where you least expect it. Today was a classic example. My hope for today was to find out something – anything – about the hippie. Now, I wanted to rush home to analyse the information gathered. Three women came in and demanded to know what today's special was. It was obvious they were regulars, and started an easy banter with Jessie. Their arrival provided our opportunity to leave.

No one spoke until we were halfway back to Millhaven. Emily was first. "You think that hippie, Trevor Griffiths, if that is his name, had something to do with Blaine's death. Do you want to tell me about it?"

"I'm not sure what to make of it. Maybe after we look at your files this afternoon, I'll have a clearer picture of what happened. But, today tends to confirm what my gut has told me for a couple of days now."

As we entered the city, Emily's phone rang. The one-sided call I heard told me it related to her work. "Sorry, Sonny, work calls. Could you drop me there please?" We were only a couple of blocks away so, a few moments later, I dropped her out front. "Sorting this out shouldn't take long. Do you still want to look at those old files?" Of course I did. "I'll give you a call when everyone goes home."

Back in my city office, I tackled emails and messages before making a start on today's notes. A few minutes after five o'clock my phone rang; Ben, not Emily. "Anything special you might like for dinner tonight?" he asked.

"Fish and chips … my tastebuds have lusted after them all day. Will Sam join us for dinner?"

"No, not tonight."

"In that case, plan on three of us. I think Emily is coming." Expecting Emily to join us might be a bit ambitious on my part, but I hoped she could. With the last couple of paragraphs added to my notes, and still no call from Emily, I was stuffing everything I wanted to take home with me into my tote bag when her call came.

"I'm alone at last. If you come around now, we can go

through those files." I parked out front. She let me in and led me through to their files room.

"About what date are we looking for?" I recited the date of the April downpour, and warned it might be a few days later before a body was found. "Okay, this is the right time period. Let's see what we have." She flicked across the files, reading the label on each one as she went.

As I watched, my heart sank. She flicked past too many files for us to be in luck. Then, I felt excitement stir. She ran her hand back across the tops of the files to where she started, mumbling to herself as she did so. I wanted to shout, 'let me look', but I bit my tongue.

Then, a few clear words. "There is only one possibility … a bit later, but maybe…" She hauled out a hefty folder and slapped it on the bench in front of me. "I'm not sure about this one. It's about a week after the downpour, but it's the only possibility around then." As she opened the file and turned to the photographs pocket, she added, "Our problem is, a body might be nothing more than supposition on our part."

She up-ended the pocket. A cascade of photographs spread across the bench. Her keen eyes spotted the corner of a photo poking out from under a few others. As she dragged it out, she yelped, "Eureka…! I think we have Mr Griffiths."

It was all there; photographs matching Jessie's drawings of his tattoos. Emily snatched up a photograph and studied it. "Ooh, I see what Tina was on about. Maybe it's as well Jessie didn't see this one."

Yep, it was the tattoo covering most of the man's chest and midriff area. We exchanged looks. I couldn't help myself, it was out before I could stop myself. "I wonder how that impacted his social life. Did it help things along, or kill any attempt stone dead?" Emily dissolved into giggles as she gathered up the photos and shoved them back into their pocket.

"Sonny, do we agree this is the hippie and one-time mate of Lyle Rogan, a man who disappeared only a few months after Thomas Blaine's death."

"We are in agreement. What does the file say about what happened to him?" Too engrossed in what she was reading, she didn't answer. I waited patiently –for as long as I could stand it. When she slammed the file closed, I tried my luck again. "Was there anything useful in the file, anything which tells us what happened?" Still no response forthcoming.

Emily had her phone to her ear and a conversation in progress. *...I was only going to look at the one of Blaine's body, but maybe bring them both .... Okay, come to the deliveries entrance and I'll let you in.* The call ended, she turned to me, her face flushed with excitement. "We might have struck gold, Sonny, but we have to wait for Ben to arrive before we know for sure."

She checked the CCTV monitor before rushing from the room to return a few moments later with Ben in tow. "Sonny, come on; this way. We'll take everything to my lab." I fell in behind Emily and Ben and almost had to 'double-time' to keep up with them as they rushed along the corridor.

Within moments, I watched Emily place two bullets on the landing of her expensive-looking microscope and start twiddling knobs. A blurred image swam across the computer screen attached to the microscope. As she twiddled things, the image focused and became clear. Ben leaned in close to the screen while Emily continued to peer through the microscope's eyepiece.

"No, it's not that one," Ben said as he stood up and stretched his back. "Which one was that?"

Emily didn't answer. She was busy fiddling with things and the image on the screen blurred again. Then, I realised she had swapped one of the bullets on the landing and was adjusting the focus again. The image sharpened to show clear images of two bullets.

I saw Emily stiffen. Ben swooped in close to the screen again. "It's a match," Emily squeaked. "They match!"

"Which one, Emily … which one is the match?" Ben demanded. Then Ben and Emily had their heads together. Excluded from their murmured conversation was too much for me.

"Perhaps you might like to share with me. This is my case too," I said a tad louder than necessary in the tiny lab. They spun around to face me, the shocked looks on their faces morphed into embarrassment.

Chapter 30

We were three for dinner. Sam did not appear. The fish and chips disappeared off plates in record-breaking time as we adhered to the house rule of no shop talk while at the table …. and all of us were impatient to talk shop. Emily and Ben picked up the coffees and started towards the lounge room. I redirected them to my office where each sought a comfortable perch for the long session ahead.

I opened proceedings. "Where would you like to begin and who should do that?"

"It might be best if you take the lead, Sonny. Start from the beginning of your case," Ben suggested.

Nothing suited me better. I launched into a succinct overview of my investigation. I drew a timeline on my whiteboard as I went, adding significant facts or events as I came to them in my delivery. I began by covering the background which led to Lucy's alienation from Tanwood. "So, it's not difficult to understand how unhappy the situation was at Blaine's farm for Lucy and her father before she left for boarding school when aged about thirteen, or why she never returned here until a week or so ago." The story of how Lucy and her father managed to maintain contact over the years until his death tugged at heartstrings. Details of how she found out he died so long after the event brought tears to Emily's eyes.

From there, I moved the story back to the night of Thomas Blaine's death. "On the night of Blaine's death, Rita and the child were supposed to be in town. It wasn't until they returned to the farm a few days later, they found out he was dead. Despite Tanwood locals 'knowing' mother and child were in town somewhere, they were nowhere near Millhaven. They were in Rogan's shack on Bob Joyce's property further up the valley. Connor Joyce can attest both Rogan and Rita were there on the night of the storm. Rogan did leave the property briefly during the storm, but wasn't gone long enough to drive to Tanwood and back in that brief time. So, it's possible he didn't go far, maybe to meet someone."

As I scribbled the next entry on my timeline, Emily recalled the event. "And then, Rogan waited a respectful period of time – until after the coroner's hearing – before moving in with Rita. When was that?"

"Thomas was killed in January. Proceedings dragged on until late March. Rogan moved in with Rita early in April." Both Ben and Emily nodded and I continued. "Then, a further heavy storm occurred a couple of weeks after Rogan moved in with Rita. Strange as it seems, Connor Joyce says Rogan was at the shack the night of that storm and helped Connor with some straying cattle. He also states he encountered Rogan in the early hours of the morning when Rogan returned to the property after having been elsewhere, and not on his way to the Homestead as he claimed he was."

"Why would he be at the shack when he was living with Rita?" Emily's brow furrowed as she considered what I'd told them. "If he left the property during the storm, where did he go, and why?"

"Just prior to that storm, Blaine's neighbour, Ned Edwards, heard a blazing row at Kirk Michael Farm between Rogan and his hippie-looking mate, who visited the farm on occasion. Ned heard the word 'money' mentioned during the argument. That was only a couple of weeks after Rogan moved onto the farm. The hippie never visited the farm after the storm. The only hippie seen around Tanwood appeared to be a mate of Rogan's. On the day prior to the April storm, the hippie was seen being aggressive and making threatening comments to Rita in the store car park. They haven't seen that hippie since the storm, and he still owes the store a few dollars."

"A description of the bloke gathered from those at the Tanwood store complex matches photographs in a file of an unnamed body discovered further downstream about a week after the downpour occurred. The body was not in good condition when found. It was assumed the man had somehow gone into the river and drowned, and his body was damaged as it washed downstream. Although the case was closed, a post-mortem was carried out to ensure a complete record before the file was archived. The post-mortem revealed the man did not drown. There was no water in his lungs. He was dead when he went into the river. What the post-mortem did find, was evidence of a gunshot wound to the head, and the slug still rattling around in the cranium."

"This afternoon, that slug was compared to a bullet test fired from Thomas Blaine's rifle and the bullet extracted from Thomas Blaine's body. Striations on the slug from the hippie's skull are identical with those on the bullet which killed Blaine. Therefore, the rifle used to shoot Blaine was the same rifle used to murder the hippie. As Blaine's rifle was considered the weapon with which he took his own life, it was taken into evidence from the crime scene and remained in the evidence locker at the police precinct when the hippie was shot in April. Blaine was shot through an open window by someone standing outside the building. The heavy rain, combined with the general condition of the area around the house, obliterated any sign of footprints or any other activity."

"Christ, Sonny, do I have this wrong? I'm hearing that the hippie shot Thomas, and later was shot by Rogan. Did Rogan meet the hippie that night? Isn't it possible someone else was involved; a third party? Do we know the hippie even had a rifle?" Ben asked.

"I don't know, Ben. Did the police find his campsite? Did they find a rifle? Perhaps your file on the dead hippie might answer those questions. By the way, Ben, the bloke's name might be Trevor Griffiths. It was observed on a credit card he had in his possession but opted not to use. Whether it was his credit card or someone else's is another matter."

Emily voiced her concerns. "Why did Rogan and his brood mount such a sudden departure from the farm? It was a good eighteen months after Thomas's death before they absconded. What happened to precipitate that?"

Ben offered a response. "Rogan was growing drugs in the scrub behind his shack. It's possible a drugs deal went bad." Emily didn't look convinced, so I tried to help.

"That part of the story remains a bit speculative, although there is evidence to suggest what happened." I added another couple of entries to my timeline as I gathered my thoughts. "Rogan had another supposed 'mate'. That one dressed in black leathers decorated with numerous colour patches, and rode a big black noisy motorbike. Unlike the hippie, he visited Tanwood on only a couple of occasions, but was seen travelling the road through the valley on many occasions. Ned Edwards also overheard a row between Rogan and the bikie, during which Rogan was threatened and told 'time was running out'. A couple of days later the farm was deserted, with Rogan and his mob not seen since. The bikie was seen on the road a couple of times soon after they disappeared, but not for a long while since then."

"Forgive me if I'm being a bit thick," Emily began, "but did Rita and Rogan have a long-term strategy to own or take-over Blaine's farm? It sounds as though the Rita-Rogan relationship was alive and well the whole time and continued after Blaine's death. Sonny, you said they let the farm run down. Doesn't it suggest they didn't want it?"

"While Rogan was happy to cultivate a small plot of drugs at the shack, he didn't do a tap of work on the farm and it became overgrown. I'm wondering if he expanded his horticultural pursuits once Thomas was out of the way. There's a patch of scrub at the back end of the farm. It would be ideal for establishing another 'garden'. The unkempt nature of the property would divert attention away from the place, and the long grass helped hide what was going on. There was no income from the farm, but somehow they afforded a nice lifestyle."

"Are you suggesting I need to send the drug squad out to tramp through another patch of scrub?" Ben asked.

"Might not hurt to have a look…" A thought flashed in, helping me recall something Ned told me in passing. "Ooh, I just remembered… The scrub is still there, but it's mainly regrowth now. Remember the bushfire outbreak about two years ago…? Quite a bit of the valley was burnt – including the scrub on the boundary of Blaine's farm where it borders the national parklands. Perhaps it robbed Rogan of his 'produce' to sell – and his income."

"That's just the sort of deal-gone-bad situation we were looking for. I'll organise the boys to take a look out there tomorrow. There might not be anything suspicious growing there now, but there might be evidence of previous cultivation." Ben seemed brighter all of a sudden.

Emily remained withdrawn. I felt concerned I hadn't been clear enough about some aspect of the case. "No. No, it's not that. I was thinking about Thomas. He was a pawn in their grand scheme from the outset. A pawn who lost his life as well as his two daughters."

"Well, he lost his only daughter … if local gossip is correct." I tried to reassure Emily. "The younger child, Sarah, is reputed to be the mirror image of her father – right down to his red hair. In case you are wondering, Thomas' colouring included jet black hair to match his eyes."

"Did he know she wasn't his child?" Sometimes Emily seems naïve but, on this occasion, I had to admit it must have been hard to go on living the lie.

I wondered why Thomas persisted with the marriage and the 'happy family' pretence when he must have been aware of the truth. Perhaps I should try pursuing this with Lucy when she returns. Did Rita and/or Rogan have some sort of hold over Thomas? An idle thought danced across the forefront of my thinking. I thought it was a private thing but it appears I was thinking aloud. "Did he send Lucy away, and keep her away, to keep her safe?"

"Eh…? What's this keeping Lucy safe stuff about?" Ben demanded.

"Fanciful thinking probably… Remember, I said it looked as though Thomas was putting his life in order, as if he knew something would happen to him. I'm wondering if, when he sent Lucy to boarding school, he knew what his ultimate fate would be and he wanted her well out of it to keep her safe."

"Is she in danger now, do you think?" Emily whispered. "Hasn't the poor girl has been through enough."

Ben looked a bit stunned by Emily's question. "That's an interesting question. Sonny, when is she due back in Millhaven? You and I need to have a long talk with her. …And, I might have a different assignment for Sam while she is here."

I sent Lucy a message asking her to come into my office as soon as she returned to Millhaven. Her almost instant reply agreed to meet me at nine o'clock tomorrow morning. Ben arranged to come to my office a few minutes after Lucy arrived to give me time to explain why I asked her to come in.

*****

All the way into the city this morning, I wracked my brain for a way to initiate the conversation we needed with Lucy. As I dumped my bag on my desk, I realised I still didn't know how. The voice in my head kept suggesting the conversation was a rubbish idea anyway. If Lucy knew of any danger to herself or her father, wouldn't she have mentioned it? She never appeared nervous either here in the city or at the farm. Maybe the little voice in my head was right. It was just a fanciful notion on my part.

Then, Lucy arrived and it was time to prepare her for Ben's arrival. "Thanks for coming. There are a few things to discuss, and the local top cop has invited himself along to our meeting." I saw her stiffen at the mention of Ben. "It's okay. There's nothing to worry about. I do have a report on my investigation to give you, but it will be verbal today as I haven't prepared a hardcopy yet."

"It sounds as though you have completed your investigation. Is it possible you have all the answers already?"

"It looks that way. A couple of loose ends remain, but they should be sorted out within the next day or so. Ah, here is Superintendent Ben Richards ... and just in time for coffee." I left Ben and Lucy to get acquainted and become comfortable with each other while I worked the coffee machine.

Ben appeared keen to lead discussions, so I allowed him to do so. His first and most significant question related to any threat to Thomas and Lucy's safety. He asked her to think back to when she left home for boarding school. Lucy continued to look perplexed by his line of questioning but co-operated. Then, his questioning moved to the contact she and Thomas maintained over all the years she was absent from the farm.

"No, I never picked up on anything to suggest he might be in danger. He never even commented about how unhappy he was or how miserable his life had become, but I picked up on those clues. His choice of words told me more than the words themselves." Lucy remained unperturbed by the question, but Ben's next question made me catch my breath.

"If it was such a rotten life – such a lousy marriage – why did he stick with it? Why didn't he chuck her out?". Lucy was unfazed by it.

"I've asked myself that many times since his death. Somehow, I feel she – they – were responsible for what happened to him. I don't mean I think they killed him. It's more like they were involved somehow. The only thing was something which happened not long before they were married.

No, don't ask me what it was, because I don't know … not exactly … but I think it gave them a hold over him in some way."

"Okay; tell us what you know, or think, happened."

"Right … I think Rita was involved in something. I don't think she committed a major crime. It was more like she was where she shouldn't have been when something bad happened, and it was best if people didn't know she was there … or, perhaps, that she was involved in some way. I remember a huge row about whatever it was. Dad said she was stupid and asked if she even possessed a brain. Later that day, people came to the house and they all went into the office. While I don't know what went on in there, I think Dad covered for her in some way – gave her an alibi or something. Later, the truth came out and Dad knew he did the wrong thing and had implicated himself in something serious."

Ben considered Lucy's story in silence for a couple of moments. "So he might have provided her with a false alibi. Maybe perverted the course of justice in some way. Does that align with your thinking?" Lucy hung her head, shrugged, and then looked up at Ben and nodded.

"I swear I don't know what it was. Maybe it was my imagination; just me trying to justify why he didn't throw her out – especially after Sarah was born."

"Did he doubt Sarah's paternity?" Ben never takes a soft approach with hard questions.

"He didn't question it. He knew she wasn't his. Anyone with eyes could see she wasn't Dad's. But, he tried hard to do the right thing by the child – always said it wasn't the child's fault who its father was."

With Ben's questions ended, he left. I saw Lucy physically relax and exhale a long breath. We drank the fresh coffee I made in silence for a few minutes before I gave her a verbal report on my investigation.

"So Rogan didn't kill Dad?"

"No, we have evidence to refute that. Lucy, if I'm honest, and maybe a bit premature, I could tell you what I think some of those 'loose ends' I mentioned will show." She asked me to continue. "Remember, this is speculation … I think another person, a mate or associate of Rogan's, was hired to shoot your father – probably so Rita and Rogan could take over the farm. Then, soon after, something turned sour between to two men. Maybe it had something to do with payment for the job, or it could have been over something else entirely. I suspect, when things weren't going his way, the 'hired help' threatened to go public. It ended up causing his death. Did Rogan do away with the man? I don't know yet and maybe won't ever be sure."

"…But you think Rogan killed the bloke who shot my father to shut him up. Right…?"

"Yes … but, as I said, I have no evidence to support that."

My report was finished and there was nothing about the case to discuss. We moved onto Lucy's intentions for the future. "The notice about my reclaiming ownership of the farm appears in local and Brisbane papers today. The solicitor thought it unnecessary but wise, and assured me any challenge will not stand up in court. The other reason I spent more time than intended in Brisbane was to change my surname back to 'Blaine'. It was a bit complicated because of the change to Telford while I was overseas. If I'm going to live at Blaine's Kirk Michael Farm, I should revert to my birthright. I am now once more Lucy Blaine."

Chapter 31

It's Wednesday already. The week is disappearing. With the Blaine case almost wrapped up, I intended spending the day in my city office tidying up loose ends and catching up on everything else. I expected no interruptions. That was until about mid-afternoon when Ben called. His excitement was clear from the moment he spoke.

"Emily tested the rifle we found near the hippie's campsite. It was in poor condition, but our blokes got it firing again. The rifling on the test bullet matches that on both the slugs taken from Thomas Blaine and the hippie."

"Okay, that's a start. So they were both shot with the same weapon, but the question is: whose weapon?"

"Ah well, the rifle is old, and probably was registered when purchased by one Trevor Griffiths. We confirmed that was the hippie's real name." I made a 'suitably impressed' type response, and Ben continued his gloat. "With use and age, the rifle developed a few nasty habits. Another piece of evidence was preserved at the time of the shooting. Anyone using the rifle, who was unaware of its 'habits', ended up losing a bit of skin when the mechanism grabbed his finger as it closed. Emily is testing the fragment of skin from the rifle preserved all those years ago."

"Now, if we just had something to compare it with…"

"Oh, but we do. One of my men took a quick trip up the valley first thing this morning. He brought back a toothbrush and a comb from the pocket of one of Rogan's jackets. Emily thinks she can recover DNA. Fingers crossed we get a match."

I had to wait until Friday morning for confirmation. The DNA from the rifle matched samples taken from items at the farm. Ben strode into my office just before lunchtime. Having called me with the DNA news earlier, I was surprised to see him. Everything about him screamed 'excited'. I barely said hello before he launched into the reason for his visit.

"The evidence is so clear. We had no problem getting an extradition order approved. Sam's been handling it. She called when I was on my way here to say the extradition order was through and she was liaising with the police on the other side of the country. Overnight, we got lucky. Rogan and his mob were located in Western Australia, where he is working at one of the mines. Sam and a couple of my blokes will fly across tonight to escort Rogan, Rita and the child back to Millhaven."

Lucy dropped by while Ben was here. She had been setting up the house on the farm and was ready to move in.

"I put notices in the Tanwood store and coffee shop advertising a garage sale, including lots of furniture. Just about everything is gone. A woman is coming to look at the last couple of things tomorrow. A fair bit has gone to the dump, and some of the better stuff went to charities. That's why I'm in town now. I had a couple of bags to drop off at Life Line. In amongst all that, some of my new stuff arrived yesterday and the rest should be there this afternoon. I'm hoping to be moved in by the end of the weekend."

"I hope to finish your report today and wrap up the case for you. What should I do with it when it's ready?"

"Mail it to me at Kirk Michael Farm if you like. The reason I dropped in was to ask you to lunch at my place on Sunday week. I'm hoping the two of you and Emily can come. Ned will be there too. He is going to be busy over the next little while helping me sort out the farm and bringing it back into production. You could bring the report with you when you come if you prefer."

Anxious to return to the farm before the rest of her furniture arrived, we accepted her invitation to lunch and she left. As she clattered her way down the stairs, Ben said, "By the time we meet for lunch, we might be in a position to tell her the end of the story. I'd prefer we didn't share too much yet about what's happening … not until it's all confirmed. The other thing I meant to tell you before Lucy arrived was about the drug squad visiting the farm yesterday. The bushfire did a good job on that patch of scrub, but they still found evidence of cultivation and even the remnants of a sophisticated irrigation system. Rogan's list of charges grows longer by the day. See you tonight for dinner." I said I would cook some sort of pasta dish, and sent Emily a message to join us.

After a disrupted morning, I left town early to work at home for the rest of the afternoon. Lucy's report was completed as far as possible. I hoped to add a final chapter before going to the farm for lunch. As I finished tidying the Blaine file, Ben and Emily arrived within minutes of each other. The sauce for tonight's dinner was done. All I had to do was cook the pasta. It gave us time for a drink before dinner. As I believed there would be plenty to discuss tonight, I thought it prudent to have dinner out of the way early.

With no time wasted on eating and clearing away afterwards, it was quite early when we settled in the lounge room with our coffees. Emily opened discussions. "It's amazing the way everything came together over the last couple of days. I can't believe that, after such a long time, Thomas Blaine's murder will receive justice. Lucy's moving into her old home is a nice touch given everything that's happened."

I knew how she felt. It was a whirlwind wrap-up of the case in the end, but I held other concerns. "I hope a successful closure of the case puts to rest any 'ghosts' for Lucy so she can settle in to the old church without being haunted by unpleasant memories."

"You know, it's funny in a way…" Emily said quietly. "A church is a place of secrets; secrets parishioners share with God, or His representative on earth. Over its lifetime, a church is privy to many secrets. In the case of Blaine's farm, the secrets continued long after it ceased being St Michael's parish church."

Insightful as usual, Emily voiced my thoughts while working on Lucy's report this afternoon. "You're right. Saint Michael's probably kept many secrets over the years, but the secrets Kirk Michael Farm was home to were as bad, if not worse, than any the church knew. Those of recent times are 'unholy' secrets compared to their earlier counterparts."

Ben, looking thoughtful, nodded as I finished speaking. "In spite of the world our work takes the three of us into, what happened at that farm is almost impossible to comprehend. To think a couple could plan so meticulously to destroy the lives of Thomas Blaine and his daughter – and how they did it is difficult to take on board."

"It's going to be a long hard road ahead for Lucy as she tries to rebuild her life and re-establish the farm, but I think she has what it takes," Emily said. "While the death of her father is hard to live with, knowing how and why it happened might help make coping a little easier."

The evening had taken on a morbid atmosphere. I felt compelled to change the subject. "So Ben, what's going on with Sam? Have you worked out why she is not 'our' Sam lately … and why didn't she join us tonight?"

"She didn't come tonight because she is busy with the extradition stuff for the Blaine case. It appears taking her off the Blaine case investigation and putting her in charge of organising the extradition did the trick. You will find Sam is back to normal. While it took a bit of digging, I found out what caused her behavioural change. Eliminating the cause helped."

"Was something we were unaware of going on in her life the problem?" I had to ask, although I wasn't sure Ben wouldn't say, even if he knew.

"When a homicide occurs in a regional area, a homicide squad is dispatched from Brisbane to investigate. With the crime rate escalating in the southern metropolitan area, especially homicides, all the homicide officers are too busy at home to deal with regional incidents. There was talk of setting up another small squad to deal with regional issues. When not busy with regional homicides, they would strengthen the force in the metropolitan area. Sam heard about a possible new squad and thought she should be part of it."

"I don't imagine Pete would be happy to lose her. She is a good detective, Ben, but is she ready for such a squad?" I asked.

"No, and it's more complicated than that. It seems she had worked on Pete to put in a good word for her. His response was vague at best. She saw my investigation as a chance to prove herself … and ended up almost stuffing things up in the process. After a few words to Pete about the inappropriateness of Sam's reporting to him on my case, he realised he was partly to blame. He had a hard conversation with her. She now knows she is not as ready as she thinks she is, and Pete would not put her forward for any position should the squad be formed. Once the message hit home, and she realised how inappropriate her behaviour was, the real Sam re-emerged."

"If she is still in Millhaven, will she come to Lucy's luncheon with us?" Emily asked.

"An awkward situation avoided. She will return to duties at Ralston prior to the lunch date."

*****

The three of us arrived at Kirk Michael Farm in Ben's car. Already the place looked so different; no long grass, a handful of cows in one paddock, and the shrubs around the house trimmed. Inside, the transformation continued. As Ned later confided, this was how the living area used to be when Valerie was alive. The kitchen was revamped, with the new stove and wall oven taking pride of place, and the office door stood open.

A scrumptious baked lunch with all the trimmings, followed by panna cotta for dessert, had me feeling like a carpet snake looking for somewhere to hibernate. After lunch I handed over my report – and invoice. Lucy took them straight to the office. When she returned, she handed me a cheque. "Lucy, this is too much. My invoice was for less than this."

"You deserve more. I don't have words to describe how it feels at last to know what happened. Although it is horrendous to think about the events of that night, it is beyond relief to know Dad didn't commit suicide. I can't explain it, but the suggestion of suicide made me feel guilty. Guilty I wasn't here for all those years, and wasn't here when things became so bad, he took his own life. In many ways, he is still with me, here in this house. He saved so much of our life together for me, a part of him will always be here with me. For the first time in nearly four years, I feel settled and at home at last."

We made appropriate noises about how much more relaxed she seemed before she continued with what I believe was a well-planned speech. "Sonny, I'll read your report later. I assume it reiterates all you and Ben have shared with me, but I'm wondering if you were able to add that final chapter you were waiting for."

"I'll leave it to Ben to give you an overview of the final chapter."

After taking a deep breath, Ben began cautiously. "We did manage to track down your step-mother … I'm sorry, that just doesn't sit well with me. I'll start again. We tracked down Lyle Rogan, Rita and their daughter, Sarah, and brought them back to Brisbane to stand trial. There were reasons for not returning them to Millhaven. On their arrival, they faced a preliminary hearing and have been ordered to stand trial on charges of murder, aiding in the commission of a murder, and various drug related offences. Sarah is in temporary foster care while her long-term future with her grandmother is organised."

"Good. Then that's an end to it." Lucy's answer stunned me for a moment before I realised there was nothing more needed saying. Her demons were laid to rest, as were the unholy secrets which, for so many years, governed the lives of those who lived here.

As we sat on my back deck that evening, watching the sunset hues darken into night, Emily broke the silence that prevailed since our return from Tanwood.

"I admire Lucy's strength of character. She is so ... so 'together'. And, I think our group might have acquired a new member. Maybe not a regular one but, whenever she is in town, I feel sure Lucy will be joining us."

The End

About the Author

Neive Denis is the creator of the series featuring the Private Investigator, Sonoma (Sonny) Whittington. Neive Denis is the pen name of a writer who was lured from her usual genre to focus on the mystery and excitement that are a part of Sonoma Whittington's world. Neive came into being specifically for this series and, for the moment at least, intends remaining faithful to only stories from Sonny's case files.

This series tells of the intrigue and scrapes – some on occasion life threatening – that are part of the life of Sonoma Whittington, an Australian Private Investigator based in a Central Queensland coastal city. However, Sonny doesn't confine her escapades to Australia, and that provides Neive with an opportunity to weave some of her other areas of interest into Sonny's hair-raising adventures.

See more about Neive Denis and her work at

www.neivedenis.com

or contact her at

contact@neivedenis.com